THE

SECRET NORTH

KA NEWBORRN

Ka Newborrn.com | Knowbelle Press

ISBN-13: 978-1-7354511-1-4

Library of Congress Control Number: 2020911835
Printed in the United States of America

For Geneva, Camille and Jerry

"All around the constellations are stars glowing and twinkling without being attached to a design."
C. Erickson

"Be softer with you. You are a breathing thing. A memory to someone. A home to a life."
Nayyirah Waheed

"And through an open window where no curtain hung I saw you."
Marty Balin

THE SECRET NORTH

Odette

Outside, the sun and wind fused pastel predictability into the August sky's afternoon canvas, leaving it up to Odette to enhance an insufferable composition with texture, form and abstraction.

Daylight deferred to darkness as she stared, with awareness uncommon for a six-year-old, at the framed piece of world affixed to the easel of her kitchen window. Backlit by a wash of pink factory lights and refinery smoke, an apartment complex bordered an incline of trees that stood entangled in rusty pipeline roots.

Feeling wistful with the passing of each moment, she closed the window shade and combed her surroundings for delights to bind her to the safety of immediacy. Like an envelope of instant oatmeal emptied into a mug of water piping hot from the tap, or a ticket to the land of television, where spun sugar girls bared their teeth in celebration of short shorts, baby fresh skin and "bouncin' and behavin'" hair. And there was always the frenetic burst of dancing induced by rhythms found buried in Mama's record collection.

"Ah ha ha ha ha," she chuckled in her throatiest Suzanne Pleshette impersonation, resting the half-eaten mug of oatmeal on the television set and batting her eyelashes coyly. "Stop it. Stop it, Bob, I can't stand it!" Clad in her mother's orange satin robe with arms stretched out to the world, she spun, twirling away from the television and into the family room closet where she grasped the handle of the dented trunk that housed her small collection of Barbie dolls. Soon Superstar Ken, Malibu Christie, Fashion Photo Barbie and SuperTeen Skipper were lined up neatly on the couch beside her.

"Go to your room, you're grounded!" barked Superstar Ken.

"But Ken," SuperTeen Skipper whined, "Fashion Photo Barbie just got her driver's license. We're going for a ride in her pink Corvette."

"Fashion Photo Barbie is a bad influence!" Superstar Ken glowered, placing his pink plastic arm around Malibu Christie's brown shoulders. Malibu Christie nodded and flipped her synthetic black hair in agreement. "It's not fair!" wailed SuperTeen Skipper.

Using her thumb and index finger, Odette clumsily rotated SuperTeen Skipper's head from side to side, showing off the straight pins that she had stuck into the doll's ears earlier in the week.

"You pierced your ears without our permission!" Malibu Christie added tersely. "We have rules in this house! You barely have breasts! I have big ones!" Odette twisted the doll's plastic torso suggestively.

SuperTeen Skipper looked to Fashion Photo Barbie for support, but the buxom doll smirked indifferently. "Fine!" she spat defiantly. "I'm going to my room!"

"Who cares?" Superstar Ken answered distractedly. He turned to Malibu Christie. Their lips met as they stretched out their plastic arms to each other and embraced.

"I'm running away!" SuperTeen Skipper announced. Superstar Ken and Malibu Christie ignored her.

Dancing madly in circles with the emotion of the moment, Odette stood up, grabbed SuperTeen Skipper by the hair, and crouched down into the cobweb and dust bunny filled space behind the television set. "No one will ever find me here," she whispered.

Odette traversed the cobwebbed space for what seemed an eternity, fighting for footing as the gusty winds of the dust bunny storm gave way to a full-fledged tornado. She accidentally stumbled into a nest of hissing, dust covered electrical cord snakes and screamed as one lunged out and bit her on the ankle with its brass prong fangs.

Clutching her ankle and fighting back tears, she felt a waxy surface at her feet and looked down. A playing card blanketed in dust rested halfway under her foot near the antenna plug.

A woman's voice called from the card. "Hello, Odette"

"Who's there?" Odette responded. She knelt directly onto the card and gently brushed the dust from its surface, revealing an elegant and composed Queen of Clubs.

The Queen's voice was smooth and regal. "They just don't understand," she offered sympathetically.

"No, Your Majesty," Odette agreed, rubbing her ankle. "I wasn't bothering them. I was just walking."

The Queen was gracious. "I meant Superstar Ken and Malibu Christie, not the snakes," she clarified. "The snakes are here to protect me. They won't bite you anymore, now that they know you're a friend. Give me your hand."

The little girl reached beneath the plane deep inside the card until her clammy hand firmly grasped the Queen's lightly sketched one. She completed the ritual by jumping up into a spontaneous dance, scooping her plastic companions into the dented trunk and closing the closet door behind them. Her reality was now intertwined with a little bit of magic and an illusory veil of the finest design. She was free to visit whenever she wanted; the Queen of Clubs was the gateway. She was free to travel to distant worlds and look behind the eyes of different girls; all it took was solitude.

Odette slept peacefully that night. When morning came, she opened the window shade. Dusk deferred to sunlight as she stared, with awareness uncommon for a six-year-old, at the framed piece of world affixed to the easel of her kitchen window. A castle was bordered by an overgrown ridge of butter-hued flowers and wild fruit brambles. Beyond the flowers and brambles sprawled a herald of trees illuminated by a rose gold halo, roots curved gracefully about the base of a warbling stream, the atmosphere thick with dark, moody clouds. Her soulful eyes were no longer blind to the perception of what is beautiful and validated in splendor, or what is beautiful and left alone to decay.

SCEPTRELIND, HJULDER
1979

Ester

From the time that she was old enough to crawl, Ester wanted to grow up to be a famous Luminatrix like her idol, Lilith Brisbane.

"Daddy!" she shrieked from the family room sofa after dinner one night. "Lilith's interview is starting right now! Turn it up!" She perched herself on the sofa arm while her mother cleared the dinner dishes. Her father picked up the remote control and raised the TV volume.

Onscreen, a sinewy young woman with blazing red hair layered stylishly about her shoulders sat at a restaurant table as a reporter pointed a microphone in her direction.

"Thank you so much for agreeing to speak to me on such short notice, Miss Brisbane," the reporter began. "You must be exhausted, having only returned to Glaivelind Forest last night."

"Team caffeine for the win." Lilith's smile was charming and casual as she raised a demitasse of espresso to the air in an impromptu toast. She tossed her hair out of her face before downing the contents of the cup and turning her attention to a passing server. "May I please have another?"

"Anything for you, Lilith!" The young server sported a hairstyle identical to Lilith's. She grinned shyly before taking the cup away.

"Not a bad looking young lady, that Lilith Brisbane," her father remarked.

"Shhhh!" Ester screeched.

The camera panned the length of Lilith's body. She wore dark sunglasses and was dressed in a simple black cashmere sweater, dark denim jeans and vintage crocodile boots.

"She eats seaweed and wild mushrooms for dinner!" Ester chimed excitedly. "She spends two hours a day in inversion boots and an hour jogging. Mom!" Ester barked in the direction of the kitchen. "How come you never make seaweed and wild mushrooms for dinner?"

"And yet you look so rested, like you just stepped out of a spa." The reporter leaned in close. "Must be rough, coming home to a riverfront castle the likes of yours on thirty acres in Glaivelind Forest."

Lilith pushed up the temple of her sunglasses with her index finger and crossed her legs at the ankles. "The Kaspare River sang me a lullaby when I got home last night. And drinking the best bottle from my wine cellar before bed didn't hurt, either."

The reporter chuckled and turned to the camera. "Do you have plans to see your fans while you're home?" Lilith dabbed her eyes behind the sunglasses with a paper napkin. "I'd do a million meet and greets if I could, but I can't. I'm leaving tomorrow."

"Fill us in about your latest cases," the reporter gushed.

"The Jonas Case was first," Lilith began. "Jonas was a mechanical engineer and all-around, proverbial ray of sunshine. His father disparaged him as a child, so he developed a nasty inferiority complex. For three straight months he corrected my grammar incessantly, even when I was right. And I generally am. But I never stopped him because it was the only thing that seemed to relieve his chronic constipation."

The server reappeared and placed a fresh demitasse on the table. Lilith thanked her and turned her attention back to the reporter. The reporter giggled. "So, the takeaway from the Jonas Case was a lesson in constipation, Miss Brisbane?"

Lilith downed the espresso and smirked. "Men are fragile and need to be right, even when they're wrong. Be kind to them. Handle them with kid gloves. And don't waste your money on expensive toilet paper."

Peals of laughter ensued. The reporter giggled freely and carefully dabbed away a tear. "Carry on, Miss Brisbane."

Lilith paused reflectively. "Then there was the Brady case. Brady carried the weight of the world on his shoulders. He took care of his alcoholic parents as a child and never really had a childhood of his own. His parents never nurtured him, never paid him any attention at all, really. He constructed his own societal rules and passed them off as having an elevated sense of self control. He was a bit of a sociopath, really."

"Then what happened?" the reporter asked. "What was the lesson?"

Lilith ran her fingers through her stylish haircut. Coughing, she turned away to bring the paper napkin to her eye again and absentmindedly removed her sunglasses. Her right eye was swollen shut in a painful shade of blackish purple. She turned her focus back to the reporter. "I'm so sorry. What was the question?"

The reporter looked at Lilith's eye and sharply drew in her breath.

"What is it?" Lilith smiled, momentarily oblivious. "Oh!" Suddenly aware of what the reporter was reacting to, she pushed her sunglasses firmly into place. "The uh," the reporter stammered awkwardly, "lesson learned from the Brady Case, Miss Brisbane?"

Lilith cursed silently behind the cover of her left hand. She had not meant to reveal so much. "Roll with the punches?" she smirked.

The reporter changed the subject. "You've been nominated this year for an outstanding achievement award. Tell us how that makes you feel."

Lilith's stomach screamed. "I'm incredibly honored."

"You must be crazy with the excitement and anticipation of it all."

"Not really. I've already won, just being included in such a talented group of peers."

"Is there any advice you would like to give to any aspiring Luminatrixes watching right now?"

Lilith straightened up in her chair and angled her shoulders to the camera. "Your bodies and minds hold the key to the evolution of our planet and, ultimately, the universe."

She paused to light a cigarette with an art deco torch lighter and raised it to her lips, inhaling. "Take care of yourselves. Rest. Study hard in school." Smoke poured out of her nose. "It takes a tireless commitment, but your dedication will make a difference."

Ester's life in Sceptrelind was a provincial one. She lived with her parents at 7 Storyville Lane in a reddish brick house with a white door, matching shutters and lattice window boxes filled with snapdragons. Manicured shrubs lined the cobblestoned front walk.

Her parents took an avid interest in her schoolwork and encouraged her to outperform her classmates.

"Are you almost finished with your elemental analyses of Andromeda?" her father asked at dinner.

Ester sipped her milk. "Oh, yes, Daddy!" She dabbed her mouth with a napkin and mopped a tiny spill from her papers. "Dr. Baton says I have the most accurate estimations she's ever seen, and she's very, very old."

"Are you enjoying the extragalactic microlensing kit that

Daddy bought you for your birthday?"

"Oh, yes, Mommy!"

"That's my girl," her father said proudly. He looked across the table and winked.

A week into the school year, Dr. Baton arranged a conference with her parents and informed them that Sceptrelind's curriculum wasn't challenging enough for Ester. Excited by their daughter's prodigious tendencies, they immediately began to research boarding schools.

Mr. Myling wanted Ester to study in Barterlind because it was the financial superpower and free from the biases of organized religion. Mrs. Myling wanted Ester to study in Phialind because it was the global headquarters of the clergy and impressive in structure and discipline. Confident in the fact that her father knew best, she gave her mother a reproving smile and gently informed her that the prettiest, most famous Luminatrixes always had Barterlind educations.

The night before she left Sceptrelind and never looked back, her father appeared to her in a dream. He pulled a snapdragon from the lattice window box and lovingly tucked it into her hand. "Who's my hummingbird?" he asked. "Who's my wise little owl?"

She tried to answer him, but no sound came out of her mouth. He faded away before her eyes, and the snapdragon crumbled into dust.

GLAIVELIND, HJULDER
1991

Ester

"Why does the water turn red, Elspeth?"

As she bathed, the trees cast their haunted eyes upon the Kaspare River and tried to scare the stygian water into turning red. The riverbank trembled under the wind's touch. The lingering embers of sun burned out.

Her handmaiden was silhouetted inside a hollowed oak. In the darkness, it was hard to distinguish where her wizened face ended and the tree bark began. The branches were fused at the top in the shape of a flame, as if the foliage had once been charred. By fire or anger, she couldn't tell. But it left her feeling cold.

The water slid between her fingers like liquid onyx and the crisp air kneaded her nipples into arrowheads. She drew her knees up to cover herself, but the trees leered at her anyway. She held their gaze for a few moments. When she turned her eyes back to the water, she was immersed in a fountain of blood.

Elspeth stiffened inside the hollowed tree. She was used to avoiding the question by now. She chose her words carefully.

"It's nothing."

"You know something."

"I can't see anything."

"You weren't born blind."

"The scientists say it's just an optical phenomenon."

She sat motionless in the void of red.

"Perhaps you miss your family," Elspeth offered.

She lowered her eyes briefly and thought about her parents.

"What about the hunger?"

"Just a few more minutes before dinner, child."

She knew it wasn't what the girl meant, but she didn't care. And why would she? With the trees always boring their yellow eyes into her back, why should she speak at all? Shivering, she pulled her woolen shawl tightly around her shoulders and rose from the hollowed oak. The riverbed warbled between her toes.

"Are you ready for the birds, child?"

She nodded.

Elspeth called into the night sky with a polished agate recorder. A cloud of bird elves flocked to the riverbank in response. They carried a purple towel in their beaks.

Gemstones leaked from her spiraling coils as she emerged from the jet black water. She draped herself with the towel and patted down her hair and skin. Her caramel skin flushed with carmine in the night wind as she patted her herself dry.

Sitting down, she dabbed violet oil behind her knees and stained her cheeks and mouth with pomegranate seeds. She arched her back and allowed Elspeth to massage some of the oil into her hair and secure the loosened bits of pearl and crystal. The bird elves laid out a white peasant blouse, a pair of faded jeans and her favorite necklace, a moonstone pendant carved into the shape of a hummingbird. She slipped on the garments and lifted her hair. Elspeth fastened the necklace.

The bird elves frolicked as she devoured a plate of root vegetables and a glass of mead. They rocked their tail feathers along the ground and flew in a playful circle dance.

"The trip to Earth." She looked up at the sky. "The stars. The planets. It does fill something inside."

"You have everything you could possibly imagine right here."

A lone bird elf abandoned his dance, perched himself upon her left shoulder and slowly licked her face. She winced and brushed him away.

"But it's unsettling."

In the distance, a thread of silver trailed across the sky. It rose from the pastoral valleys of Phialind, cruised westward towards the iridescent skyscrapers of Barterlind, and glided southward into the oat-colored flatlands of Sceptrelind, where it coasted amid a cluster of unassuming homes. But that was temporary. It would crest into Glaivelind Forest before morning, when it was time.

"It's only a feeling. It isn't real. Close your eyes to it."

"The way you did?"

"Feed on it. Fill yourself. Let it nourish you."

"Like a parasite draining a host?"

Elspeth held her tongue as they sat together and listened to the sky. The girl was right. She had closed her eyes to it and was subsequently enslaved by blindness.

It wasn't so bad, really.

At least there was safety in it.

Lilith

"Shit!"
Lilith stared in disbelief as the left heel of her red suede boots snapped off in a jagged patch of cobblestones a few yards from the Myling family residence in Sceptrelind.

She hadn't expected rain, especially the likes of this, streaming down the sides of her face and saturating her smartly-tailored, loden green cashmere coat. Her fragrance was alluring, much like that of a wet dog. She pushed her sopping hair out of her face and turned up the collar, but the coat remained lifeless and soggy.

On a day like today, she observed while gazing at the blanket of grey sky, Barterlind would be flooded with hover cars. Sceptrelind was so hickish.

She bent down to retrieve her heel from the angry, pointy-sharp cobblestone teeth. Spotting it, she wrenched it free and shoved it into her pocket. "Nine hundred bucks for these fuckers and the heel snaps off after two days," she growled silently. The cobblestones growled back. Her stomach chimed in harmoniously.

Just two days before, when Lilith and Ester had been

interviewed tandemly, a live audience of squealing fans had admired these very boots. She had managed to hide her jaded nature behind an impeccably groomed exterior. She had listened politely while her younger, up and coming colleague described her rudimentary experiences.

The same impeccability extended to her etiquette, ensuring a careful tongue when placed in front of an adoring audience. No one would guess that she was paying Ester Myling's parents a visit with the intention of telling them that their daughter was in trouble and needed to get the fuck out of this business before it was too late.

It was a tradeoff and an unfair one at that. It was a ruse designed to thwart your attention from the fact that you were being cheated out of your mind and your body. All the castles, loden green cashmere coats and red suede boots in the cosmos were insufficient compensation.

She had sensed something different about Ester as soon as they started working together. The universe didn't revolve around the thoughtful young woman. She was a fragment of it. A rare, bright and precious one. Lilith respected this and instinctively wanted to protect it.

Staying in the Luminatrix business would be suicide for Ester. Lilith felt certain of this. During the interview, Ester had described an unfinished series of Earth cases. She was too sensitive for such a heavy load and would most likely snap, much like her nine hundred dollar kicks. Hjulder would be only too happy overlook this casualty in exchange for two cents' worth of evolutionary insight. That was a steep price to pay for someone else's cheap shot. The sooner she put an end to it, the better.

She glanced down at the address scribbled on the waterlogged strip of paper, then looked back up at the house. 7 Storyville Lane appeared smaller and lonelier than she had anticipated. She cursed again, knowing that it would be damn near impossible to make a good impression while wearing wet cashmere. Lightning flashed, followed by a lagging, distant thunder clap as she approached the unadorned front door, which was the color of sun bleached bones. She hesitated then knocked, gathering up what remained of her dignity and courage.

She waited nearly thirty seconds without a response. "Hello?" She cupped her hand to a window just to the right of the door. "Mrs. Myling?"

She waited a few seconds and knocked again, but again nobody came. She tentatively turned the knob and was surprised to find that the door yielded and slowly creaked open.

Another lightning bolt sliced the night sky as Lilith stepped into the doorway. "Hello?" She stepped out of her boots and waited for a response. "Mrs. Myling?"

The house was dark except for the flickering light from a blaring television in a room off the hallway. Lilith peeled off her coat and hung it on the rack next to the door. Holding her elbows in apprehension, she took a few steps forward and peered into the room. She was suddenly face to face with herself.

"Tonight's rebroadcast is an evening with Lilith Brisbane, Hjulder's best and brightest, and Ester Myling, a rising new star with an exciting career ahead."

The host's voice was at once presentational and vapid. It belonged to Clyde Briberis, a popular tabloid reporter from Barterlind, and it was a voice Lilith would recognize anywhere. He had been a stage actor at one time but started covering news stories when the theater fell out of vogue about two decades before. He was the vainest man that Lilith had ever encountered. Which was saying something. Before the cameras started rolling, he barked at his crew for a solid hour until he was convinced that his hair, makeup, lighting and camera angles were spot on.

In the light from the television screen, Lilith could make out the kitchen from the hallway. The cold tile felt good beneath her feet, which were still burning from the pinch of her silly boots. She groped around the wall until she located a light switch. There was a note on the counter.

Back in two weeks, Lumen. Please water the plants and fetch the mail.

She opened the refrigerator and peered inside. A sizable platter was covered with tin foil. She lifted a corner of the foil. Underneath, she found a roasted chicken with cornbread dressing and gravy. Her eyes lit up. Her stomach screamed.

"I always admired you, Lilith, from the time I was a little girl," Ester's canned voice chirped from the family room. Lilith looked through the wooden bars of the kitchen partition to catch a glimpse of the program.

"Your appearance does not precede your accomplishments. Yet here you are, so beautiful!"

Lilith pushed her dripping, matted hair from her face and scowled. She should've never worn a tank top and red jeans to the interview. Despite the fact that a tailor had sewn the side pockets of the pants down to make her figure look narrower and her bones were sticking out everywhere, she looked like a bona fide hippo in front of the camera.

"When I was a little girl I begged my mom to let me have seaweed and mushrooms for dinner just like you!" Ester gushed in fangirl mode. "Do you still run for two hours each day? Are you still into inversion therapy?"

Lilith set the platter of chicken onto the counter. She pulled off a drumstick and brought it to her nose, inhaling. Six biscuits were lying in a plastic bag behind the space in the refrigerator where the platter had been. She snatched up the bag and set it next to the platter.

"Yes, please share your secrets for staying fit," Clyde grinned, staring at Lilith's breasts. Earlier that year, three hooligans had roughed him up in front of a popular bar in Phialind and knocked out four of his teeth. Lilith heard the scuffle outside and ran out to see what had happened. The perpetrators had scattered when she came out onto the sidewalk. Maybe she had screamed, maybe not. She only remembered kneeling beside him on the concrete and observing his mangled, bleeding mouth. "Wiwif!" he had cried in way she found grotesquely comical. "My teef! Fine a fucker a fucked up my teef!"

A large clump of cornbread dressing fell from the chicken and onto the counter. Lilith stared at it and tried to determine how many calories it contained.

"I fight tooth and nail for it, Clyde." She raised an eyebrow and winked. She caught him off guard with the comment, but he recovered his capped smile with a quickness. His profile was at a perfect angle in the lighting, which was positioned at the sides and from the back to give him a subtle ethereal quality not afforded his guests. He smoothed the side of his hair with his hand and began again.

"Tell us about your latest cases, ladies. Lilith, we'll start with you."

"Ester should go first." Lilith heard her voice drift from the television set. "I've been through so many before. I'd like to hear a fresh perspective."

Forty calories. Fifty, tops. The dressing was greasy, and a far cry from the raw vegan diet that she preferred. She might allow herself to make sparing exceptions, but chicken was just plain wrong.

A chicken wasn't an animal that Lilith would typically choose to consume. They were full of yellow fat and their skin was pocked and rubbery. Nor could you enjoy their blood. It was poison, everybody knew that.

Deer and elk, on the other hand, were creatures she might consider. They ran free in the wild with graceful, lilting energy. They were lean, sinewy and full of the spirit of the forest. The taste of their blood would nourish more than just her body; she could relate to the shapes of their souls.

"Lilith! Lilith!" the audience roared. She brushed her hands on her red, tailored jeans and slyly pushed the younger girl in front of the camera.

Maybe just a biscuit, she thought. They had been stored separately from the roast chicken, but not really. Biscuits were made with chicken eggs. Egg yolks were brimming with fat. Egg whites were brimming with mucous. But, supposing for the sake of supposing you were breaking it down to percentages. Eggs were only a binding ingredient, perhaps fifteen percent of the composition, if that. Biscuits were mainly flour and salt.

"I know how everyone likes a juicy love story, but I really don't have a romantic case to speak of just yet." Ester's voice was timid yet confident amid the barreling crowd. "But I'm still working on the Jana Case. She wasn't ready to accept me. I have to finish it."

Salt wasn't really an issue. Despite the hoopla about sodium restricted diets, salt was a friend to anyone with a raw foods lifestyle because it helped one's body maintain a steady mineral balance, and, when consumed with adequate fluids, prevented the onset of dehydration. Coarsely ground, non-iodized sea salt was best, of course, but that flour. It was white.

Clyde's powdered face perspired with lust. "Tell me more about this Jana Case," he said, raising a penciled eyebrow, "and why you didn't invite me to watch."

Lilith felt her cheeks darken. Despite herself, she actually felt embarrassed for him.

All of the nutrients in white flour had been bleached away, leaving just a sticky, intestine-clogging paste behind, but at least it was wheat. Wheat was a grain and therefore passable in tiny amounts, although generally not allowed when adhering to a raw foods regimen. She could make an exception.

Ester remained patient. "As I said earlier, the context wasn't romantic, but it's a very important case. Others were involved. A man named Lasse. A woman named Margaret. They're all connected to my future."

Except for the fact that wheat was the most indigestible grain there was, and if she were to make an exception for grain, the only tolerable ones would be oat groats, quinoa or millet.

"What did you say was the purpose of being there, again?" Clyde was losing interest. He caught a glimpse of his refection in a monitor and tilted his head.

Her favorite way to enjoy oat groats was by crushing them and blending them with herbal coffee substitute, agave syrup and ice to make a smoothie. She could make an exception for oat groats, but these biscuits were made of white flour. White flour was difficult to justify, but it was wheat. Wheat was a grain and thereby passable in small amounts, and while it was generally not allowed in a raw foods regimen she could make an exception. Wait a minute. Hadn't she just gone over this in her head? It had turned out to not be alright, right?

"Well, that's just it. I'm not finished with the Jana Case yet, but it's going to be prolific."

"Earth mama Jana?" Clyde was condescending.

"That's right," Ester said evenly.

"What about Margaret and Lasse? Will they be important cases, too?"

"No. But their children will be."

"Heavy!" Clyde pursed his lips.

"The Joseph Case," Lilith snapped, irritated by the way the smug, third-rate actor-turned-douchebag was treating Ester. "I lived in his house for eleven months. He stayed in the basement all the time working on chemical experiments. He forbade me to go down there because his projects were top secret. He hardly ever came upstairs. He said he didn't need a job because he'd invested his lab tech earnings in the stock market and turned a giant profit."

Chicken or biscuits, biscuits or chicken? At times like these it was best to simplify it to protein or carbohydrates. Cruciferous complex carbohydrates won over fatty animal protein every time, but then again, lean game was leagues ahead of the gluey white starch of simple carbohydrates. "Fuck!" Lilith snatched up the drumstick and bit into it greedily. The grease spread like a virus on her clean tongue and stormed her senses like a sniper's bullet.

"One day, Joseph's friend, Peter, stopped by the house. He brushed past me and went into the basement where Joseph was, despite my protesting. I could hear them arguing; it was intense and angry. It worried me, so I opened the door a crack and yelled down the steps to see if everything was okay. Joseph snapped at me. He said they were fine and told me to drive to the store to pick up something for dinner. I hadn't planned on going out; we lived in a rural area and the closest grocery store was ten miles away. Anyway, I got into the car and drove to the market. I took my time picking out food. I wasn't looking forward to coming back to a fight."

She ran out of the kitchen and down the hallway to the bathroom. A digital scale decorated with a fluffy pink cover lay on the floor. She stepped on it and waited for the results to register. 108. She stepped off and tried five seconds later. 108.5.

It had to be a mistake. The drumstick was the only thing she had eaten all day. Her penultimate meal of thirty-and-one-half kernels of popcorn had been consumed the evening before. A carefully rationed amount of popcorn could never cause a weight gain overnight, but it was salted popcorn, and the sodium could contribute to water retention. However, salt was your friend on a raw foods diet. The minerals were important, but popcorn wasn't raw and didn't require mineral supplementation, so now she was paying for the thrill of the moment. Additionally, she really hadn't needed the extra half kernel; she had told herself that at the time. The thrill and the salt were both long gone, but here she was, consequently overweight some twenty-four hours later with no one to blame but herself. She stripped naked and stepped back on the scale. 106. She turned the scale forty-five degrees to the right and tried again. 105.5.

Hot tears streamed down her face as she put her clothes back on and wandered back into the kitchen. The chicken basked in the spotlight of the counter as the television audience clapped. Lilith sniffed it longingly. Then she carefully replaced the aluminum foil and returned the platter back to the refrigerator. Holding her stomach, she walked to the family room and collapsed wearily into the couch. She stared at the television and tried to ignore her fatigue.

"When I arrived back at the house about an hour and a half later, Peter's truck was still in front of the house. I went to the basement door and called out to Joseph. He said he was busy. I made dinner. A half hour later, he came up the steps. I asked him if Peter was staying for dinner. He told me that Peter had run off after the argument. So I asked him why Peter's truck was still in front of the house. He stammered a bit, then told me Peter had a few shots of whiskey and was too drunk to drive. Joseph drove off in Peter's car later on that night. He came back on foot, when I was almost asleep. When the police came by a few days later, they told us that they had found Peter's body a few miles away, and wondered if we knew anything about it. Joseph stammered again, but they had a search warrant. He tried to keep them from going down into the basement, but they pushed past him anyway. They found his meth lab and a good deal of Peter's blood. They took him away in handcuffs. I never saw him again."

Lilith laughed wryly as she sank deeper into the Myling's couch and reached into her pocket for a vial of cocaine. She collected a bit with a practiced scoop of her pinky finger and snorted.

Clyde Briberis was milking the moment for everything it was worth. The audience was gasping with the shock and thrill of it all. Ester appeared painfully distracted. Despite the uncomfortable looking studio chair, she pulled her legs close to her body and sat with her hand over her heart.

"Leave, Ester!" Lilith grumbled to the image on the screen. "Come on, kid! Can't you see it's going to kill you? Do you really want to go back to some Earth mother who isn't ready for you? Do you really want to get involved with her creepy friends and their degenerate offspring?"

"That's our go getter!" Clyde crooned. "The experiences that you ladies endure may seem hurtful, dangerous even, but think of all the good you're doing for our planet. You're helping Hjulder advance, and why should you complain? I mean, something had to pay for those boots! Great boots, Lilith! May I? Nice! Money well spent! Look at how sturdy these heels are. So solidly made." He moved his jaw a strategic centimeter to the left. "What was the lesson of the Joseph Case, Lilith?"

"Wanna know the truth about the Joseph Case?" Lilith spoke loudly over the sound of the television, snorting more cocaine from the vial and indulging a two-dimensional Clyde in an obscene hand gesture. "I'd be glad to share! For starters, cocaine is a much better choice than crystal meth." She rubbed her puffy red eyelids and paused to light a cigarette. "And second, when spilling blood, be very, very particular about the animal you choose!"

She watched the television until the end credits rolled. It was useless to wait any longer. The note on the counter said the Mylings were out of town. It was unlikely that she would stop by to see them again. Sceptrelind was a one-horse town, and she had things to do.

"Sorry, Ester," Lilith mumbled. "I tried. I really did." She walked over to the coat rack and slipped into her soggy coat and boots. She extended a shaky hand, closed the door of the cozy house behind her and set out lopsidedly, heel in hand, into the violence of the night.

Jana

"Daughter, I'd like to have a word with you at this very moment, if you don't mind. Where are you now? Where do I really come from?"

When she overheard Jana's musings for the first time, Gladys Montgomery stood right where she was and dropped her Pyrex bowl. Eggs and glass shattered across her shiny kitchen tiles like fireworks.

"Who did it?" she demanded. Her circle skirt swirled around her calves as she fled to the kitchen table, buried her head in her hands and wept.

"I never said I had her yet," Jana explained. "But it doesn't mean she can't answer me."

Gladys continued to cry. Her daughter's clarification was of little consolation. She couldn't digest the words completely, but one thing was perfectly clear: her hopes of becoming Audrey Hepburn someday were forever out of reach.

Her new powder blue cardigan with the rhinestone buttons and contrasting yellow ribbon trim was powerless against the likes of this blast. This alone was more than enough of an excuse to flee the kitchen and retrieve the nerve pills on her bedroom dresser. She stood up with a flourish, brushed off her skirt and dramatically crunched an eggshell with the sole of her yellow kitten heel. "Pick that up, will you?" she drawled. Then she bounded up the stairs and angrily slammed her bedroom door behind her, leaving her twelve-year-old daughter to clean up the mess.

A few hours later, Harlan Montgomery's car engine clattered up to the driveway. Refreshed by her nerve pills, Gladys floated down the staircase to greet him at the door.

"How was it?" she asked.

He kissed his wife and hung his hat on the coat rack. "My meeting, my business."

Emptying his pockets, he placed his keys and a silver dollar onto the coffee table before collapsing on the sofa and picking up a copy of *The Citizens' Council*. He glanced at the headline.

"You hear the news about Brown versus Topeka? Them boys in Arkansas better get on back if they know what's good for them. That's all I can say."

Gladys put a hand to the back of her hair. With a low voice, she told her husband what had transpired in the kitchen earlier that day.

Jana had no understanding of how to relate to her father because he was a caricature.

Living under his roof had left her more than familiar with his halitosis, his flatulence and the dusty smell of his clothing, but when it came to his personality, one note and one note alone was accessible to his family and community, like a trilobite stuck nosediving in limestone. A conscionable human being would have long revealed his inner workings to his family, but it never happened with him. Not even by default or accident. He was a perfect stranger. An enigma. And not a good one, either.

Relating to a caricature was stressful enough; being the

daughter of one was worse. It was a loaded responsibility that required consistent foresight and strategy on her part, which was a lot more than she had signed up for at birth.

Sometimes she let her guard down and wasn't as careful as she needed to be. It was a slippery slope because she didn't know who she was facing. To her eyes, his puffing on the church stage was an attempt at deflecting from a state of inner weakness. Was he dangerous? The weak ones always were.

Existing within his domicile was like living hand to mouth in the purest sense. She always had to think ahead and protect herself. The collective majority of her twelve years had been spent in a pattern of self-government. It was exhausting. It was like being a lifelong orphan but worse. Orphans knew exactly where they stood. She envied them.

"There'll be no immaculate conception under my roof," Harlan told his daughter as the family sat down to a dinner of leftover ham. "God's got his sights set higher than you. Just eat."

Jana glared. It came as no surprise that her mother had, in her usual manner of cowardice and deference, redacted the story to make her words more palatable. A daughter with a Madonna complex, however misguided and delusional, was noble. A heretic daughter? Not so much.

"I never said I was carrying the Messiah, but my daughter's a star, too. A different kind, though." She spit a clove into her napkin.

Harlan was unnerved. It was downright unsettling to dissect the logic of having to make a child before it existed. Any six-year-old would understand it, and his daughter was twice that age. But he would sooner die than admit she scared him. The world was spinning out of control as it was. The way things were heading these days she could disgrace him. Ruin him. Grow up and steal his followers, even. There was no room for interpretation; he had to protect his legacy. God would understand. He was the reverend, after all.

Miles away from the confrontation, Gladys was enjoying a pleasant buzz brought on by her last two nerve pills. Her eyes wandered to a patch of congealed yolk that Jana had missed on the tiles.

"Satan!" Harlan challenged. "You can't have my daughter. She's mine."

At least she was as skinny as Audrey Hepburn. She stared at her uneaten portion of ham and smiled. Perking up, she glanced at the liquor cabinet in the adjoining room and wondered if there was any vermouth left. Her rhinestone buttons sparkled. It was going to be okay.

"What does the devil have to do with it, Dad? He can't make souls. I'm pretty sure he didn't make the stars, either."

He was losing, and that called for putting on a show. He seized Jana's glass of milk and poured it into her plate for effect. Then he gnashed his teeth and pounded on the table, upsetting a sauceboat of gravy in the process.

"You can't have my daughter, Satan! She's mine! She's my property. She belongs to me!"

Harlan stood up from the table. Fingering a corner of the white linen tablecloth, he pulled menacingly. Ham, peas, gravy, and plates flew in the air before landing onto the black and white tiles in an explosive heap. Gladys flinched momentarily and shielded her clothing from harm's way.

He turned to his wife. "We can't send her away to get help. People will blame us. I'm the reverend!" He turned his back and looked to the sky for an answer.

A stray wedge of ham and a single pea landed next to the patch of yolk. *Ham and eggs.* The laugh track inside Gladys' head roared ferociously. Her mouth twitched.

"Harlan." The syllables of her husband's name felt like an alien grade of velvet in her mouth and nothing like the compact, rigid-minded man had she had married.

"She's not allowed to talk or leave. Ever again. You hear me?"

"Harlan," Gladys willed her face to appear concerned and smiled at her success. "She has to go to church. She has to go to school. She has to buy dresses. Ribbons!"

"You can make her dresses, Gladys."

"Do you expect me to make her ribbons, Harlan?"

"Dad?"

"Shut it! Both of you. I said, not one more word!"

She was mostly silent after that, but her beet-faced father continued to strut and preen inside the chapel that marked the cornerstone for the town's spiritual activities. She did, however clear her throat audibly when she witnessed her father staggering out from behind an abandoned building with a meticulously painted woman. As plain as day, she had watched her father remove his hand from the woman's behind. Harlan, however, chose to overlook this particular expression of mutiny. Throat clearing didn't count, really. Especially where whores were concerned.

Gladys' patience with her daughter's gestational theatrics was waning. She dug a fingernail into Jana's ribcage whenever she caught her caressing her stomach and vowed to draw blood if absolutely necessary. In truth, her mother had little reason to be concerned; any amateur talent that Jana possessed was eclipsed by the spectacles that unfolded on the church stage.

Every outburst that occurred during the Sunday services competed to outdo the next. The milkman spouted glossolalia. The occasional snake sought freedom from the wire cages on the altar. The latter incited even the most sullen of children to attention, but Jana remained unmoved. She kept her head bowed and tuned out her surroundings. Little by little, her hands crept back to her stomach.

One day, a water moccasin snake escaped from the cage and

slithered down the aisle. Jana glanced at the snake nervously and shifted in her seat. Gladys felt her fidgeting and poked. The crowd brought its hands together in a burst of gratuitous clapping.

"Brimstone! Fire!"

Harlan's words sprayed the front row of the congregation as the snake crawled on its belly towards the back of the church at an alarming speed. Alarmed parents grabbed their children and clustered towards the middle of the pews for safety, but Harlan spread his arms in triumph and ran into the aisles.

Touched by the Holy Spirit, the audience fainted and slumped to their seats. Gladys eyed her daughter's traveling hand and jabbed her in the ribs again.

"Ow! Mom, stop it!"

The room fell silent. Everyone turned to stare in Jana's direction. The snake found its way to the entrance of the church and wriggled out the open front door.

"Chokehold of desire!" Harlan spat. He locked eyes with his daughter. A baby in the back row wailed in discontent.

After the service, the family shared a picnic lunch under a maple tree on the marshy bank bordering the river. Jana watched her father wave to a young couple he had married earlier that year. The woman was about eight months pregnant. She breathed heavily and knelt down with great difficulty as her husband spread a tablecloth onto the grass a few yards away.

Jana unfastened the basket of chicken, parted a nest of napkins and helped herself to a drumstick. "Is desire really meant to be a chokehold?" she asked, frowning.

He snatched the drumstick out of her hand and closed his eyes before turning to his wife. "Must I," he began in a controlled voice, "be subjected to her blasphemy every single day of my life? Why can't you do something?"

Overpowered by the cloud of acrid breath, Gladys breathed into her napkin discreetly.

An elderly man leaned against a cane and nodded in their

direction. "Great sermon, Reverend!"

Harlan tipped his hat. "Thank you, Mr. Percy!"

Jana took advantage of the diversion by reclaiming her chicken. "I don't experience desire that way." She bit into the drumstick hungrily.

Harlan grabbed a wing from the picnic basket and pointed it at his daughter. "Stop it." His breath was metered.

"It's because I'm a girl, isn't it? Nothing I ever say or do matters so long as you can blame me for it, right?"

"Actions have consequences. For instance, if you painted your face and ran around town naked it might be difficult for you to find a respectable husband and provide a first born son."

"Because that would be wrong?"

"Yes."

She held her father's gaze and cleared her throat emphatically. She glanced at her mother. Gladys stared at the maple tree and sipped from a thermos of lemonade.

Harlan shrugged and bit into the chicken wing. "Yet you speak to the devil and pass him off as your bastard child. That, daughter, is worse. A whole lot worse."

The rest of the town looked forward to the sound and spectacle of Reverend Montgomery's weekly sermons, but Jana was only in it for ice cream.

After the picnic dinner, Gladys packed up the basket and spread the blue cotton picnic blanket across the front seat of the Montgomery's Ford sedan. Jana crawled into the back seat and waited for her parents without speaking to anyone. Harlan basked in the attention of the townsfolk with the swollen pride of a blowfish.

The transmission clattered as the Ford crawled away from the church. Jana watched the clusters of antebellum homes lining the sage-colored river pass by like pages in a storybook and wondered why she had been born into the life she lived.

They passed through the bluff, under the hill and into an outlying area of swampland. Shotgun houses rested among the willowy grass blades turning cool with the promise of sunset.

A small bonfire smoked to the side of a house where a sinewy black woman hung wet laundry from a tree branch. Her flowing skirt and matching headdress were made of moss colored linen.

Her regal neck curved demurely into graceful, sculpted shoulders. She gathered her skirt off the ground with one hand and selected a sheet from a wicker basket. The fluidity of her motions transformed her arms into wings. Jana was transfixed.

A boy and a girl, about four and five with reddish brown complexions that reminded Jana of her mother's homemade gingerbread, ran from the direction of the neighboring house, shrieking with peals of laughter. They sobered when they saw the Ford and retreated to the folds of the woman's skirts.

The woman stopped what she was doing and stood tall and serene. She put her arm around the girl and held her hand out to the boy. The girl hid her face. The boy stared at the Ford through unbelievably long eyelashes and sucked his fingers.

Gladys put a hand to the back of her hair and pretended not to notice. Harlan focused on the steering wheel. Jana waited until the boy made eye contact with her. She leaned against the window and waved gently. The boy continued to hold onto the woman's hand, but Jana thought that she could see the slightest tinge of raspberry flushing through his cheeks and nose. His lips curved ever so slightly as he raised a trembling hand in response.

The car lurched forward abruptly.

"Watch it, Dad!"

"You're the one who needs to watch it." His knuckles were white as they gripped the steering wheel.

"Watch what?" Jana prodded.

Holding the steering wheel in one hand, Harlan turned around in his seat and squarely grasped Jana's throat with the other. She gasped for breath and clutched both hands around her father's wrist in an attempt to free herself.

"Satan!" he spat. "What demon possessed you, Gladys? I've told you before she didn't come from me! I know she didn't come from me!"

"Harlan, stop it!" Gladys slapped the back of her husband's head as he veered into the path of an oncoming tree and wrenched his hand from her daughter's throat. Jana collapsed against the back of the seat, coughing.

"What demon possessed you, Gladys?" He mumbled to himself before gazing at his wife. "Was it that flower man who stayed at Ledford's Inn during my retreat coming up on thirteen years ago? What was his name again, Linden Woods?"

"What?"

"That horticulture fellow named Linden Woods said he wanted the town to take their hard earned money away from the church and start a flower society and an aviary. He was staying here at the time of my Tennessee retreat. Widow Ledford said you made him a peach pie."

"What exactly are you accusing me of?" Gladys' tone was terrible.

"Calling birds and planting flowers and sprouting the seeds of Satan himself." Laughing aloud, he narrowed his eyes at Jana in the rear view mirror. "She ain't one of us! Our hair's brown and hers is blonde! That flower man had blond hair too!" Gladys shook her head furiously.

Jana placed her hands gently across her belly. "It's okay if you don't look like me. I don't mind."

Exasperated by the onset of yet another gestational ranting, Gladys prayed. "Sweet Jesus," she began. "Mary, full of grace."

"Because your hair is illuminated by pearls and crystals and styled by a mermaid who lives underwater. Your dresses are made from gold moss and vines. And when you turn in profile to face the magical moons that always surround you, the birds cannot fly. They can only stumble beneath the weight of their hearts because your radiant beauty intoxicates them. All the boys want to dance with you. Sometimes you waltz, sometimes you move to a drumbeat, but you don't have to stay with them if you're unhappy. You can always leave."

Gladys turned her ear towards the back seat. She didn't fully understand her daughter's rantings, but listening to them was oddly calming.

"I can't talk to her," the reverend whined. "Did you teach her this? Where does she get this?"

"And I'm tired of wearing dresses all the time. You'd think I was going to visit the White House," Jana added defiantly. "You can wear pants if you want to. I don't think it's a sin."

The reverend looked lost. Suddenly aware of his failing façade, he remembered his purpose and angrily drew his body upwards, pulling the car to a curbside halt in front of Stack's Ice Cream Shop.

A freckled boy on a bicycle passed on the side of the passenger window, waving and ringing his bell. Gladys dabbed her eyes with her handkerchief and quietly cleared her throat. Feigning a smile for the boy on the bicycle, the reverend gritted his teeth so tightly that Jana suspected they would crumble and break.

"Serpent!" her father mumbled as he turned off the ignition. "What else have you got to say for yourself?"

By closing her eyes and slowly exhaling, Jana hoped to will away the onset of her tears and regain the air of confidence that always marked a victory over her father and rendered him futile. She succeeded. She brushed off her dress. "I sure would love some ice cream, Dad," she answered, managing a tiny smile. Harlan glared as his wife and daughter got out of the car and walked to the door of the shop. He cursed under his breath and followed them inside.

Sleigh bells sounded as they walked into the front door. Stevie

Stack looked up from polishing the stainless steel appliances that lined the counter, set down his rag and smiled dazzlingly as the Montgomery family approached him. Harlan ordered a banana split and slid into an adjacent booth with his wife. Jana sat at the counter and ordered a double dip strawberry cone.

"When you gonna run off and marry me for good, Miss Jana Montgomery?" Stevie Stack murmured in a low voice, eyeing the peculiar blonde girl with the mess of frizzy curls who sat before him. He tucked his chin into his neck, widened his eyes like a puppy dog and wrinkled up his forehead before handing over her ice cream.

She wondered who had told him he looked cute when he did that. She also wondered if he made a point of remembering to use that face with every girl he came into contact with, or if it was instinctual by now. He was like a statue sculpted from marble: finely chiseled but devoid of detail beyond the surface. She could see the pitifully predictable wheels turning at half speed behind his eyes and wondered why she bothered being polite.

He was the son of Arnold Stack, the shop's owner, and a tenth-semester junior and former football scholar at Mississippi State University. During the summers, he returned to Natchez and helped his father in the shop. Most of the local girls seemed to swoon beneath his advances.

"Let's see, Stevie," she patronized. "I have to start and finish high school. Then there'll probably be a post graduate year or two to compensate for my back of the woods education. By then I'll be ready for my scholarship to the university. After that, I'll be heading off to medical school. That sure is a long time for a fine fellow like you to wait."

"Aww, Jana," he rattled. "No one needs all that school. Elope with me tonight." He abandoned his dishrag and walked around the counter. He dropped to his knees at Jana's feet. He took her hands in his, indulging the chance to tuck his chin into his neck, widen his eyes like a puppy dog and wrinkle up his forehead yet another time. Jana prayed for a miracle.

There was a knock at the side door. A black man opened it and stood in the doorway, carrying a large bundle of napkins and tableware. He was approximately thirty years old, and had pouty lips, full cheeks, and long, curly lashes.

"Hi, Stevie. Is your father here today?"

Stevie nodded stiffly and turned towards the back room.

"Hi, Lonnie."

A voice that was neither rude nor friendly boomed from the back room. It was followed by an older version of Stevie. Arnold Stack had a receding brown hairline streaked with grey and a tidy moustache. "I wasn't expecting you 'til Wednesday."

Arnold glanced around the room and saw Reverend and Mrs. Montgomery seated at a booth, finishing up their banana split. "Hello, Reverend. Gladys." He waved in acknowledgement and smiled. "How's the banana split?"

"Mighty fine as usual, Arnold." Harlan smiled in response. Feigning satisfaction, Gladys raised her eyebrows and pretended to take a bite.

Arnold rubbed his hands together and turned his attention back to Lonnie. "That's right, Lonnie," he repeated. "I wasn't expecting you 'til Wednesday after closing."

"I work fast," Lonnie said. "I finished the linens already. I thought you could probably use them early."

Arnold Stack walked up to Lonnie and took the bundle from him. He placed it on the counter and began to critically inspect the linens, hem by hem. "They do all look good to me, Lonnie. You sure are quick with a needle and thread. Well, I'll be. All right then."

He moved away from the bundle and took a key out of his pocket. "All right, Lonnie, you just wait a minute and I'll go get your money." He turned to face the booths. "Reverend!" he cried out jovially. "I'll be right back. I want to talk to you."

Harlan stood up and folded his napkin next to the empty dish.

"I'm afraid we have to get going. It's getting pretty late."

"So soon?"

"I'll see you on Thursday." He walked towards the counter. "Come along, Jana," he said in his best company voice. "Your precious Stevie will have to wait." He placed his hand lightly on her shoulder. "Come on."

Jana eyed her father with alacrity and ignored the grinning fool behind the counter. She did, however, nod politely to Lonnie when he cordially acknowledged the Montgomery family as they walked to the door. Gladys' eyes widened ever so slightly. Harlan's hand was still resting on Jana's shoulder. His fingers turned into claws.

"What's going on in your life right now, baby girl?" Jana thought to herself. "Do you have friends to keep you company, or are you lonesome? Do you have enough to eat, or are you hungry? Do you dream at night? Are you safe?"

At school, proud cheerleaders pirouetted front and center in the hallway as her rounded shoulders grazed the stale cinder walls. Rumor had it that she wasn't the reverend's real daughter, which essentially relegated her to the lowest rung of social hierarchy. She didn't care. Partially hidden behind a lioness mane of blonde tangles, she hung her head, clutched a pile of books to her chest protectively and sat at the back of the classroom, daydreaming.

When she came home, she paused briefly at the refrigerator for a snack before retreating to the privacy of her bedroom. It took her all of twenty minutes to complete the facile school assignments. After that, she scoured her bookcase and lost herself inside a collection of horror stories. That was when the real lessons began.

In H.P. Lovecraft's The *Outsider*, a ghoul escaped the confines of its tomb, only to glimpse its terrifying reflection in a mirror, return to the shelter of the tomb again, and find it locked. The lesson? When you discover who you truly are, there's no turning back.

Ambrose Bierce's *A Vine on a House* was another favorite. Time and ambivalence conspired to hide the uxoricide of a one-footed woman, but a rogue vine growing in the likeness of her body ultimately betrayed her husband. The lesson? The truth always comes out eventually.

Not that her bend was entirely sinister. She liked a good fairy tale, too. In The Brothers Grimm's *Aschenputtel*, two sisters amputated their own toes to fit into a golden slipper. The lesson? Princes over selves, it seemed. But no matter the story's end, the compromised footing of women was invariable.

Life lessons brought the need for comfort, and Jana had favorites for that as well. She faithfully read a chapter from Kahlil Gibran's *The Prophet* every morning before going off to school. The Bhagavad Gita was something she hoped to discuss with anyone who had the capacity to isolate religion from philosophy. Regrettably, she didn't know of any such being.

Gladys watched her daughter disappear into her room every day with a new stack of books and decided that it would be best to support her interests in the best way she could. She knocked on Jana's door one evening, arms loaded down with a stack of *Ladies' Home Journal* and *Redbook* magazines.

"I thought you might like these since you like reading so much." She put a hand to the back of her hair and sat down on the pink bedspread. "The pictures are pretty, too. I thought you might like looking at the dresses and the lipsticks."

Jana looked down at the magazine cover at the top of the pile. Suzy Parker was dressed in a fashionable grey suit. She wore a casual white scarf tied at her neck, tortoiseshell sunglasses and a matte red smile. Jana looked back at her mother. Everything about her seemed so appropriately polished.

"Thanks, Mom. I thought I wasn't allowed to wear lipstick."

"Not around your father, but I think some of these dresses would be pretty on you." She looked at her daughter's matted curls. "And some of these hairdos are very smart."

Jana put her hand to her hair and felt the knots forming at the base of her neck.

"Can I, uh, bring you a sandwich or something?"

"No thanks, Mom. I had an apple."

"Well alright then. I guess I'll see you at dinner." Gladys stood up to leave. She looked uncomfortable.

She closed the door behind her mother and flipped through a magazine. Changing her mind, she went to her bookcase and pulled out her copy of The Bible.

Her father's angry, fear-based sermons seemed antithetical to her idea of mysterious desert sabbaticals fueled by visions, vibrations, and fragrant clouds of frankincense and myrrh. In her mind, The Bible meant gathering herbs and baking loaves from ancient grains, or catching trout in the river, roasting it over an open fire and sharing it with newfound friends. Harlan had it all wrong.

It was just before sunset. Through the descending clouds, she thought she could just make out the light of the star that had illuminated the wise men's path.

Three men had loaded their camels with cumbersome gifts and traveled over the mountains. They were hungry, smelly and had likely engaged in multiple fist fights before their task was complete. They found a miracle nestled deep in a cave—hidden from Herod's cronies by a spider's web concealing the entrance. If the North Star was an oracle that somehow led to treasure, she, too, could follow its lead. Surely there were other miracles waiting to be had.

She was vaguely aware of the sound of her father coming home and the faint clattering of dinner plates. A waft of roast beef came and went, as did the repetitive clattering of a martini shaker. Eventually, her surroundings ebbed away, and the Mississippi sky grew solemn and black. She dreamed of sparkling sand.

A few hours later, she was awakened by the faint hooting of an owl and rose out of bed to investigate. Outside her window, the stars were pinpointed like needles on a compass. In that moment, she knew exactly what to do.

She opened her bedroom door as quietly as she could and tiptoed to the staircase landing. Olive-littered glasses and an empty gin bottle were abandoned on the cocktail table. Based on the density of snores emanating from her parents' bedroom, she estimated that her father had consumed three martinis. Judging from the size of the mess that hadn't been cleared from the living room, she deduced that her mother had finished four.

She tiptoed down the stairs and into the kitchen. Working quickly, she stuffed a paper bag with apples, carrots, and pecans. She wondered if Audrey Hepburn drank herself to sleep every night.

She closed the front door silently. Placing the bag of food down on the doorstep momentarily, she paused at the base of a tree and pried away a tall branch. With her fingers curled confidently around her newfound staff, she proudly tapped the ground and set off on her way.

It wasn't cold outside, but she was grateful for her sweater. The thick cotton protected her shoulders from the tree branches as she followed the North Star and sauntered off the road. She clawed her way through thick, wooded brush and stopped to rest in a small clearing.

The tree branches wavered as she enjoyed her modest meal. Pleased to have a visitor, the river beckoned like a naughty temptress.

Three wise men once bathed in a river just like this.

Taking the bait, she stepped out of her dress and dipped a toe into the shimmering water.

The mud that squished between her toes was surprisingly warm. She arched her back and eased her head down. Her hair grew heavy under the water's murky caress. She rolled onto her stomach and took a few more steps. Her fingers grazed a ropelike plant. She pulled and it came loose in her hand. She held it up to her nose, sniffed it, and put it her mouth. She chewed and chewed, but it was very rubbery, so she released it and watched it briefly float at the surface before sinking back down to the bottom.

She thought it would be pleasant to stay naked for a while but knew that she needed to leave. She crawled back to the clearing, stepped into her dress, and knotted the hem around her thighs.

Her newfound cleanliness heightened her sense of vulnerability as the landscape grew dense and wild. She had expected a journey of solitude but soon realized the woods were teeming with life. The sounds and movements were subtle, but the vibrations were deep and supernatural. All attempts to quicken her pace were futile. Vines and branches coiled around her ankles, seized her shoulders and slapped her in the face. She hacked at them with her walking stick. It snapped into two useless pieces. The oppressive humidity of the atmosphere filled her lungs and left her gasping for breath.

Tree branches intertwined themselves in her hair. She removed them and wrapped the sweater around her head. Uncertain of her bearings, she circled around for a few moments before locating the star again and reclaiming her path. The faint trace of a small cabin became visible in the distance.

She plowed on in pursuit of another clearing, only to trip over a decaying log that housed a sleeping water moccasin snake. It lunged forward, bit her on the arm, and slithered off towards the water, leaving her alone with the sound of her cries and the indifferent warbling of the river.

Lonnie

"Moose?" Lonnie looked up from his sketchpad and towards the ladder that led to the bedroom loft. He slowly rose from the kitchen table and walked over to the pot of stew warming on the stove. He stirred it with a wooden spoon and tasted it. He wrinkled his nose and added a touch of salt. Dinah Washington wailed from the record player. He swayed his hips to the beat.

"Moose!" Lonnie bellowed. He took two wooden bowls out of the cupboard next to the stove and placed them on the counter. He filled the bowls with stew and started towards the table. He placed them on the kitchen table and turned towards the loft. He jumped in surprise at the sight of Moose descending from the ladder. "Why didn't you answer me? Aren't you a bit big to be creeping around?" He patted his chest. "Don't you know how delicate I am?"

"I answered you the first time," Moose was indignant as he climbed down the ladder. "But you didn't hear it." He walked over to the record player and turned it down. "Nobody told you to blast that hyena so loud until I can't hear myself think and you can't hear me answering."

"Then put that depressing Bessie Smith back on and stop complaining," Lonnie said. "And have some of the dinner that I slaved over a hot stove to make while you're at it. But first, take a look at my new creation."

"Stew?" Moose was sarcastic. He lifted the Dinah Washington record off of the record player and replaced it with Bessie Smith. "Tell me Lonnie, are we really having stew again?"

Lonnie smirked. "If you wanna eat the bacon, you'd better learn to bring some home. Now bring your behind over here and take a look at my work."

Moose eyed the sketchpad. "What's that? Designer tablecloths for Arnold Stack?"

Lonnie pursed his lips and rounded his shoulders.

"I didn't mean that," Moose apologized. "I was just teasing. I'm sorry." He walked over to Lonnie and enveloped him in his arms. They kissed.

Lonnie took him by the hand and led him back to the table. He handed Moose a sketch. "It's perfect for the lavender organza I have. It's a bias cut, and the skirt is a little bit straighter than what they're wearing now. Trust me, by the time the sixties roll around, all the ladies will be wearing straight skirts. I know I can sell it. Look." He pulled a magazine from a stack of papers, flipped through the pages and rested on an image of Jane Russell. "Now picture the dress coming to life. Picture it on her."

Moose briefly studied the picture of Jane Russell and looked back at the sketch. "A bias cut organza gown?"

"Yeah."

"On that behind?"

They giggled. Lonnie put spoons next to the bowls while Moose continued to flip through the magazine. He stopped at a full-length photo of Suzy Parker. "I can picture your design on a beanpole like this."

"On who?" Lonnie asked. He sat down at the table and peered over Moose's shoulder. "Oh. Her." He rolled his eyes.

"What'd I say now?" Moose looked puzzled. "I just think the line of a bias cut gown would fall better on someone with less, uh, stature."

"No you didn't just put my dress on Suzy Parker," Lonnie continued. He turned up his nose and pursed his lips.

"Who's Suzy Parker?" Moose asked.

"That's Suzy Parker," Lonnie answered. He narrowed his eyes into a witchy glint. He shook his head and crossed his arms to his chest.

"You don't think she's right for the dress?"

"Nope. Wrap her bony ass up in a white sheet."

Moose raised an eyebrow and studied the picture. "What about her hair? Dippity Do?"

"Nope." Lonnie mockingly raised a hand to the back of his razored cut and pretended to shake it out. "A white pillowcase will be fine."

"How about her face?" Moose goaded, thoroughly enjoying himself. "Max Factor makeup? False lashes?"

"Cut out some eyeholes." Lonnie puckered his lips. He put his hands on his hips and swayed to the music.

The mood was jovial as they ate. Lonnie was flipping through the magazine and Moose was dishing out a second helping when they heard a cry for help followed by a weak rap at the front door. They stood up abruptly.

"What's that?" Moose said. He walked over to the nearest window and pulled down the shade. "You didn't latch the door, fool!" He sounded harsher than he had intended.

Lonnie tried to conceal his fear. "It's just a girl, Moose!"

Moose eyed the closed door with suspicion. "Doesn't matter. Get the rifle!"

Lonnie walked briskly towards the back room.

"Somebody help me, somebody please help me!" the voice

called out with urgency. Moose stood to the right of the door. Lonnie returned with the rifle in his arms. He pointed the barrel towards the door and stood off to the left.

Moose opened the door to the darkness. A girl lay there. She appeared to be about thirteen or fourteen. Her head was partially wrapped in a filthy, tattered cardigan sweater. Blonde matted curls littered with twigs peeked out from underneath. Her eyes were circled and wild. Her face and legs were dirty. Her dress was torn. She clutched frantically at her left arm.

"Jesus Christ!" Lonnie said. He lowered the barrel.

Jana swallowed and tried to ignore the dizziness she felt, the ringing in her ears, and the fact that her eyes wouldn't focus. "Please help," she croaked. "I've been bit."

"What are you doing here?" Moose asked. "Who are your people?"

"Across the bluff," Jana murmured. She stood up halfway and stumbled back to her knees.

He knelt beside her and gently examined her arm. Swollen puncture wounds were visible through her torn sleeve.

"Help me get her inside."

Lonnie stared at the matted hair littered with twigs. "We don't know her," he protested, arms crossed in front of his body.

Moose slid his fingers up her neck and felt for her pulse. "Aren't you going to help me?"

"Maybe we shouldn't be doing this."

"You'd rather let her die?"

"What if someone finds her here? What if she needs a hospital? What if her people are right behind her and see her with us at one o'clock in the morning?" Lonnie narrowed his eyes and took a step back.

Moose shrugged and dropped Jana's left side back to the ground. "Fine." He crossed his arms to match Lonnie's. "Go on and let her die, then."

Lonnie pulled her up by her right side. She moaned. "I didn't say that! I was just asking what we should do!"

"Well, I tell you what she's going to do," Moose snarled. "She's going to die right here if you keep sitting up here acting foolishly and then what're we going to do?"

Lonnie stood firm. "Her folks come around looking for her and your flaming ass is going to be hanging from a tree. Then what're you going to do?"

"What would Jesus do?" Jana whimpered. She started to wheeze.

Feeling ashamed, the men scrambled to pick her up. They carried her over to an easy chair by the record player and gently sat her down. "Everything will be just fine, miss," Moose said. Jana nodded her chin and closed her eyes. Moose grasped her chin between his thumb and forefinger. "But you have to stay with us. You hear me? Stay awake. Okay?"

Jana nodded.

Moose untied the cardigan sweater that was wrapped around her head and picked a few twigs out of her hair.

"I'm going sit here with you, and Lonnie's going to get a knife and we'll get you fixed up, okay? But you have to stay awake."

Her head fell back. The ceiling clouded over. When her eyes focused, Lonnie came towards her with a knife, a wooden spoon, a piece of elastic, a bucket of steaming water and a washcloth.

"I'll suck out the poison, but I'm not cutting anyone," Lonnie said. He washed Jana's wound with steaming water and tied elastic above her elbow. He handed Moose the knife.

"It's okay," Moose repeated. Jana whimpered. "Just relax." He looked at Lonnie. "That blade's clean?"

Lonnie nodded. "I stuck it in the fire." "Get the moonshine," Moose ordered. "And a glass."

Lonnie obliged. Moose cradled Jana's head and tilted it back. He poured a generous shot of the whiskey and urged it to Jana's lips. "What's your name?" he asked.

"Jana," she murmured.

"All right then, Jana. Just take a little sip to ease the sting."

Jana eased her head up and wrapped her lips around the Mason jar that Moose held. The whiskey stung the back of her throat. Her eyes filled with tears and she began to cough.

"That's it, a little more. I know you can do better than that! That's it. Now you're going to feel a little pinch," Moose warned. "Just a little pinch."

Jana flinched at the feel of the hot metal on her skin. Lonnie held her steady as Moose cut.

"Bite down on this." Lonnie placed a wooden spoon between her teeth. "Bite down hard, okay?"

Jana bit as hard as she could while Moose carved an "X" into her forearm. Her eyes screwed shut with pain.

Lonnie took a big swig of moonshine and swished it around his mouth. He fastened his lips to the bleeding wound and sucked and spat into the glass repeatedly. Jana shivered and continued to bite down on the spoon. Moose washed the wound with whiskey and dressed it with a strip of muslin.

Jana's eyes began to focus. She took in her surroundings for the first time. She felt the cotton padding of the chair with her fingers. Her eyes shifted back and forth between Moose and Lonnie.

"Where did you say your people were?" Moose's voice resumed its edge of suspicion.

"Across the bluff." Jana felt the dressing on her wound. "They're asleep."

"They're asleep, huh?" Lonnie scolded. "Well it's very late, Jana. You should be asleep, too. What're you doing out here alone at this hour?"

A glimmer of recognition overcame Jana as she tried to focus on the eyes of the man who had sucked the venom from her arm.

"I was following the North Star."

Despite the unfocused eyes, Moose sensed her embarrassment. "Why were you following the North Star?"

"I was looking for treasure." She coughed.

A faraway look washed over Lonnie's eyes.

"The summer after my daddy died of tuberculosis, I was playing in the house with my sister when a tornado hit. Our terrier, Daisy, smelled it and tried to warn us. She pulled at the hem of my momma's dress with her teeth. Momma shooed her away at first, but Daisy continued to growl and knocked a bowl of peeled turnips onto the floor. Then the sky turned green. Momma told us to get in the cellar.

The three of us huddled between the rows of preserves and canned goods for what seemed like ages. Daisy wriggled from person to person, wagging her tail and licking the tears from our cheeks. We thanked her for saving our lives and rewarded her with a jar of tomato preserves. She licked it clean. We laughed at her crusty red snout.

When the spinning stopped, we ascended the ladder and found a pile of sticks and broken glass in the spot where our house used to be. Momma held out her arms. My sister ran into them. Then I looked out beyond the horizon and saw a double rainbow.

I had never seen one before and almost didn't trust my eyes, but I said to my momma, 'See? Everything's gonna be alright.' Then I started running towards it as fast as I could.

Momma hollered, 'Get back here and stay with us!' And I yelled back, 'I have to hurry and find the pots of gold before somebody else does!' And my foolish ass ran off in the direction of the double rainbow. Dust flying in my eyes and ears, falling over sticks, pipes, and rusty nails. Trying to save my momma's heart by finding some damn pots of gold."

He trailed off.

"Did you find them?" Jana asked.

"What do you mean?"

"When you got to the end of the rainbow. What was there?"

Lonnie didn't answer.

Moose nudged him. "Stop blubbering over that tired old rainbow story and fix this girl a plate. That moonshine's probably burning a hole through her stomach."

Lonnie disappeared into the kitchen and returned with a heaping bowl of stew. Jana savored every mouthful and accepted a second helping.

"Do you always eat this late?"

"We wait until all the work is finished. When Moose is done with his papers and I'm done sewing my napkins."

"Napkins," Jana said. She squinted at Lonnie. "That's where I saw you. You were at Mr. Stack's last Sunday."

"Yeah, I make his napkins and tablecloths."

"So you're a seamstress?"

"Table designer," Lonnie scoffed. He stuck his nose in the air.

Across the room, Moose placed the stylus at the edge of a record. Bessie Smith's *After You've Gone* filled the air between them. All surroundings faded away as Jana listened to the music.

She turned to Lonnie. "Who's singing that?"

"You've never heard Bessie Smith before?"

"Bessie Smith?" Tears welled in her eyes. She paused. "It's like she's putting a candle up to her heart so you can see inside."

"That's why it's called the blues, baby," Moose said.

"What's blue?"

"Don't you know the blues?"

"I'm not allowed to listen to music."

"Why not?"

"Because its roots are in the devil's kingdom."

Lonnie laughed. "Who told you that?"

Jana sighed and licked her spoon. "Some big dummy I know. But I guess I'll be the first one to burn in hell because I feel like I know what Nessie's saying."

"Bessie," Moose corrected.

"That's right. Bessie." She tried to steady herself and wobbled.

Lonnie showed Jana the sketch of the gown. "Look at this dress. Now imagine it coming to life on Jane Russell. What do you think?"

She hesitated. "On that behind?"

Lonnie closed the sketchbook and rolled his eyes. Moose winked.

"Are you a table designer, too?" Jana looked at Moose.

"No." Moose said. "I'm a schoolteacher."

"A schoolteacher?"

"Are you surprised?"

She pulled herself up a little bit. "How did you become a teacher?"

Moose laughed. "Well now, Miss Jana," he said sarcastically, "the truth comes out. You think all Negroes are laborers by trade? Uneducated boors?"

"I didn't mean it like that." Jana began. "You went to college? In Mississippi?"

Moose looked proud. "I went to Lincoln University in Pennsylvania. It's a respectable and wonderful school. As a matter of fact, it's Langston Hughes' alma mater."

"Langston Hughes?"

"He's a poet. Do you like poetry?"

"I like to read." Jana managed a tiny smile. "HP Lovecraft, Edgar Allan Poe, Ambrose Bierce."

Moose looked impressed. "A gothic at heart, are you, Jana?"

"I guess so."

"Well I pegged you as more of a poet. You know. Following stars and all."

"I read lots of things. Where are your books?"

"Mostly up in the sleeping loft. I use that space as my office, too. I sit on the mattress and grade papers."

Jana looked at the layout of the house. "Well, where's the other bed?"

Moose stammered. Lonnie interrupted. "I sleep down here on the easy chair. I don't need much space."

"I guess not," Jana agreed.

A long pause followed.

Moose broke the silence. "Didn't you say you lived over the bluff?"

"Yes." She paused. "I guess I'd better get back home now."

"How are you feeling?"

"Much better. Thanks. Thanks an awful lot to the both of you, sir."

"Moose. I'm Moose and this is Lonnie. You know how to get home from here?"

"Retrace my steps in the woods, I guess."

Moose held out his hand. Jana grasped it. He led her to the window. "Do you see that dirt road to the left?"

"Yes."

"Follow it a quarter mile and turn left at the fork. That'll lead you back to the bluff."

"I never took that road before."

"It's a shortcut. It will lead you home. Sure you're feeling okay?"

"Yes sir. Thank you. Thank you for everything."

Lonnie handed her the torn cardigan. She buttoned it up and waved goodbye as she wandered up the road towards home.

They heard a knock at the door three nights later. Moose watched in horror as it started to open by itself. He felt at his side for the rifle and crept to the door.

"Who's there?" He growled and tried to sound menacing, silently cursing Lonnie for forgetting to lock the door again.

"It's me, Moose." Jana smiled and held out a paper bag. He didn't smile back. "What can I do for you?" His tone was crisp. "I don't think you left anything here."

"I just wanted to thank you again."

"You're welcome." He started to close the door.

"Wait!" Jana interrupted. "I've got bacon! And I wanted to ask you a question because I think you might be a good teacher. There aren't any good teachers who can answer questions worth a lick at my school."

"What's this I hear about bacon?" Lonnie made his way down the loft ladder and saw Moose's wide frame blocking the door. "I thought I heard something about...Oh." He stopped. "What's she doing back here?"

"It seems our visitor let herself in because somebody forgot to latch the door again."

Lonnie winced. "Oops."

"Please," Jana pleaded. "I won't stay long, I promise. She held out the paper bag. "I, I just brought the bacon as a thank you."

Lonnie put his hand on Moose's shoulder. "It's okay." Moose glared at his lover and stepped aside.

Jana walked in and handed the paper bag to Lonnie. He peeked inside and pulled out an oblong slab wrapped in foil.

"Thank you, Jana. I'll fry this up right now." He handed the paper bag to Moose and headed to the stove. "Get the moonshine, Moose," he called. "And the good glasses!"

Jana sat in the chair next to the record player and listened to the music.

"Is this Bessie Smith?"

"Billie Holiday."

Moose pulled two books out of the bag and held them at arm's length to read the titles out loud. "The Prophet." He picked up the second. "The Bhagavad Gita. They're teaching you this in school?"

"No. I found these on my own. Have you read them?"

Moose shook his head. "I'm more familiar with Jacob, Moses, and John the Baptist, but this does look interesting." He opened the front cover of The Bhagavad Gita. Jana Montgomery was written in copperplate letters.

"That's nice penmanship you have."

"Thank you."

A waft of bacon frying filled the room. She paused.

"I wanted to ask you some questions about these books. Maybe if I leave them here you can read them and we can discuss them later."

"No." He held the books back to her. "Thank you for the bacon, but I'm not taking anything else from you."

"Come on, Moose," Jana pleaded. "What's the good of having a book if it dies with me?

She hung her head and walked to the door.

"Oh, alright. Leave them here, then." Moose said.

"Thanks, Moose!"

Lonnie called from the kitchen. "Sit down while I fix you a plate, Jana."

"I ate already. But I'll see you later. Maybe?"

Her heart was buoyant as she opened the door. Moose and Lonnie waved goodbye as she set off in the direction of the bluff.

Stevie

"Hey, Pop?"

"Yeah, Stevie?"

"Could you bring some more napkins out here?" Stevie Stack called from the ice cream counter and into the stockroom where his father was doing inventory.

"Look in the drawer next to the register." Arnold Stack checked off items in his notebook.

"I already did. It's empty. Do you have more in the stockroom?"

"I'll check."

Arnold walked out of the stockroom a few minutes later, tying an apron around his waist.

"Dammit, I guess they're all at the laundry."

He walked to the drawer next to the register and checked it. "Lonnie's supposed to bring some by tomorrow after closing, but I'll bet they're ready to go. He usually finishes ahead of time."

"Call him," Stevie suggested. "Ask him if he'll bring them over now."

"He doesn't have a phone," Arnold continued. "But you got legs and you can walk to his place and get them. We open in an hour. I'll take care of things by myself until you get back.

He opened the register and handed Stevie a silver dollar.

"Here. It's that little log house about a mile and a half up past the thicket beyond Shack Row. Give him the money and bring back the napkins." Arnold whistled and turned back towards the stockroom.

"You want me to walk through Shack Row?" Stevie's tone was incredulous. "What kind of Pop are you?"

"The thicket road goes around Shack Row, not through it. And nothing bad ever happens out there anyway, boy. Lonnie and his brother have a nice place, too."

Arnold watched as Stevie continued to sulk. "What's the matter, Mr. Football Hero? Afraid?"

"I'm not afraid of anything," Stevie spat back. "Lonnie's the one should be carrying the napkins back, is all."

"And how is he going to know to carry them here if we can't call him on the phone to ask, Stevie?"

"A telegram?"

"That'll take a couple a days, Stevie. By the time he gets it he'll have already delivered the napkins by tomorrow evening."

"Then I'll walk over there and tell him to carry them back."

"It doesn't take two men to carry back a stack of napkins, and you have to walk back any way."

"Well, why don't you pick me up at Lonnie's in your car and then he can carry them back by himself?" Stevie felt triumphant.

"Interesting idea, Stevie. So who's going to watch the shop?"

"What do you mean?"

"If I'm driving to pick you up from Lonnie's, I can't be minding the store at the same time, can I?"

Stevie reflected. "No," he finally answered, crestfallen.

"So, I'll ask you again. Who's going to watch the shop, Stevie?"

Stevie knit his brow in concentration. "Can't you just drive out to Lonnie's, get the napkins and drive back here again? I can watch the store by myself."

"And leave you in charge of the register?" Arnold laughed. "That's the dumbest thing you've said all day!"

Arnold continued to laugh as a glaring Stevie pulled his apron off and threw it in a crumpled ball onto the counter. "Don't be too long!" he called after his son. Stevie bounded out the door and stalked off in search of Lonnie's house.

Lonnie's house stood in a clearing of red clay a few yards from the edge of the thicket. Stevie wiped his feet on the front doorstep, leaving bloodied trails of mud behind. He knocked on the front door. "Lonnie?" he called. There was no answer. He knocked harder and tried to peek through the curtain at the window. "Are you in there, Lonnie? It's me, Stevie Stack. I came for the napkins. Hello?" Stevie tried the doorknob. It was unlocked. The door swung open. "Hello?" He stepped into the doorway and looked around.

The small living space was neatly swept and sparsely furnished with a worn easy chair, an ancient sewing machine, a record player, a crate of records and a purple braided rug. A wicker basket heaping with scraps of material rested to the side of the sewing table. To the right of the main room was a kitchen area furnished with a large wooden table and a coal pipe stove. Magazines and sketches of dresses and books were casually strewn about.

A neatly tied bundle of napkins and tablecloths rested on the chair. Stevie scooped it up in his arms and started to leave. Suddenly remembering the silver dollar, he set the bundle down on the table. He fumbled through his pockets, found the coin and placed it on the table. He started to pick up the linens again when two books lying on the table caught his eye. He picked one up and brought it closer to his face.

"The Bhagavad Gita," he stumbled. "What in the world?" He glanced at the second. "*The Prophet*. Kahlil Gibran? I don't remember any preaching about that prophet in Sunday school." He opened the copy of The Bhagavad Gita.

"Jana Montgomery?" he cried out, reading the inscription. "What's her book doing over here?" He opened the copy of *The Prophet* and found the same signature. Bewildered, he tucked the books under his arm, scooped up the linens, closed Lonnie's front door behind him and headed back to the shop.

Sleigh bells jingled as a frowning Stevie walked back inside. He set the bundle of linens down onto the counter. His apron lay in a ball where he had left it earlier. Arnold stopped sponging the counter and walked over to the bundle of linen to inspect it.

"If your face freezes that way, you're out of a job. Did you remember to pay him?"

"Yeah," Stevie fingered the books and hesitated.

"Well, what is it then?" Arnold continued. "You need to take a break or something?"

"Jana Montgomery," Stevie began.

"What?" Arnold undid the twine around the stack of napkins. One by one, he began to fold them. "You see her today?"

"Did the reverend ever talk to you about his family visiting Lonnie's house?"

"Not that I recall. Why do you ask?"

"Are you sure about that?" Stevie persisted.

"The reverend's a fine man. Why would he need to visit Lonnie's house? I reckon he stays away from Shack Row."

"Well like you said, Pop, the thicket road to Lonnie's house goes around Shack Row, not through it."

"Polly wanna cracker?" Arnold Stack mocked. "I don't even think he knows Lonnie. Lonnie can't attend our services."

"I did what you told me and got the napkins," Stevie began. "Lonnie wasn't home, but the door was unlocked so I went right on in." He handed his father the books. "I found these lying on the table next to the napkins. They got Jana Montgomery's name inside."

Arnold opened the covers and stared at Jana's signature. Stevie drawled on.

"Even if he could read a little bit, and I don't think he reads, does he? Anyway, he probably can't write either, so I know he didn't put her name in the books, so they must be hers. But how would he know Jana Montgomery? Do you think he stole them?"

Arnold fumbled for an explanation. He laughed and started sponging the counter again. "C'mon, Stevie," he said. "I wouldn't put it past the reverend to collect a few family items for charity. Charity is what being a preacher is about."

"I don't think he'd be preaching this, though." Stevie squinted at the cover of The Bhagavad Gita and tried to repeat the title. "Sounds like voodoo to me."

"Focus on the counter, Stevie." Arnold's voice was dismissive. "I'll ask the reverend about it tonight." He put the books in his apron pocket and turned towards the stockroom.

"What do ya'll do in those meetings, anyway?"

Arnold snatched a cloth from the pile and regarded his son impatiently. "Fold those napkins and put them away." His voice was steely. "Go on!" Stevie glared.

Arnold walked into the stockroom and closed the door behind him. He picked up the telephone resting on the metal desk and began to dial. "Reverend?" he whispered into the mouthpiece. "Arnold Stack, here. Yes, we're still on for tonight. I was just wondering if you could make it a bit early, before the rest of the fellows get there. No, there's nothing wrong, nothing wrong at all." He traced Jana's signature with his fingers. "There's just something I'd like to share with you, is all..."

Afternoon passed into evening, and there was no sign of the reverend. Gladys clicked her lilac fingernails against the dinner table and watched the chuck roast gravy congeal around islands of carrot and potato. Jana sat across from her with a book sprawled in her lap. She strained to read the print as the evening grew darker.

Gladys sighed and unfolded her napkin. "Go on ahead and start. I don't know why your father is running so late. I hope there wasn't an accident."

They looked up from their plates a few moments later when they heard him at the front door. He walked into the kitchen tracking red mud onto the floor. He was flushed, and he smelled bad. He sat down at the head of the table and placed a parcel at the side of his plate. His eyes glowed.

"What do you men talk about so late that you can barely make it home for dinner?" Gladys asked. "And why were you walking off the paved road and tracking mud all over my floor?" She straightened her spine and tried to appear self-righteous.

He heaped his plate with food. "God forbid I track up the floor on the first day you bother to mop it in a year," he said. He looked at his daughter. Jana braced herself for diatribe. He said nothing. An odd smile crept over his face.

"I work hard, too." Gladys was tense.

A tinge of panic settled into the base of her spine as her father continued to stare at her. The odd smile deepened. She buttoned her sweater and hugged her shoulders. The chuck roast felt heavy in her stomach.

Gladys cleared her throat. "What were you doing so late at the meeting?"

He buttered a biscuit and addressed his daughter. "Stevie Stack asked about you, Jana. Wants to know when you'll be done with school so he can marry the reverend's daughter. He sure is impressed with you. So is his father."

Jana put her fork down and willed her chair to stop swaying.

"What's gotten into you, Harlan?" Gladys squeaked. Something had snapped inside her husband, and she could almost see a viscous substance oozing from the gash. She slid a hairpin from her tidy updo and held it firmly between her thumb and forefinger.

He glanced at the hairpin in his wife's fingers and smiled. "And you brought her into this world, Gladys." His eyes were cold. "Tell me again, how is it that such an angel came to grace your womb? Our hair and eyes are brown."

He turned his attention back to his daughter. "You know who else admires you, Jana? Lonnie. Would you even think that Lonnie would have an appreciation for a fine young woman like you? Times are changing. Isn't that right, daughter?"

He dabbed his lips with his napkin and turned towards his wife. "This roast is delicious, Gladys. You really put your foot into it this time."

Gladys turned to her daughter. "What's this about?"

Tears rolled freely. This was too much. She didn't deserve this. She didn't understand.

"No."

"Oh, yes."

"Jesus Christ!"

"Christ wasn't there, daughter. But some other gods were. What were they called again?"

Jana stood.

Harlan motioned to the white parcel. "Don't you want your present?"

Jana sat. Her fingers shook as she untied the string and unfolded a Klansman hood. Her blood splattered books were inside.

His laughter was low-pitched and subtle at first, but it steadily filled the room with its poison until Jana was unable to breathe.

Gladys rolled her head around noiselessly like a useless pendulum. When the tears finally came, she held her palms over her ears to drown out the sound of her husband and transported herself back to the day she was in labor with Jana.

There had been flowers, and she had arrived at the hospital

with a bottle of perfume. Then Jana pushed her way into the world. After one whiff of her daughter's body, she couldn't get enough of the smell. Consequently, the atomizer bottle had remained forgotten at the bottom of her purse. It was funny what the mind chose to remember.

The laughter gradually increased in volume, and the pitch rose steadily until the house was flooded with the emasculated shrieking of a cornered hyena.

Gladys held her arms out towards her baby, but Jana pushed them away. She bolted through the living room towards the front door. Gladys stood up to follow.

Harlan grabbed his wife's arm and twisted it behind her back. "Where in the hell do you think you're going, Gladys?" He slapped her and pushed her to the floor. "We're going to have a martini."

Of course her husband could never truly understand her daughter. He didn't recognize her scent. That was why he was so ugly. That was why he rejected her. She held her cheek in her hand and remained on the floor. There was no rush to meet him at his level. It didn't get much better up there.

Outside, the sidewalk tottered like a see saw, and the humidity made it nearly impossible to breathe. Jana fell and hit her head on the pavement. She got up again but stopped to vomit as she ran through the thicket beyond Shack Row.

Her eyes were swollen shut by the time she reached the doorknob.

"Moose?"

She rattled it blindly. It was locked.

"Moose?"

Gutted by a feeling of loss beyond her comprehension, she sank to her knees at the doorstep.

"Moose!"

When the vomiting stopped, she was paralyzed by a raging fit of dry heaves. She continued to cry out for Moose until her voice cracked into broken, bloodied whispers. The whispers eventually stopped, but she continued to spit blood throughout the night. As she sat on the ground outside the front door, she thought she could hear the sound of muffled sobs on the other side. But she couldn't be sure. Curling up into fetal position, she fell asleep in the doorframe with her cheek to the pavement.

He never answered.

Russell

Eight-year-old Russell North woke up every morning to the aroma of sausages frying, biscuits baking and coffee brewing on top of his mother's potbelly coal stove. Inspired by the sunbeams outside his window and the scope of his imagination, he captured a wealth of images with the paper and crayons that his parents left next to his feather stuffed, feed-bag mattress.

He liked drawing himself best of all: a smiling, chocolate brown face with exaggerated shoulders and legs dressed in multicolored garments and holding oversized red and blue gemstones. Sometimes the gemstones rested in patches of bluegrass. At other times, they winked from the summit of Black Mountain, outlined in a flintlike edge of green. Sometimes his mother had knee-length hair, an O-shaped ruby mouth, and mittenlike hands that rested at the end of short, bedazzled arms pointing to gemstones in the mountains. At other times, her mouth was a toothy wedge of crescent moon.

When he stumbled out of the outhouse and into the kitchen, his parents greeted him with kisses and asked him to recall his dreams. After breakfast, his mother plastered the walls with his drawings while his father started his walk to the coal mine in

Lynch, where he would cheerfully remain until dark. They enjoyed this peaceful, simple routine until the morning the potbelly coal stove exploded and his mother was killed in the fire.

The casket was a pine box that his father sanded down and left him in charge of decorating. Russell started by painting a background of mountains and an expanse of bluegrass. Then he painted his mother with hair down to her knees and an O-shaped ruby mouth. It occurred to him at that moment that the painting was silly, disproportionate, and unbefitting of her beauty, so he hastily covered the entire casket with a coat of scarlet paint, which effectively reduced the images beneath the surface to painful looking bruises. He left the casket and wept. When he returned and it was quite dry, he dipped a paintbrush into a yellow pigment and spelled out, UNFAIR in sprawling letters that covered the entire length.

The handful of people who came to pay their respects ignored the charred smell emanating from the casket and focused on the letters instead. Aunt Alice rolled herself to Russell's side and firmly grasped his hand as his mother's body was lowered into the ground.

Later on that afternoon when family and friends had gathered at her home for the repast, she called him into the kitchen. "Sit down here while I fix you a plate," she said, motioning to the table. He did as he was told and settled into an ancient chair made out of splintered green wood. She heaped a plate with greens and smothered pork. She cut a piece of freshly baked cornbread from a cast iron pan. She set the plate down in front of Russell and poured him a glass of milk. Her eyes filled with compassionate tears. "You bet I'll make sure that baby has enough to eat." She adjusted the cushion of her wheelchair to fit more comfortably and hoisted the weight of her body upwards. Her face contorted with pain.

Russell and his father moved into her house the following morning, having extracted the meager belongings that had not

been destroyed from the smoldering foundation where their kitchen once stood. His father resumed his work at the coal mine the following day. Aunt Alice sent Russell off to school with the remaining smothered pork and greens packed into his lunch pail and a fresh cornbread for his teacher, Miss Hornbeam.

His father sank into a deep depression and got into the habit of asking him to bring him glasses of corn liquor from the Mason jar supply at the side of the house. Russell poured as carefully as he could, but a bit of the liquor spilled down his fingers. He instinctively raised them to his lips to taste. Aunt Alice laughed at the sour face that he made but proceeded proactively. "You'd best remember that taste for the rest of your life," she advised the grieving boy as he watched his father heading to work in a visible state of intoxication. "You don't wanna turn into a drunk like Ronald."

The following morning, Aunt Alice sent Russell to school with a basket of biscuits, a jar of pork gravy and a note asking Miss Hornbeam to give the boy extra homework to divert his attention from problems at home. That same afternoon, two local authorities showed up to the schoolhouse barn while the students were taking a vocabulary test. The class looked up in alarm as the men removed their hats and spoke in hushed whispers to Miss Hornbeam, who silently clasped her left hand to her mouth and turned in Russell's direction. She closed her eyes and calmly informed the class that school was dismissed, and the tests would be completed the following day. She took Russell by the hand and walked him home, where Aunt Alice was thanking a coal miner for returning her brother-in-law's belongings.

Miss Hornbeam stayed at the house that night to console Russell. Aunt Alice busied herself making dinner. She scooped grease into a large cast iron skillet and dipped pieces of chicken into egg and flour. She stirred milk into the leftover egg and flour mixture and rolled it into biscuits. Miss Hornbeam swept the wood floors, covered the table with a yellow cloth, and placed a centerpiece of freshly picked field flowers into an empty Crisco can.

The two women quietly discussed the funeral arrangements in the kitchen while Russell attempted to study his vocabulary lesson in the back bedroom. The scent of chicken frying and biscuits baking lured him into the kitchen. He unleashed his rage at the sight of the yellow tablecloth, and smacked the centerpiece to the floor with his fist.

Miss Hornbeam hung back hesitantly, but Aunt Alice rolled right up to his side and held out her arms. "It's all right, baby," she reassured gently. Russell gave way to a torrential outpouring of tears. "Unfair," he sobbed, his shoulders shaking violently," Unfair! Unfair! Unfair! Unfair! Unfair! Unfair!"

"Come and have some chicken and biscuits, baby," Aunt Alice pleaded.

"I want it to be fair!" Russell howled. Miss Hornbeam offered a handkerchief.

"Unfair is dead, buried and laid in the ground," Aunt Alice kept her voice from trembling. "You can't change that your momma and daddy are dead. Maybe you could change things to make it fair for the rest of us who are still here. You're a smart one."

"You're at the top of your class with vocabulary," Miss Hornbeam added, "but you need to work on your arithmetic."

———————◆———————

A decade later, his acceptance letter to Kentucky State University arrived in the mail. Aunt Alice took a long, hard look at the boy's clothing and decided that it was entirely unacceptable. She planned a day trip to the Sears department store in Louisville, where Miss Hornbeam would help him select a wardrobe befitting his future. Russell was awestruck by the generosity of his aunt and excited about the opportunities that awaited him.

Four years later, he was practicing his valedictorian speech in front of his dormitory mirror when he suddenly felt dizzy and needed to sit down. Overcome with drowsiness and unable to focus, the sounds of campus activity faded away as he closed his eyes for a few minutes. When he opened them, the walls were adorned with the crayon pictures drawn from the scope of his childhood imagination. Enormous red and blue gemstones were strewn about the room, casting prisms in the afternoon sun.

A hummingbird fluttered in figure eight motion and came to rest on a red gemstone. A tall, broad-shouldered man with rich ebony skin extended a hand in its direction. The hummingbird flew towards the man, trailing a visible thread of silver, and came to rest upon his finger.

"Who are you?" Russell stammered.

The tall man paused eloquently before he responded, filling the air with a lyrical peace.

"I'm Paul."

"What are you?"

Paul's eyes were warm and reassuring. He followed his gaze to the hummingbird that had left the perch of his finger and flown out of the open window. "I'm a beacon of clarity to be revealed at various crossroads in your life." He paused. "Sometimes I am available for counsel."

"What counsel are you here to give me?"

Paul stood up and brushed away silver threads from his tailored blue suit. "Maybe you can see to changing things to be fair for the rest of us still here."

"How can I do that?" Russell asked.

"Columbia Law School," Paul said soberly. He grabbed a gemstone into each of his hands and disappeared in a swaddling of red and blue light.

In January of 1967, Russell graduated from Columbia Law School and passed the bar exam. Later on in the year he was contacted by the NAACP and asked to provide legal services.

In 1972, He traveled to Washington, DC to attend a benefit gala for the Taborian Hospital. He was on his way back from the men's room when he noticed a peculiarly beautiful woman with untamed blonde hair wearing a lavender bias cut organza gown. Sensing a familiarity about her eyes, he walked through the sea of party guests to introduce himself.

They spent the rest of the party on the terrace watching the stars and admiring the lilacs in the surrounding garden. Russell talked about growing up in Harlan, Kentucky, attending Columbia Law School, and how his work had brought him to Mound Bayou, Mississippi. Jana talked about growing up with a father named Harlan in Natchez, Mississippi. Somewhere between Mound Bayou, Natchez, and the tale of two Harlans Russell remembered where he had seen those eyes before.

She had been an Anaheim-based pediatrician working for the State of California. Details about her work and private life leaked to the press after she terminated her pregnancy illegally. He didn't fully understand why she was targeted as a scapegoat. Extortion, probably. Protesters and activists alike made a stink, but the damage had been done. She was harassed incessantly and disappeared off the face of the earth a short time later. The state legislators never tracked down the perpetrators.

He remembered the sullen air reflected in the photos of her that ran in the newspapers a few years before. And here she was, leaning against his arm enjoying a buzz brought on by a well-shaken martini and the last of her valium. In his mind, the logistics were utter nonsense. To his heart, they were perfection.

They married six months later. Calvin was born soon after. Jana mailed a wedding invitation and a birth announcement to her mother. She never heard back. She continued to send letters and photographs to her mother throughout the decade, all seemingly ignored, until the final letter was stamped *DECEASED* and returned to her.

A year later, he was contacted by a high-profile law firm in Philadelphia and asked to join as a partner. He moved his family into a large house in Gladwyne. Later on that week, Aunt Alice called and told him that Miss Hornbeam had passed away. He spared no time or expense in making funeral arrangements, hiring a company to pack up her belongings, and moving her into his home.

Margaret

Margaret sprawled face down on the couch wearing a full face of makeup and the white cotton dress and nylon stockings she had put on the morning before.

Sunlight turned the black cloud behind her eyes to a fiery shade of red.

An empty bottle of scotch rolled at her feet. She kicked a patient file out of her path and walked to the bathroom, head pounding. She sat on the toilet and buried her head in her hands, trying to drone out the sound of the television blaring in the kitchen downstairs.

Gin.

She rinsed her face in the sink and regarded her greying blonde curls, puffy eyes and sagging belly in the full length mirror affixed to the door. She felt in the pocket of the dress for her cigarettes. It was empty. She cursed.

The telephone rang from a table in the downstairs hallway. She carefully made her way down the mosaic tiled staircase, only to trip and fall over a pile of red and white polka dotted Toss Across bean bags that Bela had left in the middle of the floor. She cursed again, got back on her feet and picked up the receiver. "Yeah?" she answered gruffly.

She raised her voice in order to hear herself over the television. "What, Lasse?" she began, rubbing her ankle. "You finally got a customer this month? Well, it's about fucking time. Hold on, Lasse. Bela, turn that down right now."

She spotted a half-smoked cigarette lying in an ashtray. She raised it to her lips greedily and felt in her pocket for a match. "What do you mean she doesn't have all the money? Not my fucking problem, Lasse," she continued as she lit the cigarette. "You're the talent, you figure it out." Smoke poured from her nostrils. "I really don't give a rat's ass if you take a cut at all; business is business and I charge what I charge, goddammit. Bela! I mean it! This is long distance!" She closed her eyes and rubbed her right temple with her fingers.

"You're supposed to do all of the work; you're the talent. It's an abortion, not brain surgery. You think you'd get it through your skull by now. I'm running this show. I put, Bela! Put that down right now! I put up the goddamn money to get us in business, I own the building, and I get sixty percent for every broad you bring in the joint! A deal is a deal!" Margaret started to slam down the earpiece, thought the better of it and brought it back to her face.

"Once a trick, always a trick, Lasse. I took pity on you and gave you a chance to save your pathetic joke of a podiatry practice and make some real money. This isn't a charity ball. This isn't a goddamn bargain basement. If she doesn't want to be pregnant, she'll find the dough. I want my full cut, Lasse." She started to cough and continued her ranting.

"Women are liberated now. Why doesn't she have the money? She just came here from China and can't get a good job because she's not an American citizen and barely speaks English? You fucked her, didn't you?" Margaret laughed. "I'm a philanthropist at heart; that's why I'm standing my ground. She wants to be an American citizen? Is that really what you think of me, Lasse? Oh, well. I've been called worse. Then ask Nixon for the money. He likes those Chinese. Oh, well. Like I just said, I've been called worse. Threaten me one more time, and see what happens. You're just the talent, you fucking trick. I can replace you in a heartbeat. I'm sick of your shit, Lasse!" Her hands trembled. "Hold on, I'm switching phones."

She walked to the refrigerator and licked her furry teeth.

Gin.

She pushed aside bottles of ketchup, barbeque sauce, and a jar of Tang looking for the pitcher of orange juice. Then she saw Bela seated at the kitchen table, holding the pitcher and draining the last of the contents into his sticky glass. He dug a spoon into his bowl of Trix and looked up at Margaret. "Morning, Mumma," he beamed toothlessly. Margaret glared.

She picked up the telephone hanging from the kitchen wall. "I mean it, Lasse," she barked into the mouthpiece. "You know what I'm capable of whenever you pull this shit!" She leaned against the open refrigerator door and fixated on the jar of Tang. "Remember a few years ago? Remember that folkie pediatrician, Jana Montgomery? You fell hook, line and sinker for that nutcase. She came up short, pardon my pun, and I made her pay. Hell hath no fury like the scorn of a concerned citizen like me, Lasse. I will tip off immigration. I will tip off the Senate. I will turn her ass out to the Archdiocese. I'm hanging up now. You get me every bit of my usual split or I'll send her back to the mainland! Don't think I won't, Lasse. Don't fuck with me." She slammed down the receiver.

Bela cleared his throat. "Morning, Mumma," he repeated. Margaret rolled her eyes. "It's Margaret," she scowled. She glanced at the portable TV resting on the edge of the table. "What the hell are you watching, anyway?" She grabbed the Tang out of the refrigerator and slammed it onto the counter.

"Bette Davis," Bela sang. He grabbed the sugar bowl and heaped a staggering amount onto his cereal. "I've written a letter to Daddy," he continued, "because he sent me his picture." He picked up a piece of yellow construction paper decorated with red glitter, purple stars, and gobs of excess glue. *Daddy* was spelled out carefully in the center.

Margaret's stomach lurched at the sight of the overly-sweetened cereal. "That's disgusting," she muttered. She grabbed the empty pitcher from the table, dumped in an unmeasured amount of Tang and thrust it under the kitchen faucet. Her knees crackled as she stooped down to open the cabinet below the kitchen sink. Her puffy eyes rummaged through a sea of empty liquor bottles as she retrieved a near-empty bottle of gin.

She mixed a cocktail and was immediately reminded of cigarettes. She found her purse and opened it, but there were no cigarettes inside. A quick check of her wallet revealed two pennies and several dog eared receipts.

She passed gas and sipped her gin and Tang. "Elvira's coming in an hour. I'll call her and have her stop at the bank before she gets here."

"It's Sunday!" Bela screeched. He jumped up from the table, shook his behind to the ground and hooted with delight. "It's Sunday, and you farted," he sang, reveling in the knowledge that the bank was closed, the housekeeper had the day off, and he had outsmarted the likes of his drunken mother.

Margaret's eyes narrowed at the sight of the horrid little entity dancing before her. "I see," she said. "Come here, Bela, I wanna talk to you." She took a sip from her cocktail. Bela frolicked to her side.

"I hear you're the hottest thing this side of the second grade since sliced bread," she began. "Your teacher, Mr. Aldrich says you're in a special reading class with a bunch of older students and reading from a fifth grade text. You must be pretty proud of yourself."

Bela shifted his weight from side to side and beamed.

"How about a little vocabulary quiz?" she continued. A sardonic grin crept over her aging face. "Why don't you bring Mr. Wiglet in to sweeten up the pot a bit?" She winked.

Bela perked up at the mention of Mr. Wiglet, his beloved ceramic piggy bank. Confident in the knowledge that his adeptness at vocabulary earned him consistent prizes from Mr. Aldrich's candy jar, he ran through the house and up the stairs to his room to retrieve Mr. Wiglet and the fifth grade vocabulary book. He placed them on the kitchen table and panted to catch his breath.

"Want to hear the words I memorized for my lesson?" he asked sweetly, "I know them all by heart."

"No," Margaret mused. "I already have a word. Epiphany."

"Epiphany," Bela mimicked. "A-P-"

"This isn't a spelling lesson." Margaret shrugged. "It's more of an existential one. Epiphany," she repeated. "Do you consider your life to be a good one, Bela?"

Bela knit his brow. "Yeah?" he answered hesitantly.

"Well, I should think so," Margaret snickered. The glaring sunlight had worsened her headache, and she walked over to the kitchen drapes to close them. "Let's see," she pointed out. "You get hungry and I feed you. I consistently provide you with clothing, and you wear it out like there's no tomorrow. You come home every night expecting a place to sleep, and I provide you with a bed." Margaret paused for a moment to finger a snag on her nylon stockings. "I even give you indoor plumbing, color television, and a vast array of reading material, all of which are non-essential luxuries," she growled.

Bela clutched Mr. Wiglet firmly against his body and rubbed his eyes with his right hand. "But I'm six years old."

"Excuses," Margaret spat. Bela wiped his face in uncomfortable silence and stared at Mr. Wiglet.

"How much am I giving you for allowance these days?"

Margaret asked. Bela lit up with importance.

"Two dollars a week," he answered proudly, sticking out his bony chest.

Margaret shook her head in disbelief and folded her arms across her chest. "Unbelievable," she continued. "Not only do you have the privilege of unlimited access to these amenities, you get paid to do it." She sighed dramatically and burst into a fit of hiccoughs.

Bela grabbed his sticky glass from the table, ran to the faucet, and filled it up with water. He handed it to Margaret who drank it down in one gulp and promptly resumed her ranting.

"How much money do you have in Mr. Wiglet?"

"Thirty-six dollars."

"And I assume you know what day it is."

"April 9th," Bela rattled proudly. "Daddy told me in the letter. It's the anniversary of Paul Robeson's birthday and the fourth anniversary of Dr. Martin Luther King Jr.'s funeral."

Margaret looked up in surprise. "Allow me to welcome you back to the here and now. Today," she slurred, "is the sixth day before Tax Day."

Bela's smile disappeared.

"And according to my calculations, you earned ninety-six dollars in allowance last year."

Bela picked up Mr. Wiglet and clutched him tightly.

"That means you owe thirty-two dollars in taxes."

Bela clasped Mr. Wiglet under his left arm and inched backwards, fearful eyes glued upon Margaret's demonic gaze.

"And no son of mine is going to prison for tax evasion!"

Bela ran.

An overturned kitchen chair hit the linoleum with a dramatic crash. Margaret chased him through the living room, up the staircase, and eventually cornered him in front of his bedroom door. She flung herself against the door dramatically, arms stretched out at her sides. Bela reached for the doorknob and burst into tears.

"An epiphany," Margaret wheezed, "is having a sudden and absolute understanding of something." She wrenched the ceramic pig from his grasp. "Have you reached an epiphany about life today?"

"It's not fair!" Bela hyperventilated as he reached for Mr. Wiglet. He gasped for breath and fell to the floor, screaming.

"Good work, son. You get an A."

Panting, she walked down the stairs and into the foyer. She grabbed her coat from the hook next to the front door and instinctively felt for the keys to her Lincoln. Mr. Wiglet jingled as she tucked him under her armpit, tail exposed.

"I'll bring your change," she called up the stairs. "I'm just going down the street to Johnson's." She closed the door behind her.

"It's not fair!" Bela howled. He drooled and pounded his heels into the carpet. Margaret ignored his screaming and hummed as she walked to her car.

Margaret

Eighteen-year-old Margaret's parents consistently demonstrated that life would be better if she were a boy.

Her father doted on her younger brother. He complimented the unbecoming ducktail that the boy insisted on at the barber shop. He praised his banal attempts at artwork inspired by paint-by-number guides and cereal box renderings. He encouraged the boy's fascination with anything and everything pertaining to race cars.

"I should have been born a boy," Margaret confided to her mother one evening as she opened the refrigerator door and retrieved a jar of peanut butter and a loaf of bread. "Then I, too, could live out my existence with an astounding lack of taste and everybody would still kiss my ass."

"Language, young lady. Language!" her mother admonished. She wiped the refrigerator handle behind Margaret with a Lysol-saturated cloth.

"Where's Dad, anyway?" Margaret huffed. She opened a drawer and selected a butter knife. "I'm starving. Why do we have to wait for him to start dinner on the nights that his trials run late?"

"Manners, young lady. Manners!" Her mother's tone was simplistic. She waited until Margaret had walked to the opposite side of the kitchen and sat down at the breakfast nook before carefully wiping down the drawer handle. "Your father," she recited, "is a very important professional man who works very hard to support us. It isn't easy being a lawyer, you know."

"Then why are we so piss poor if he's such a big time hot shot?"

Her mother followed her to the breakfast nook, cloth poised and ready for battle. Margaret shielded her face and cursed.

They turned their heads at the familiar sound of the garage door opening and the engine of a sedan turning off. Her father entered the back door adjoined to the kitchen, carrying a weathered briefcase in one hand and a Mc Donald's bag in the other.

His voice faltered at the sight of the empty table. "You didn't wait for me, did you, girls? Bobbie Jean? Maggie Mag?" He opened the bag and stuffed a French fry into his mouth, crumpling the bag shut hurriedly and retreated up the stairs to the shelter of his office.

"It's Margaret, asshole." Margaret replied calmly to the sound of the office door slamming above.

"Temper, young lady. Temper!" Bobbie Jean sang. She followed her husband up the staircase, leaving her daughter alone, fuming, and shredding her sandwich to bits with her fingers.

———————————

Three weeks after she turned eighteen, Margaret's parent drove to Pensacola High School to attend their daughter's college counseling session. During the drive, they practiced aloud the profuse apologies and futile excuses that they would offer the guidance counselor on behalf of their daughter's putrid attitude and volatile behavior. They entered the principal's office with a painful air of deference and humility, and scrambled desperately to recall the carefully rehearsed performances that had coursed through their minds only moments before.

The guidance counselor seemed undaunted by Margaret's personality. After all, he said, she had earned the highest SAT scores in her school district and had aced all of her classes with a seemingly minimal show of effort. He told her parents to be patient with her. They thanked him bleakly and retreated to their Buick with a stack of college catalogs.

Later on that afternoon, after her parents had driven away and she was fucking him in his office, Margaret told the guidance counselor that she planned to major in biology because she needed further insight into how she could have possibly been conceived from such mutant and substandard parents.

Four years later, while working as a laboratory assistant during her senior year at the University of Florida, Margaret examined the sandpapery status of her cuticles and ragged, unpolished fingernails, and decided in that instant to become a prostitute. She set her sights upon moving to Toronto after graduation, with the rationalization that the Canadian tax structure and emphasis on independent business would enable her to seek out a living with minimal legal interference.

She decided to take a vacation before relocating to Canada and decided on Philadelphia. She was interested in visiting the College of Physicians and wanted to tour the Mütter Museum.

After arriving by Amtrak into Market East Station, she checked into a hotel in Rittenhouse Square. She spent the next two weeks exploring the Mütter Museum, Franklin Institute, and other attractions of interest before realizing that she had overspent her stipend and was almost out of money. She purchased a newspaper and settled into a diner for a breakfast dinner and a quick perusal of the want ads.

Within an hour she was standing in front of a brothel adjacent to Independence Mall. Rats frolicked openly around the overflowing trash dumpster that marked its address. The numbers painted on the door were barely visible in the absence of streetlamps. She took a deep breath, carefully tossed back her hair, and brazenly walked inside.

When she took a cab back to the motel six hours later with fifteen hundred dollars, a bottle of Dom Perignon and an established cult following throughout the entire Delaware Valley, she took a hot bath, toasted her newfound success and reconsidered her travel plans.

Within three weeks, three quarters of the Independence Mall clients had followed her to the three bedroom row home that she rented in Rittenhouse Square. Within a month, half of the Independence Hall prostitutes were within her employ. Within six months, her advertisement in the trades had tripled her business. She hired a staff to book appointments, keep house, do laundry, and purchase sheets, condoms and antiseptic.

One afternoon, when she was alone in the house reading approximately three hours before her first appointment was due, the doorbell rang. She walked over to the intercom to answer it. A professional and courteous male voice responded. He told her that a friend had recommended the place and asked permission to come upstairs to see her. She asked him to recall the name of the friend, but he couldn't remember offhand. Her suspicions were piqued. She began to explain to him that hers was a strictly by-appointment establishment but rashly brushed aside her intuition in lieu of greed, secure in the fact that the vast majority of the Philly mob, a greater portion of the City Council, and the Camden, New Jersey Chief of Police were all regular customers–giving her a heightened sense of immunity.

He was disarmingly agreeable and offered no resistance to her rules. He complimented the décor of the house, addressed her as "ma'am," and graciously obliged to pay the ridiculous price that she demanded, adding an additional fifty to what they agreed upon.

He was an easy lay: diminutively endowed, conservative and relatively quick. It was only after he had been thoroughly satisfied that he withdrew a pair of handcuffs from his jacket and cuffed her to the bedposts, read her rights and used her telephone to call for backup. Seven officers came to assist. Bolstered by the sight of her naked body rendered powerless by the handcuffs, they took turns raping her as they burst about the townhouse opening cabinets, cutting up mattresses and overturning bookcases in search of money, drugs, and anything else of interest.

They found a bag of marijuana and a sheet of rolling papers in the top drawer of her filing cabinet. They rolled a joint and smoked it in front of her, passing it around jovially and urging it towards her lips although she pursed them carefully shut. They found one thousand dollars hidden in a tin of crackers and thanked her raucously for the generous donation to the Policeman's Ball Fund. They allowed her ten minutes to use the phone before taking her to the station. She called her lawyer and her gynecologist.

The following morning after her secretary had posted her bail and picked her up from her gynecologist's appointment, Margaret summoned the remainder of her staff to pick up their belongings. She relocated to an apartment in West Philadelphia and went into seclusion.

She cut her waist length blonde hair and dyed it black. For the sake of anonymity she avoided Center City altogether, opting to meld unnoticed among the Penn students that lived in her new neighborhood.

Having one hundred thousand dollars secured in investments made it unnecessary to seek employment. She spent the majority of her days at the University of Pennsylvania Archaeology Museum and evenings at the University of Pennsylvania Biomedical Library.

By 1970, she had graduated from University of Pennsylvania Medical School, completed an internship at Hahnemann University, and secured employment as a psychiatrist for the City of Philadelphia. Her arrest record had been overlooked due to her unmitigated success in rehabilitating prostitutes, drug addicts, runaways, and the homeless in the service programs she'd completed during medical school. Her good name had been restored but she was anxious to make more money.

The abortion side business had begun as a result of a phone conversation with Lasse Eriksen, a former john with a struggling podiatry practice in Anaheim, California. "The Grass Roots movement is really fucking me over," she had confided to Lasse over a bottle of scotch and pack of cigarettes. "Who can maintain a decent psychiatry practice with the city taking all of my money and self-help books popping up all over the place? *I'm OK-You're OK, The Power of Your Subconscious Mind* - can you believe such shit?" She exhaled smoke through her nostrils.

"You think you have problems," Lasse had grumbled. "It's hard enough to get patients because I'm a dwarf, but podiatrists are a dying breed. Back in the age of Joan Crawford and spike heels, I had a customer base I could rely on. Now all the dames are wearing earth shoes. My practice is in the toilet."

"I feel so sorry for you," she chided, "and your long days filled with crooked toes and fallen arches. I deal with broads who were stupid enough to get knocked up. One of them tried to give herself an abortion with a coat hanger."

Lasse paused. "You know, you may be on to something."

"What? Coat hangers?"

"Don't be coarse," he admonished. "It would be easy to do, not to mention a steady supply and demand with very few competitors."

Margaret tossed the idea around in her head for a while. "It would be easy enough to get a space and equipment, but no. You wouldn't dare. Any decent doctor could do it but not a junkie like you."

"Is that a challenge? Decent doctor my ass! I could do it with one arm tied behind my back."

"Well then, Lasse, want to put that talent where your mouth is?"

"Fine. I will."

A partnership was forged and an enterprise was born. Margaret purchased a small building in Orange County with a pseudonym and overseas bank funds. For IRS purposes, Lasse continued his podiatry practice in the building, collecting a forty percent cut for every abortion that he performed. Margaret continued her psychiatry practice in Philadelphia. Within a year, she met Magyar.

Magyar was born on Csepel Island. His parents were steelworkers, but the theater was their true passion. Despite a lack of money, their home was a constant refuge of social gaiety and entertainment. They put on skits with marionette puppets that Magyar's mother made out of homemade plaster, wax drippings, scraps of material, and artful paint jobs. His father would lead the neighbors in their reenactments: generally raunchy, drunken rants about the demoralization of culture as they knew it due to the infiltration of Stalin and the Red Army.

His family immigrated to Philadelphia after Stalin's death. His father took a job in the naval shipyards and moved the family to a small apartment on the southwest side. His mother took a job as a seamstress. Magyar began school immediately, adapting to the English language with ease, mimicking his speech patterns after his classmates.

On the morning of his ninth birthday, his parents met him in the kitchen with a frosted birthday pastry and word of a surprise waiting for him. He was instructed to get dressed quickly. When he had scrubbed until his ears were raw and yanked on a pair of pressed pants and a sweater, he was told to be on his best behavior, or the usher at the cinema might turn him away.

Cabin in the Sky was the first talking picture that Magyar had ever seen. He was impressed by the performances of Ethel Waters and Eddie Anderson, and enchanted by the ebony smoothness of Louis Armstrong's skin and voice. He fell in love with Lena Horne on the spot. It was the turning point that incited his lifelong interest in black cinema and jazz music. It influenced his decision to pursue an acting career.

With the support of his parents, he moved to New York after graduating from high school. He secured bit parts in small features and saved enough money with his work as a part-time entertainment feature editor for *Look Magazine* to enroll in Uta Hagen's acting class at the Herbert Berghof Studio. After being enrolled in class for a few weeks, Hagen told him that his acting style and stage presence were lacking in charisma, and his talents were misdirected. He was devastated. On that same day he received a phone call from his father. He told Magyar that his mother was terminally ill with cancer and wouldn't survive the year.

Magyar quit his job, packed his bags and returned to Philadelphia to remain by his mother's side during her final days. After her death, he worked for the *Philadelphia Inquirer* as a jazz and film critic, spending the majority of his time frequenting clubs and becoming a permanent fixture of Philadelphia's jazz and blues scene.

It was during this time that he was first introduced to Paul Robeson. They became fast friends. Paul introduced him to many actors and musicians who had been arrested and monitored by the government under the Smith Act. Magyar empathized and adopted their cause as his own.

He joined Robeson in organizing a relief fund for the families of the actors and writers rendered unemployable by the Hollywood Ten, still reeling from aftermath of the House of Un-American Activities Committee more than a decade later.

Magyar's father was infuriated by his son's political leanings, telling him that he had not risked the lives and future security of his family and established himself as a success story in the land of the free and the home of the brave to have his ungrateful, traitor son scratching the back of the very same regime from which they had so narrowly escaped. Magyar openly shunned his father's capitalist dreams and newfound Republican affiliations by calling him a marionette man. His father berated Magyar's affiliations with the Smith Act dodgers and budding Civil Rights Congress by calling him a red darky.

One morning, a member of the House of Un-American Activities Committee came to the naval shipyard and subpoenaed Magyar's father to testify about his son's involvement in an anti-government demonstration that had resulted in mass violence, the death of a police officer and the hospitalization of several others. Magyar's father clasped the crucifix around his neck, blinked back tears and dutifully obliged.

Magyar was arrested for murder, sentenced to life in prison, and ordered to undergo weekly psychiatric evaluations due to his political prisoner status. Margaret was appointed as his therapist.

After one session with Magyar, Margaret was convinced that their mutual attraction was much stronger than the ethical boundaries of a doctor-patient relationship. They quickly developed an inseparable bond. Despite her cast iron exterior and rational sentiment, Margaret overstepped the boundaries carefully delineated in her mind by falling in love.

Discovering that she was pregnant complicated the matter further. Margaret wanted to terminate the pregnancy but decided against it. She sullenly carried the pregnancy to term and delivered a healthy baby boy after two hours of labor. Bela's umbilical cord was cut and he was immediately placed into her arms. Fighting back tears, Margaret stared into all of his wrinkled hideousness and resisted the urge to hand him back to the obstetrician.

Bela

"Who else was a working performer during the McCarthy scare besides Butterfly McQueen and Hazel Scott?" he called from the bathroom.

Margaret exhaled her cigarette smoke and shifted in her chair at the kitchen table without looking up from her patient files. "The microwave beeped."

"I asked you a question. Harry Belafonte?"

"Get in here and remove your food. Now."

The toilet flushed. "You're my mother. Aren't you obligated to help me out?"

"Obligated?"

She set her papers aside, stubbed out her cigarette and walked to the microwave. She removed Bela's breakfast burrito and threw it out of the window as he entered the kitchen.

"Hey! What did you do that for?"

"You're running late. Aren't I obligated to help you out?"

A long pause followed.

"I really don't need this abuse."

A solitary wry snort ensued. "Then call the cops."

"I only have morning classes on Tuesdays and Thursdays, remember? Drying out before noon certainly hasn't made you smarter."

"Well aren't we fastidious." She reached for the coffeepot on the counter, refilled her mug and glanced out the window. Bela's breakfast had landed on the gas meter in front of the neighboring house. "Canada Lee," she added smugly. "That's checkmate to you. Oh, yeah, and you got a letter." She motioned vaguely in the direction of the next room.

The envelope waited for him on top of the television in the den. He picked it up and admired the antiquated penmanship before he opened it. Inside was a meticulously hand-crafted map of the theater district in Prague, a yellowed newspaper clipping commemorating the Oscar win of Hattie McDaniel, and a brief note describing the current political climate in Eastern Europe. He blinked back tears and vowed to meet his father someday. Then he gathered up his backpack and slipped out the front door without acknowledging his mother.

The majority of Temple students rode the train to Columbia Station, but he preferred to exit at Girard and purchase his lunch from the SuperFresh Market on the corner. From there, he walked past the Catholic school for girls at the corner of Broad and Oxford.

He watched them with rapt fascination. He was intrigued by the coltish grace of their scabbed, ashen knees peeking out from tartan plaid skirts and the starchy contrast of their white cotton socks. Their gravity-defying hairdos glistened in the sunshine as they played hopscotch and skipped Double Dutch rope during morning recess.

When he was done with classes for the day he spent an hour or two at Paley Library, then took the Broad Street Line to South Street and walked to his dilapidated apartment above the defunct dry cleaners at 13th Street. He unlocked the four deadbolts on his front door and was instantly greeted by the smell of dust settling and a pile of unwashed laundry.

He closed the door, locked the four deadbolts, and threw his backpack down. Two messages waited for him on the answering machine. His name had been randomly drawn in a contest and the prize was two tickets to the Academy of Music. Harold, a boy from his acting class, was having a party later on that evening.

Minutes later, he scrubbed himself in the shower with a bar of Ivory soap and hummed along to a Royal Opera House recording of *Madama Butterfly*. He followed up his careless shave job with a dab of styptic powder.

He selected a pair of faded grey corduroys and a JC Penney polo shirt from his closet's meager contents, but the image in the mirror triggered memories of high school beratement. Changing quickly, he pulled on a pair of Levi's jeans and a plain white cotton undershirt. He laced his brown leather shoes tightly and hoped that no one would notice their pitifully worn condition.

Outside, he bought a pretzel from the food truck at the corner and covered it with an obscene amount of mustard. He munched peacefully, humming the melody to *Amore o Grillo* as he walked to South Street Station. He exited at Columbia and headed north. He placed his ID into the drawer of the plexiglass security barrier and waited for the guard to acknowledge him verbally.

"Go on," she shooed. She eyed the pitiful state of his brown leather shoes, snapped her gum and turned her attention back to the small television resting on top of her space heater.

He walked ahead carefully to avoid tripping over the partly-detached soles of his shoes. A small object glittered in the hallway outside the elevator banks. He knelt down to examine it. It was a blue diamond. He held firmly in his fingertips and held it up to the fluorescent ceiling bulb. It dazzled in the gray green light. He put in in his pocket and called the elevator.

He exited on the third floor, followed the sound of music to Harold's apartment and knocked on the door. It swung open on its own. The entranceway was illuminated by colorful strobe lights and littered with clusters of people drinking from plastic cups.

He pushed his way into the living room and looked around. Mixed media depictions of the Philadelphia skyline made out of cardboard, glow-in-the-dark poster paint and shellacked breakfast cereal hung from the walls. Others were painted directly onto the lime green cinder bricks and gained texture from an abstract collage of magazine scraps. Above his head, aluminum foil mobiles in the shape of crescent moons, planets and stars hung from the ceiling.

On the left side of the room, more guests sat on a weathered couch, talking animatedly. A mirrored medicine cabinet door rested, knob up, on top of the coffee table. A rolled up dollar bill was perched next to it.

There was a karaoke machine in the right corner, and a table where Harold stood and sang along to Snap!'s *The Power*. He wore a black spandex minidress with exaggerated shoulder pads and galosh buckle closures. Between verses, he pursed his scarlet lips together and blew kisses at the cheering crowd.

A small, lustrous object caught the light at his feet. He bent to his knees and gripped it in his fingertips. It was a champagne colored pearl. He raised it to his nose. It smelled of violets.

An irate voice screamed from the doorway.

"Goddammit, Harold!"

He turned in the direction of the voice. The woman attached to it eyed Harold up and down angrily.

Another object sparkled on the ground in the direction of the glass doors leading out to the patio balcony. He tried to appear nonchalant as he bent down to pick it up. It was another blue diamond.

"Karen!"

Harold abandoned his karaoke performance and leapt from the table. He jumped into the woman's arms, wrapped his legs around her waist dramatically and inadvertently splashed his beer all over the onlookers.

He picked up another pearl and followed a trail to the patio. She was standing with one leg inside the apartment and the other outside of the glass doors. Her brown shoulders were draped in wisps of gauze and her legs were covered in soft denim. Pearls and diamonds leaked from her spiraling coils and ignited into prisms. She shifted her focus back and forth between the aluminum foil mobiles hanging from the apartment ceiling and the stars in the sky outside.

She felt his eyes on her and turned to look at him. He opened his mouth to speak and swallowed instead.

"Bullshit! I'm totally generous!" Karen shrieked above the music. "I'm not being a bitch, Harold! I totally don't mind if you borrow my dresses. I just wish you'd fucking ask first!"

He ignored the pitifully worn condition of his shoes and strode purposefully towards her. The sole of his left shoe detached completely, causing him to trip and fall on his face. The party guests turned in his direction. Flames of embarrassment lapped at his cheeks.

She watched the scene unfold for a moment before walking over.

"Are you hurt?"

He rolled from his stomach to his back and looked up at her. "I don't think so."

She stood in front of him and silently removed her shoes, revealing freshly manicured, opalescent toenails. Then she walked out of the glass doors and onto the balcony outside. He stood, removed his shoes, gathered up the traces of his pride and joined her.

They didn't speak as they stood next to each other and watched the first snow of the season. Flakes of myriad patterns swirled through the landscape and dusted the streets below as if agitated by an unseen hand.

Bela finally broke the silence.

"They look like powdered sugar."

"A good listener can hear them breathing."

Bela thought it over for a moment. "What are you, some kind of pagan?"

She didn't answer.

"Well. Try not to feel too bad. We'll make a new religion. How about Barefoot and Powdered?" He made the sign of the cross, clasped his hands together and tried to catch a snowflake with his outstretched tongue. "Oh, and that was nice of you to take your shoes off for me."

"I prefer my bare feet."

"When you get tired of listening to snowflakes, will you go out to see some music with me?"

"You see music, too?"

He raised his hands disarmingly. "I promise I won't drink from my fingerbowl. If you died of a soap overdose I could never forgive myself."

PHILADELPHIA, PENNSYLVANIA
1979

Calvin

Calvin found a dead hummingbird in the landscaped maze beyond the house while raking leaves with his father on a chilly Halloween morning. He leaned his weight against his toy rake and stared at the corpse.

To his six-year-old perception, its brightly-colored foliage was far too beautiful to be associated with death, so it had simply chosen this peaceful, random spot for a nap. He gathered up the courage to move in closer and gently clasped his hands behind his back in an attempt to remain as respectful as possible.

The diminutive bird was surrounded by a mosaic of autumn leaves in shades of garnet, topaz, citrine, and amber. He exhaled and watched his frosted breath shroud the corpse in a smoky mist that trailed outward towards the grove of oaks, past a handful of wild apple trees, and beyond the withering vestiges of rose bushes, violets, and morning glories that his mother had abandoned earlier that year. A sudden gust of wind brought forth the perfumed scent of green wood, dried petals and crisp Winesap apples. Calvin believed he could also detect a subtle trace of fear.

It lingered in the air and brushed past the surface of Calvin's woolen locs, lightly stroking the back of his ears. He inhaled it unknowingly and slowly walked backward to escape the instinctive knowledge of stumbling upon something he could sense and smell but never see or touch.

A jackdaw perched at the south end of the turreted roof caught a whiff of it and cawed mockingly in response. Calvin turned slowly to face it. It circled a few times on its scaly claws and shook out its raven wings before flying off with a streamlined, ebony swiftness towards the direction of the knotted oaks.

It wafted through a crack of open window at the west end of the house and into an adjoining bathroom, pausing to admire Jana as she dozed in a bubble-filled tub. Gathering courage, it gently brushed the delicate veins of her eyelids. Emboldened by a sense of unrequited longing, it slid under the iridescent bubbles to nestle up against her. It poked out its belly until it aligned with hers and cradled its head in the space between her breasts. It soothed its fumbling hands against her hips and comforted itself with the sound of her heartbeat, gingerly extending a finger across her inflatable bath pillow to touch the luminous halo of her curious tresses.

She awoke with trepidation, looked cautiously towards the window and instinctively brought her arms to her chest and abdomen to shield her body. The sudden agitation of the water caused the mass of bubbles to separate, exposing an inky-black body of water beneath.

Crackling leaves crunched underfoot as Calvin pulled up the hood of his faded blue sweatshirt and wiped a stream of mucous from his nose with his sleeve. Across the lawn, Russell paused at his rake, wiped sweat from his brow and watched his son lovingly. Calvin knelt down and cradled the hummingbird with his fingers, then carefully placed it on top of a garnet leaf laced with yellow palmate veins.

Fear coursed through Jana's blood. She pulled the stopper from the drain of the tub and grabbed her crumpled terry cloth bathrobe off the floor next to the tub. As the water spiraled down the drain, she ran into the adjoining bedroom and fumbled around for a bottle of pills in the drawer of her nightstand.

Shaking a pill from the neck of the bottle directly onto her tongue, her eyes spotted an open can of Tab and a pack of Chesterfields on the ebony rolltop desk across the room. She ran towards it, clutching her stomach through her bathrobe. With cigarette in hand, she gulped down the last of the soda and stood in front of the window.

Calvin approached the house with the hummingbird cupped in the protective cradle of his fingers. He paused momentarily to watch the image of his mother framed through the second-floor window. Visibly shaken, she turned her back to the sun-warmed panes and listened to the sound of Calvin's sneakers crunching through the leaves. She inhaled her cigarette deeply.

"Doctor Mommy," Calvin called as he entered the back of the house through the beveled glass doors. "Doctor Mommy," he repeated, a bit more authoritatively, tracking dusty footprints across the parquet flooring in the dining room and up the creaky wooden staircase leading to the second floor. Jana sank into the desk chair, her wild eyes fixated beyond the window to the oak grove past the maze. Smoke poured from her nostrils.

A brief knock at the door ensued. The glass knob turned and the door slowly creaked open. Calvin stood in the frame with outstretched palms, urging the corpse towards his mother. "Fix it, Doctor Mommy." His eyes were wide and innocent.

"It's dead, honey." Jana avoided looking at the bird. Her voice was shaky.

Calvin walked into the room and placed the corpse on the desk. "But it's a baby, Dr. Mommy. You're a baby doctor. Use your spethacope."

"Stethoscope." Jana corrected gently. "And Mommy's not a doctor anymore." Her voice was mildly impatient.

"It's a baby!" Calvin stamped his foot. His lip twitched.

Jana placed her elbow onto the desk and held up her brow with the palm of her hand. She stood up suddenly and paced to the bed, kneeling down to pull a small tapestry suitcase out from underneath. "Mommy's going away on her trip today and she needs to pack. You know that."

"Why are you going away?" Calvin asked.

"I've just been really tired is all," Jana began. She opened the suitcase and circled the bed. "So I'm going to a retreat. A spiritual one. I need to find my way back to something I lost when I was a girl. I have to decide if I want it to be a part of my life again, honey. I think it might bring me peace." She looked into her son's eyes and searched for a glimmer of understanding. "Do you understand?"

She didn't have to search for very long. "Won't saving the bird and watching it fly again bring you peace right here?"

"You know it's dead."

"Are you sure? Does it have to be? You're a baby doctor. It's never too late for you, you can always fix it." Calvin's tiny voice boomed with authority. "I know you can still fix it! Help it!"

"Stop it!" she replied too loudly, too harshly. She backhanded the hummingbird off the desk and onto the floor.

Silent tears welled up in Calvin's eyes. He walked to his mother's side and wrapped his arms around her protectively. Humiliated, Jana knelt down to her son's eye level to return the embrace. Overwhelmed by the love that he felt for his mother and comforted by the knowledge that he could both see and touch her, Calvin allowed himself to cry openly. As his mother held him closer and tighter, he forgot all about the hummingbird and the tears he shed were exclusively for her.

Russell's heavy footfall on the staircase broke the reverie. He paused at the doorway of the bedroom, cheerfully unzipping his hooded sweatshirt. His smile faded at the somber sight of mother and son in mourning. Reminding himself to appear bereaved for the sake of his son and intrigued by his wife's sudden proficiency as an actress, he bowed his head as Calvin knelt down on the floor and retrieved the hummingbird back to the safety of his cupped palms.

"What is it? Couldn't you find the stethoscope?" Russell asked his wife. He cleared his throat and playfully raised an eyebrow. Calvin turned his back to his parents and continued to coddle the corpse.

"No, yeah," she began, avoiding her husband's eyes. "I, I dropped him. Cal, I'm so sorry I dropped him. I'll go get the, uh," she trailed off, gesturing vaguely to the bureau as she wandered in its direction.

She found the stethoscope rolled up inside an old laboratory coat at the back of the drawer. Like a sacrificial offering, Calvin placed the hummingbird gently upon the desk. Jana held the eartips in place, checked the seals and placed the disk over the tiny body.

A warbling pulse funneled at the bell. Surging through the tubing like a rising streak of mercury, it ignited the latent embers in her heart and erupted into a ball of fire. The fire spread through her chest and traveled rapidly to her fingertips, singeing them upon contact. She shrieked as she dropped the chestpiece. Alarmed, Russell ran to her side and grasped her shoulders.

"Baby! Are you okay?" He cradled his wife's face with his hands and drew her close. He looked carefully into her eyes. "Are you having an attack? Calvin, bring me the bottle in the..."

"No, no; I'm okay. Please, I'm fine. I guess I'm just a little anxious about the trip." She nestled in closer to her husband's chest, comforted by the safety of his strong, brown arms.

Russell took the stethoscope from his wife and placed it around his own neck. He examined the bird and paused for a few moments before removing the earpieces. "I'm sorry son."

Calvin looked at his parents and scratched the back of his afro. "Isn't there anything we can do?" he asked quietly.

Russell took Calvin's tiny hand into his large one. "Let's have a snack." He handed the stethoscope back to his wife before placing his hand around his son's shoulder and leading him gently out of the bedroom.

Tentatively, Jana touched the chestpiece. It was ice cold. She sat motionless in the desk chair and stared at her fingertips.

She opened the suitcase and haphazardly threw in a few articles of clothing. Walking into the adjoining bathroom, she lingered at the window and watched the smoking clouds above the oak trees. Then she went back to the desk, grabbed the stethoscope, and tucked it into her suitcase.

In the kitchen, Calvin opened the cupboard to retrieve his favorite mug: a piece of hard plastic molded into the shape of Wile E. Coyote's head. Russell filled it with milk, cleared a space at the cluttered kitchen island for his son and quietly pulled out a chair.

Calvin sat down and sipped thoughtfully. His eyes trailed upward to the chandelier above his head, then shifted to the amber, leaded glass windows in the adjacent dining room. Sunlight poured in, framing his face with an ethereal glow generally reserved for the most precious of heavenly beings.

Russell left the kitchen to leave Calvin alone with his milk and his thoughts but returned a few minutes later with an unfinished pine cigar box and a box of acrylic paints. Lining the island with newspaper, he spread the paints and brushes to Calvin's right and a cup of water to his left. The boy's eyes were filled with questions as he looked up at his father. Russell rubbed his son's head and left the kitchen to check on Aunt Alice and help his wife with her suitcase.

Calvin watched his father disappear up the staircase and turned back in his chair to give the cigar box his rapt attention. Squinting with concentration, he painted a backdrop of oak trees capped with smoking stratus clouds, and the bereaved bird in profile: green crown, yellow beak, and pale blue body.

Pleased with his progress, he swirled a clean, watery brush into the red paint and carefully dabbed on a ruby throat. He sneezed suddenly. As he brought his sleeve to his face to catch a stream of mucous that escaped from his nose, a slash of watery red pigment dripped from the brush and bled from the bird's ruby throat into the pristine coolness of the oak trees and stratus clouds. He tilted his head and reexamined the painting.

In that instant, it occurred to him that his depiction no longer resembled a ruby-throated hummingbird at all but looked like an unidentifiable animal whose throat had been gutted by a predator. He attempted to cover the carnage with an extension of pale blue sky, but the end result was a ghastly, purple bruise that effectively destroyed the essence of what he had originally tried to convey. Huffing with disappointment, he saturated the entirety of the cigar box with an angry swirl of purple. Then he skipped out of the kitchen and into the projection room to watch *Villa Alegre*.

After the show was over, he returned to the box and the paint was dry. Choosing a silver pigment this time, he seized a brush and carefully printed the word, *HONOR* across its length in uppercase letters. Satisfied, he ran to the foot of the staircase and called out for his father.

———————

The sound of a car engine made its way up the driveway. Russell took the stairs two at a time with his wife's suitcase in tow and opened the front door to greet the driver. Jana, dressed in jeans and a navy fisherman's sweater, trailed a few paces behind.

She knelt down to Calvin's eye level and tucked her matted curls behind her ears. Her eyes softened at the sight of his beauty as she kissed the top of his head.

"You know that Mommy loves you very much, don't you?" she asked.

Calvin looked at the faint creases on her forehead. He was

startled by the wounds he saw in her eyes. "Yes," he answered softly. He gently patted her hair.

She hugged him tightly. Her eyes were focused on her knees. "I'm so sorry about the bird Cal," she choked. "I dropped it. I didn't mean to."

"I know."

She gave him one last squeeze, stood up, and joined her husband at the side of the cab. Russell kissed her goodbye and closed the car door. He returned to his son's side and felt for his hand. Calvin clasped it wistfully as the cab snaked along the driveway and crunched autumn leaves beneath its tires. It grew smaller and smaller, then gradually disappeared beyond the bend of the gate. They turned away, went back into the house and closed the door behind them.

They buried the cigar box beyond the apple trees at the base of the oaks. Calvin marked the grave with a red scarf tied to a stick.

At nightfall, brightly-colored clusters of trick-or-treaters began to swagger through the neighborhood streets, swinging hollow plastic pumpkins and paper sacks from their arms and shrieking with laughter. Russell peeked out from the maze and across the neighboring yard and chuckled at the sight of a boxy Etch-a-Sketch with holes for eyes wandering awkwardly down the road.

He grasped Calvin's head in a playful headlock.

"There's still time for you to go out if you'd like."

Calvin wiped his nose. "Isn't Auntie Alice coming out of her room today?"

"She's resting."

"She rests a lot."

"She's Superwoman. She's got some powerful batteries to recharge. Let's get your costume ready. I'll get a bag for your candy."

"I don't want to go trick or treating." Calvin stared at his feet.

"Well, what would you like to do?"

Suddenly feeling very shy, Calvin averted his eyes. "Play

castle."

Russell smiled and enveloped his son in a powerful hug.

They donned long velvet capes and covered their shoulders with Aunt Alice's ancient fox head stoles. They crowned each other with tagboard crowns decorated with gold glitter and plastic gemstones. When the doorbell interrupted them, Russell met the delivery person from Pamper Dee's restaurant in the foyer and traded a wad of cash for a large paper bag.

In the kitchen, Russell plated their turkey drumstick dinners and threw away the foam containers. Then he stood on a footstool to retrieve a pair of silver goblets from the top shelf of the butler's pantry. He filled one with Zinfandel and the other with grape juice.

Waxy tapers flickered in the tarnished candelabra at the center of the Henredon table as they gnawed on their drumsticks. When they were finished, Russell refilled their goblets and brought them out to the library along with two smoking pipes: one filled with apple tobacco and the other with caramel sauce.

Calvin sat in a red leather chair and propped his feet up on the matching ottoman. Adjusting his crown, he stared at the vellum lining the walls. Russell lit a pile of sage-laced wood in the fireplace. He tossed the logs with a poker. They snapped as they grew hotter and fragrant.

Outside the leaded glass window, the red scarf was perfectly still in the distant shade of oaks. Calvin shivered and pulled the fox stole closer to his shoulders. Draining the last of the grape juice from his goblet he stared at the sky diamonds winking through the blackness and told his father that the wood was haunted.

Turning his head away, Russell felt into the pocket of his cape and inserted a pair of plastic fangs into his mouth. Eerily backlit by the candles, he slowly revealed his face to his son and grinned. Calvin gasped with simultaneous fear and delight. He continued to suck on his caramel pipe.

Russell stood up from his chair and paused at the seemingly infinite wall of leather bound books. He carefully removed a burgundy-hued volume trimmed with black and gold. He settled back into the chair beside his son, nestled his cape closely around his shoulders, poised his pipe and opened the book to the table of contents. "And now," he began, "for your reading pleasure, I give you *The End of the Story* by Clark Ashton Smith."

Calvin nestled in the chair and allowed his imagination to transport him back to the haunted wood. Old-world spirits and vampires bade their tribute to the night, consuming everything in their path with a bloodthirsty vengeance. The oaks were alive with the fire of death, the earth of centuries, and the water of mourning.

Outside the window, Calvin traced the red scarf with his eyes as it shifted lightly in the night wind. "Honor our family crypt," he reasoned softly.

"What did you say?" Russell asked, placing the book down.

The persistent hooting of an owl rose out of the silence. It flew to the closed window and screamed at Russell and Calvin. Stretching its body to full wingspan, it hurled itself against the amber glass, then flew to the lip of the wood. It circled the hummingbird's grave, perched upon it and quieted down.

"What in the world?" Russell was alarmed. He closed the book.

"It's the keeper, Daddy," Calvin explained calmly. He put his finger on a stray dribble of caramel that dripped onto the red leather upholstery, licked it clean and felt for his crown. "It knows the family crypt's out there. He's come to keep it safe."

Russell opened the book again and continued to read. He paused briefly and observed his son carefully. For a moment he thought he was looking into the eyes of a perfect stranger, but the sound of Aunt Alice calling roused him from the reverie.

Jana

Inextricably trapped between a windshield and a moving wiper blade, an autumn leaf fought against its demise with a resounding crunch. Jana observed the tragedy through the passenger window proscenium as the cab veered westbound along the interstate towards the Pennsylvania border, entered Ohio and exited onto a rural stretch of road.

Elaborate gardens marked the entrance to a secluded, gated estate. The cab maneuvered through a tall iron gate and up a lengthy driveway before coming to a full stop at a rambling, three-story Georgian mansion. Stepping out of the vehicle, the driver opened the passenger door for Jana and lifted her suitcase out of the trunk.

A group of women dressed in thick, woolly sweaters sat on marble benches outside the garden entrance. They sipped hot beverages from porcelain cups and busied themselves with pointing out stars in the night sky. The wind tousled their hair gently, and the papery skin around their eyes crinkled as they laughed freely and easily.

She thanked the driver and thrust a wad of cash into his hand. Smoothing her hair down with her fingers, she gripped the suitcase handle in her left hand and walked towards the women with a careful smile on her face.

A woman in her mid-sixties with ample hips and earnest green eyes extended her hand. Her eyes squinted slightly. "Jana?"

She cleared her throat awkwardly.

"Yes. Hello."

"I'm Norah. We spoke over the phone last week. I'm so glad to finally meet you, sister. Welcome to the Visionary Women in Christ Retreat."

"Glad to meet you, too, Norah. I'm sorry I couldn't get here earlier."

Norah smiled and patted Jana's shoulder. "Stop apologizing. Nothing gets going until tomorrow anyway. Are you tired from the drive? The kitchen's still open. Why don't you bring your suitcase to your room and go down to the dining room to get something to eat?"

Jana clung to her careful smile. With suitcase firmly in hand she waved goodbye to the group and walked up a cobblestoned path toward a pair of transomed doors.

A tall woman with olive skin and high cheekbones opened the doors for her, grasped the suitcase without smiling and strode through the foyer with giant strides. Jana practically ran to keep up as they ascended a bifurcated staircase with an intricately carved balustrade. When they reached the top, the woman stopped at the fourth door to the right and held out a large key. "This is to be your room," she said in an Eastern European accent.

She turned the key in the lock and stepped into the doorway. The stately room was decorated with antique Chippendale furniture: a mahogany poster bed with a blue velvet bedspread, a bureau, and a corner chair. Jana approached the massive bed and ran a fingertip along the velvet. In the adjoining bathroom, an oversized, clawfoot tub was flanked by yellowing, hexagonal floor tiles.

She opened the suitcase and removed a small bag of toiletries.

Working quickly, she scrubbed her face with water and pulled a comb through her hair before heading downstairs in search of the dining room.

Three women were seated together at an extended banquet table. Above their heads, an Adam style chandelier dangled from a high, crown moulded ceiling. Despite the height of the ceiling, the chandelier hung far too low for Jana's immediate comfort. She swallowed her trepidation and walked over to join the group.

The tall woman approached her and laid a napkin across her lap.

"Can I bring you anything to drink?" she asked.

Jana smiled as brightly as she could. "Chardonnay, please. Thank you."

"Are you to join us for dinner? We're to have roast chicken."

"That sounds lovely. Thank you."

The first woman to speak stared at her matted curls. "Your hair. It's so, uh, different!"

Feeling like an animal pelt, Jana balled her napkin with her fists.

"Is this your first retreat?"

The second woman asked. Jana nodded politely. The tall woman returned to the table with a glass of white wine and a bowl of mushroom soup on a silver platter. She placed them in front of Jana.

"Where are you from?" The third woman inquired.

"Philadelphia. I'm Jana North." She played with her soup and tried to appear friendly.

The first woman nibbled at her chicken. "I'm Sandy Biecker, and this is Amy Gentry," she said, gesturing towards the second woman. "We're from Nashville. Spiree Roundtree is from Wyoming."

"Thermopolis, Wyoming." The third woman clarified. She was about eighteen with glossy, black hair and held a classical guitar. Nodding politely at the mention of her name, she gently played a few chords and winked at Jana. "You know how the train is supposed to come faster when you light a cigarette? Well, maybe the food will come faster if I…"

As if on cue, the tall woman reappeared and placed a plate of raw vegetables in front of Spiree. Sandy and Amy giggled. Spiree raised her eyebrows and set the guitar aside. Amy dabbed her lips with her napkin, folded it neatly to the right side of her plate and turned towards Jana. "Are you Born Again?"

"Not exactly."

"Are you new to Christ?" Sandy prodded.

Jana raised a hand to the back of her head and scratched. "I, I uh, have been meaning to get back to it for a while. But I'm not sure."

Sandy smiled over her cup of coffee. "Well, you certainly came to the right place. Trust Him and you'll never be lost again."

"He is the way," Amy murmured. "Find him," Spiree said. She crunched on a slice of bell pepper.

Amy reached into the pocket of her denim jacket for her wallet. She handed Jana a picture of a girl with short dark hair and Amy's doelike eyes. "This is Pearl. She's fourteen. She wants to be a comedian when she grows up."

Amy flipped to a slightly older boy wearing a cowboy hat. "This is Gil. He's sixteen years old and blesses us every day with his steel guitar playing. He wants to be the next Chet Atkins."

Jana smiled at the pictures and passed them back to Amy. "They're adorable." She assessed Amy's youthful appearance. "You don't look old enough to have teenagers."

Sandy tossed her spiky wedge haircut and sighed. "Spiree and I are still single and looking."

Spiree rolled her eyes. "I'm only eighteen, babe. Remember?"

"That's right. How could I ever forget?"

"And I don't seek from external sources. My fulfillment comes from within."

Sandy rolled her eyes. "Oh, you and your silly hippie

brouhaha. Squawk all you want now, Spiree Roundtree. You'll be singing a different tune when you're twenty-eight and your biological clock is ticking."

Amy tucked her billfold back into her pocket and looked at Jana. "Do you have any family?"

Jana opened her wallet to pass Calvin's photo in Amy's direction, but Sandy intercepted squarely with her thumb and forefinger. She inspected the snapshot. "Oh!" Her shock-widened eyes rivaled the circumference of dinnerware plates.

"What a handsome little fella!" Sandy paused for an awkward moment and cleared her throat. "Is he adopted?"

Jana kept her smile carefully in place and urged a photo of Russell towards Sandy. "This is my husband at Thanksgiving last year."

"Oh!" Sandy repeated. She stared at the picture of Russell and took in every inch of his blackness. Her eyes widened even more. She passed the photos to Amy. Amy looked at them thoughtfully.

"Your son and husband are beautiful." Amy continued to study Calvin's face. "And your son has the eyes of an artist. I'll bet his pendulum swings wide." Amy passed the photos to Spiree.

Sandy cleared her throat one last time. "You bet! Just like those nice Blind Boys of Alabama who gave that gospel concert in Knoxville for those starving black children in Africa." She paused. "I just love those starving black children in Africa!" She smiled broadly at Jana. Amy winced, rolled her eyes, and stole a carrot stick from Spiree's plate.

Spiree stared at the photos intently before passing them back to Jana. "He looks like Jimi Hendrix. Does he play any instruments?"

Jana laughed. "Not yet. Maybe I'll pay for lessons when my hearing starts to go."

The tall woman returned. She set a plate with half a roasted chicken and parsnips in front of Jana and a French press in front of Spiree. Spiree refilled her cup and watched Jana devour her meal. "I predict," she said, "that your son will turn out just like

Jimi Hendrix." She paused uncomfortably. "Well. Not like *that*. What I mean is he looks like a gifted musician. I can see it in his eyes."

They finished their meals and continued to chat. Sandy lit a cigarette. Jana reached into her purse and discovered that she had left her pack upstairs.

"Shit. I left my cigarettes in the room."

Sandy took a cigarette from her pack and urged it towards her. Jana thanked her, lit it and inhaled deeply. It was menthol.

Not wanting to appear ungrateful, she raised it back to her lips, hesitated and tapped it against the ashtray at the center of the table. Spiree laughed and produced a hand-rolled cigarette from a small pouch that hung from her neck by a silver cord. "Have one of mine."

Jana shook her head and reluctantly took a second minty puff. "I shouldn't waste it."

"Take it," Spiree ordered. "Save it for later, even. I roll my own and blend the leaves myself."

Jana took the cigarette from Spiree's fingers and tucked it into the zippered pouch at the back of her purse. She glanced at her watch. "It can't be one o'clock already! Really? I'll see you ladies tomorrow. I can barely keep my eyes open."

She said goodnight and made her way through the main hallway and up the massive staircase, pausing briefly to peer at the framed photographs of past attendees that hung above the balustrade.

———————————

She sat on the edge of the oversized clawfoot tub and drew a bath. The floor was ice cold against her bare feet. As the bathtub slowly filled with water, a teardrop escaped her womb. It trailed down her thigh and dripped stealthily onto the yellowing tiles.

"That's odd," she said aloud, putting a finger to the bloodspot. "I'm not due for another week." She swiped the tile with her finger, dunked her hand into the water, and swirled until it came back clean.

The water gurgled as she eased herself into the steaming tub. She raised her legs and soaped them languorously. In the distant background, a woman's voice rose combatively. A second voice begged for peace and quiet. Mahalia Jackson's sweet contralto wafted faintly from an indeterminate direction as voices faded away.

She reached for her cigarette pack, and remembered the hand-rolled gift from Spiree at the back of her purse. She pressed it between her lips and groped on the floor around her toiletry bag for a matchbook.

Her fingers grazed the cold metal of the stethoscope instead. She pulled it out of the bag and held it for a moment before securing the earpieces inside her ears and placing the chestpiece to her belly.

An essence breathed softly in the water. It exhaled towards the surface in a halo of concentric ripples and inhaled downward through the drainpipe with a burst of black smoke bubble. Closing her heavy eyelids, Jana slid the chestpiece upwards to the space between her breasts and listened closely to the story she kept there.

JANA: (Exhausted agony) "It hurts!"

LASSE: (Mildly placating, wiping his forehead) "It's nothing really, just a little cramping."

JANA: (Wavering in and out of consciousness, weeping, detecting the odor of gin and peanut butter on Lasse's breath) "It's not supposed to hurt this much!"

LASSE: (Calling to his secretary in the adjoining room) "Hey, Ells? In the bathroom medicine chest there's morphine and a syringe. Bring it back here, would you?"

ELLS: (From the office) "Alright, Lasse." (Abandons her

typewriter and walks briskly to the bathroom to retrieve the morphine and the syringe. Walks into a back room where Jana is tossing on a creaky cot with blood-soaked hand towels wrapped between her legs. Pushes the bridge of her trifocals up against her nose and looks at the vials) "She's not supposed to lose that much blood! How much blood has she lost?"

LASSE: (Gruffly) "Just give me the fucking drugs, Ells!"

ELLS: (Offended, hands him the morphine and fans her heart with her fingers) "The language that comes out of you!" (Drags over an ancient elementary school pupil's desk, sits down next to Jana and places her hand on her forehead as she rolls onto her side and continues to whimper. Her concern turns fast to anger) "I may be an old woman but I'm no fool! She's burning up with fever! She has an infection! She needs antibiotics!"

LASSE: (Applies a tourniquet to Jana's right arm and injects the syringe, seemingly unaffected by her pain and trauma) "It's just a little cramping, that's all." (Removes the tourniquet from Jana and applies it to his own arm, tightening the rubber with his teeth)

ELLS: (Wincing) "Maybe you shouldn't be doing that right now."

LASSE: (Angry and defensive) "What the hell's that supposed to mean? You think because I'm a dwarf I can't hold my liquor and drugs?"

ELLS: (Attempting to convey the gravity of the matter, thoroughly disgusted) "Lasse Eriksen, this girl needs a hospital. She's bled through her clothing, and there's peanut butter in your beard."

LASSE: (Darting his tongue out of his mouth to remove the blob of peanut butter, refills the syringe with morphine, plunges the used needle into his arm) "Not in the Tarot cards, Ells. I'm not implicating myself. Have enough trouble getting patients as it is. Besides that, I'm off duty." (Grins with euphoria, walks over to radio and fiddles with the dial, settles on *Incense and Peppermints*. Closes his eyes, flails arms and legs in an interpretive dance).

ELLS: (Incensed) "This is preposterous! You have an obligation to your patient! You're responsible for her wellbeing! She paid for your services! Doesn't that mean anything to you?"

LASSE: (Dismissively) "She's a flat-broke, first year pediatrician who only came up with half the fee. Margaret's going to kill me when she finds out."

ELLS: (Stroking the damp tendrils framing the bleeding woman's face, gently picks up her hand) "I'm not going to let you die in this hellhole." (Standing up with authority) "I'll you to Kaspare Cohn if I have to carry you there myself!"

LASSE: (Dancing to the song blaring from the radio, rocking his buttocks and weaving his hands in front of his face) "Kaspare Cohn? What're you talking about?"

ELLS: (Removing bloodied towels from between Jana's legs and walking towards the bathroom in search of fresh ones) "Used to be the TB house. In the city. On Fountain."

LASSE: (Making the connection, stops dancing) "Kaspare? You mean Cedars. It's Cedars Lebanon now."

ELLS: (Emerging from the bathroom, placing fresh towels between Jana's legs and feeling her head again) "They won't know her there. It's clean and state-of-the-art." (Brusquely, pushing her trifocals up the bridge of her nose and regarding Lasse with disdain) "Look here, doctor, you can either idle around like some common smackie, or you can help me get her ready. I need hot water, surgical scrub and more towels!"

Growling, Lasse wandered into the bathroom and stepped onto the wooden platform in front of the sink. He turned on the hot water and filled a plastic basin resting next to the sink. Carefully stepping down from the platform, he grabbed a bottle of Phisohex that rested on top of the toilet. The towel rack was empty. He opened the bathroom cabinet and found it to be free of towels as well. He cursed and walked back into the tiny room. Ells grabbed the plastic basin and the bottle of Phisohex from his hands and placed them onto the tiny desk. Lasse started to mention the lack of towels, had a sudden idea and stormed out of the back room and into the front office.

Ells gently supported Jana's back in an upright position. She squirted some of the surgical scrub into the water, dabbed a washcloth into it, and gently wiped the feverish woman's brow. A crash emanated from the closet of the front office, followed by a string of expletives and footsteps. A few seconds later, Lasse returned to the back room carrying a black duffel bag.

"I went to Malibu earlier this week," he explained, opening the bag. He pulled out several *Playboy* magazines, a bottle of baby oil, a pair of leopard print bathing briefs, a snorkel mask, and a large purple beach towel. He held up the towel. "Is this okay?"

Ells secured the last hand towel between Jana's legs and pulled the leopard bathing briefs snugly into place. She helped the younger woman stand up and wrapped the purple towel around her body. "Get the car, Lasse," she urged.

Lasse crossed his arms. "Not in the Tarot cards, Ells. I already told you."

Jana leaned against the older woman and allowed herself to be led out of the building, down the front steps and onto the sidewalk. Ells leaned on her agate cane and rested. "Let's get a cab dear," she said soothingly.

Lasse lingered at the top of the steps. "You think a cab is gonna stop in this neighborhood? Not in the Tarot cards, Ells!" he spat.

Shut up!" Ells barked, leading Jana into the street. She fumbled about in her pocket and withdrew a steel whistle. Firmly supporting Jana's weight with one arm, she blew into the whistle sharply and waved the cane in the air with the other. Horns blared furiously as she stepped into the line of oncoming traffic. A tan, mufflerless El Camino sped past. "Idiot bitch!" the driver shouted.

"Get out of the fucking street!" Lasse bellowed. "You're gonna get killed!"

Ells secured her grip on Jana and continued to blow the whistle.

Lasse ran into the street and knocked the two women out of the path of an orange Volkswagen bus. "Okay, you crazy coot!" Lasse screamed. "You win! I'll drive! I'll drop you off!" He seized the arms of both women and led them back to the sidewalk.

The purple towel unfastened at Jana's chest. She lurched to grasp it, but her hand trembled and it fell to the sidewalk, exposing her bra and Lasse's leopard briefs. A green Dodge Dart slowed down to observe as Ells dropped to her arthritic knees to retrieve the towel.

"How much?" a greasy man with too much jewelry inquired, holding out a wad of bills as Ells scooped up the towel and wrapped it around Jana's body.

"Keep on moving, you good for nothing hooligan!" Ells scolded. She shook her agate cane menacingly.

"Granny pimp!" the man taunted, laughing as he drove away.

Ells let out an audible sigh of relief as Lasse's Mercedes pulled up to the curb. Opening the rear door, she eased Jana into the backseat. She had barely pulled the car door shut behind her before Lasse laid into the accelerator and sent the car into motion with a squealing lurch.

Lasse's head reverberated with the wane of morphine and the scent of blood. He adjusted the rear view mirror and watched as Ells took off her trifocals and rubbed her eyes. Jana laughed detachedly to herself, curling her body into fetal position and resting her head on Ells' shoulder. "Not in the Tarot cards, Ells," she mimicked, continuing to chuckle softly.

He eyed Jana derisively. "What's she laughing about?" he growled. His body twitched with morphine withdrawal. A group of trick or treaters carrying hollow plastic pumpkins filled with candy dashed in front of the car, causing Lasse to slam on the brakes. He stared at her in the rearview mirror. "The fuck you laughing at?" he grumbled, looking at Ells. "What the fuck's so funny?"

"She's fine," Ells replied. "She just needs…"

"My baby," Jana rambled deliriously.

"What?"

"She's gone," Jana babbled, nodding her head and falling asleep.

Horns blared as traffic crawled along the 5. The Mercedes crept a few feet forward and came to a stop. Ells pushed her glasses up the bridge of her nose in a futile attempt to see what was happening. The back end of a semi obscured her view of the freeway. Its exhaust fumes permeated her nostrils.

"Can't you take a side street?" Ells asked, feeling Jana's forehead. "She has a fever."

Lasse snorted. "Why don't you use your witchcraft to make the car move itself?" he added sarcastically.

"Shut up," Ells grumbled. "You know my witchcraft isn't good for that."

An hour passed. Ells cradled Jana in her arms like a baby and turned her head towards the warmth of the sun. Lasse blew his horn at the cars creeping ahead.

"Oh, fuck me," he exclaimed. He slapped his palms against the steering wheel.

"Not in the Tarot cards, Ells," Jana mocked deliriously. She lifted her head, pulled her towel open and trembled at the sight of her own blood. Ells pulled the towel back modestly.

"Keep holding on, sweetie. Just keep holding on," Ells whispered. A trace of fear mixed with the scent of blood in the air.

"It hurts," Jana whimpered.

Lasse sneered as he watched the exchange between the two women in the rearview mirror. "So what's in the Tarot cards, Ells?" he finally asked.

Ells looked cautiously at Jana and the back at Lasse, as if she already knew the answer to the question and was fearful of the outcome. "What? Here?" she asked Lasse bleakly.

"What's in the Tarot cards, Ells?" Jana asked limply. Ells carefully replaced her fear with a convincing look of scorn. "Oh, you don't really want to be bothered with that, do you?" Her eyes met Lasse's in the rearview mirror. They glared.

"Just tell us what's in the bloody Tarot cards, Ells!" Jana managed with all of the energy that she could muster.

Ells gasped and clutched at her heart. "No need to get testy," she scowled. She opened her purse and withdrew a black silk bundle. Inside was an ancient, gilt-edged deck. She placed it on her knees and began to shuffle, all the while glaring at the back of Lasse's head.

"Cut the deck," she prodded, urging the cards towards Jana. Weak but satisfied, Jana lifted a shaking hand and divided the deck into halves. Ells restacked the deck and carefully laid the cards face up on her lap.

Ells peered at the cards and held them up to her failing eyes. "Let's see," she began. "I'll translate the Celtic into English for you. Two Sceptres, Wands or Clubs. Three inverted Phials or Hearts, two remain standing. One inverted Barter or Diamond. Nine Glaives or Swords. Inverted Tower. Death. The High Priestess. Oh, dear..." she trailed off.

"What?" Jana moaned. "Death? Tell me! What happens? Am I going to die?"

Ells regarded the bleeding woman soberly. "Your time of death is entirely unrelated to the relevance of this reading. The magic of the Sceptre will always surround you. Death in the figurative sense represents change. An inverted Barter indicates a change in your career." She winced. "Your tower is going to fall. Nine Glaives will plague you throughout a difficult time. Two Phials will sustain and nourish you, even when all the others around you have dried up.

"What does it mean?"

Ells scratched Jana's back gently. "Life is a circular journey that ultimately completes itself in one way or the other. We often choose difficult paths that we perceive to be mistakes, but the truth of the matter is, there are no mistakes. Do you understand?"

"I think so."

Lasse looked up into the rear view mirror. "Are you getting blood on my seat?"

"You're a dunce, Lasse." Ells mumbled. She turned back to Jana. "Until a lesson is learned, circles have a way of reappearing over and over again. Embrace your fate or it will remain unresolved. Look to your family."

"I don't have any family!" Jana burst into tears.

Ells gathered up the cards and wrapped them up with the scarf. "What about the father?" Jana shook her head vehemently and sobbed.

Tears of sympathy welled in the older woman's eyes. "Oh, my dear, I am sorry to hear that!" She reached for Jana's hand. "It might not be with him, but you will have a family someday, I assure you." She continued to comfort the younger woman and hold her hand. Gradually, the traffic eased, and the car made its way towards the hospital.

Lasse stopped the Mercedes several feet away from the emergency room entrance. "You can make it from here, right? I have to call Margaret."

"Go away!" Ells snapped. Jana leaned against the old woman's shoulder and allowed herself to be led through the main entrance, past the front lobby and into a waiting area.

The walls were pasted with cardboard Halloween decorations. A group of tables were clustered to the back of the room behind two sofas. A receptionist looked up at the sound of their entry, picked up a telephone, and helped Ells ease Jana into a wheelchair. "Someone will be right with you," she said, handing Jana a clipboard with paperwork attached. Exhausted by the course of the day, Ells sat down on a sofa and nodded off.

A boy was drawing with crayons and paper at the table adjacent to Jana's. He was around six years old, and had red hair that stood straight up to the sky. He looked feverish. Clutching a crayon drawing in his hand, he approached Jana and smiled shyly.

"I'm Finn," he said. "What's your name?"

"Hi, Finn. I'm Jana." She extended her hand and tried hard to conceal her discomfort. "What's this?" she asked, looking at the paper in his hand.

He handed the drawing to Jana. She stared at the waxy depiction of leafy green trees with giant brown trunks shrouded in a dark blue sky. A large yellow moon loomed in the upper right hand corner. A multicolored castle with multiple spires surrounded by a gate was drawn in the distance.

"Who lives here?" Jana asked.

"It's a healing forest," Finn explained. "Sick kids and..." he looked at the bloodstains in Jana's lap and paused, "...ladies who need to be healed go there to experience the magic." He smiled and exposed the gap where his front teeth had once been.

"It's beautiful." Jana said softly. She urged the picture back towards the boy. "Thank you for showing it to me."

"I made it for you," Finn said. "That way, when you get there you'll know you're in the right place." He took Jana's hand in his own and patted it. Then he sat back down at his table, picked up a crayon and started a new drawing.

Moments later, a woman with a short white afro wearing a white medical coat with a low slung belt came into the room. She appeared to be in her early sixties and held a chart. "Jana Montgomery?" she asked. "I'm Dr. Nell." She approached Jana's chair and held her hand.

"Am I going to die?"

"Not on my watch." Dr. Nell took Jana's pulse before wheeling her into an adjacent room.

———————————————

"Would you like to see her?" the receptionist asked Ells a few minutes later, rousing the older woman from her nap. She nodded and followed the receptionist through the partition door and down a corridor to a small room where Jana was being prepped for a transfusion. Dr. Nell looked up at her and smiled.

"You're welcome to stay with her if you'd like," she said. "It might keep her calm to have family nearby. Are you her mother?"

"My ride is waiting for me, I'm very sorry." Relieved that the younger woman was in capable hands, she started to walk away but hesitated.

"Wait!" Ells fumbled with a clasp behind her neck. A Celtic cross carved from moonstone dangled from a silver chain. She placed it around Jana's neck and fastened it. Twitching slightly, Jana clutched Finn's drawing in her hand as Ells kissed the top of her head.

"Seems fitting you should have this, being that it's Samhain." Ells explained, leaning in closer. "So you'll always be able to find your way safely. God hold your hand through the Celtic New Year, and throughout the circle of life." Leaning on her cane, she pushed up her glasses and bowed her head for a moment. Then she walked out of the room and quietly closed the door behind her.

———————————————

She was vaguely aware of being helped out of the wheelchair. When she regained consciousness, she was lying in a shallow metal tub filled with warm water and clutching the crayon drawing. "Can you ease your legs up a little?" Dr. Nell asked gently.

Jana obliged.

"You're a very lucky woman. All that bleeding was caused by gashes to the outer cervix and vagina. You shouldn't have any problems whatsoever if you choose to have children in the future. Your blood count is stable now. Heat will ease the cramping. Has the sedative kicked in yet?"

Jana closed her eyes and nodded. She hung her head to the side and stared at the drawing in her hand. Comforted, she swirled the picture along the surface of the bathwater and watched as the waxy paper sunk to the bottom.

She spent the evening resting comfortably in a private room. The following morning, dressed in clean clothing that the receptionist had given her, she thanked Dr. Nell and waited for a cab.

Dr. Nell gave her a brown paper bag filled with antibiotics and painkillers. "Take it easy for the next few days. If you have any problems, get in touch with me immediately."

"I will," she lied. She hoped the painkillers would make it possible for her to return to work that very afternoon.

She waited ten minutes before donning a pair of dark sunglasses and walking towards the rear entrance of the hospital. She stepped outside, hoping to duck into a cab unnoticed but found herself accosted by a moderate-sized group of people blocking the back entrance.

"Dr. Jana Montgomery?" A voice shouted. Despite the dark sunglasses, a flashbulb blinded her. Dazed, she stared ahead.

The more obtrusive members of the group were holding microphones. "Dr. Montgomery! Is it true that you illegally terminated your pregnancy a few hours ago? Are you aware that the procedure is illegal? You practice as a pediatrician in the state of California. Given the circumstances, is it a conflict of interest to continue in your career?"

"Baby killer!" An elderly man holding the hand of a little girl screamed at Jana. "Baby killer," the little girl mimicked, sticking her tongue out at Jana. Several rosaries were thrust in her face. Hail Marys rang from multiple directions.

"Over here, Dr. Montgomery! Sources say you were raised in a loving, Southern Christian home by a pastor father and God-fearing mother. Is this the example they taught you, to kill the innocent? Do they condone murder?"

"Over here, Jana!"

"Hail Mary, full of grace!"

"Dr. Montgomery!"

Jana inched backwards. By now, the staff, led by Dr. Nell, had come to the door to rescue her from the commotion.

"Get out of here before I have you arrested for trespassing! All of you!" Dr. Nell screeched. She grasped Jana's shoulders and pulled her back into the building. Shutters clicked as she braced herself for one last flash of blinding light.

Everything went black. When she opened her eyes, she was naked in a river of scalding black water. Burning mud shackled her ankles in a death grip below the surface. Despite an impenetrable thickness of trees sprouting around her, she could see the faint lights of a castle in the background.

A silhouetted figure stood at the edge of the mossy, tree-lined bank. It was swaddled entirely in gauze. Black spiraling coils gleamed with pearls and crystals.

"Help me!" Jana barked. "Help me!" She tried to run, but the mud grabbed the hair at the back of her head and stopped her in her tracks. Losing her balance, she gasped and swallowed. The black liquid scalded her throat as she continued to flail and scream. Her nipples were blistered by the heat.

She rolled onto her stomach and clutched at seaweed leeches in an effort to leverage herself, but the plants bound their tentacles around her neck and tried to strangle her. With her last bit of strength, she pulled herself loose and collapsed in a fit of coughing. She fought to overpower the seaweed leeches and keep her head above the stinging water. "Are you my daughter?"

The figure turned around slowly. Jana couldn't see the face through the shadow of impenetrable trees. It took a few steps forward and calmly extended an arm. Jana flailed her blistered fingers in desperation.

She had almost grasped it when an unseen vortex yanked her away. She tried to scream but found herself sinking into the burning mud instead.

Carmine water sloshed out of the large clawfoot tub and onto the yellowing hexagonal tiles as her eyes and body bolted upwards. Agitated, the stethoscope slid from the space between her breasts to her navel. Horrified, she threw it across the tiles with all of her strength and briskly pulled the chain on the stopper. The water turned obsidian black as it gurgled down the drainpipe.

She dressed quickly and swallowed two Valiums without water before making her way to the dining room. A sizeable crowd clustered around a breakfast buffet. Jana took her place in line and tried to stop her hands from shaking.

"Over here, Jana!"

Sandy, Amy and Norah waved to her from the far end of the table where they had dined the evening before. Jana was relieved to see that the low-hanging chandelier seemed far less menacing in broad daylight. She loaded her tray with scrambled eggs, sausage and coffee, and walked across the room to join the group.

"Did you have pleasant dreams?" Amy asked her.

"I don't remember. How were yours?"

"Slept like a log. Have you met Norah?"

"Yes. How are you this morning?" "Thirty-six attendees this year! I'm so excited!" Norah said, buttering a biscuit. "I've never seen a turnout like this before. When I started back in Corpus

Christi nine years ago, we had a group of three."

Jana took a bite of scrambled eggs and wiped her mouth with her napkin. "Congratulations, Norah! Has anyone seen Spiree?"

"She's fasting." Amy munched on a piece of bacon. "She's going to meditate in the garden until the art session begins."

"Have you seen the studio, Jana?" Sandy asked.

"Not yet." Jana sipped her coffee.

"Do you draw or sculpt?"

Jana exhaled. "Russell and Calvin are the artists. I just observe."

"You just remember that you came here to express yourself," Amy said. "I'll bet you discover talents you never knew you had."

"I don't know about that," Jana sniffed. She watched the others enjoying their meals and picked at the food on her plate.

The studio was set up in a greenhouse. Four long tables covered with white paper were set up in the center, and easels lined the perimeter. A kiln rested against the wall, along with an abundance of art supplies.

Multiple pockets of women huddled together and chatted as they sketched charcoal images of the garden landscape. Jana smiled self-consciously and remained a few paces behind while Amy and Sandy ventured ahead to select canvases, brushes and paints.

"Good morning!" Spiree burst into the room. She was red-eyed, barefoot and wearing a t-shirt, jeans, and a necklace made out of feathers and bones. She carried a bulky mass wrapped in burlap.

"Intriguing neckwear, young lady," Amy remarked as she opened a bottle of turpentine and placed it onto one of the paper covered tables. "Did you make that yourself?"

"Of course." Spiree looked proud. She set the burlap mass

down on the table next to Amy. "It was the last time I ate flesh, when I was twelve years old and my Grandpa shot a pheasant. I was used to my parents hunting for meals, but this time it was different. That pheasant was majestic. I could sense its instincts, its determination, even. It had a purpose all on its own. Who were we to take that away? So I told my family that consumption wasn't a righteous destiny. They shrugged and told me to clean my plate anyway. I did as I was told, but that was the last time. Later on that evening, when everyone was asleep, I dug its remains out of the garbage and prayed for its soul. Then I made this necklace."

A chill swept through Jana.

"You been smoking those funny cigarettes again, Spiree?" Sandy's voice was disapproving.

Spiree ignored her and wrapped her arm around Jana's shoulders. "You okay, sister?" she asked. Jana nodded and sat down. Amy and Sandy looked on in concern.

"I, I'm fine. It was just the smell of turpentine, that's all."

Spiree relaxed. "I know what you mean." She removed a burlap cover from a large block of clay. "I could never work with turpentine. It makes me sick, too."

Jana glanced around the room and looked at the kiln.

"We can sculpt clay together if you'd like," Spiree offered.

There was a bundle on the floor next to the kiln. She walked over to it and pulled back the newspaper. A slab of dusty white marble lay beneath. An unknown force coursed through her body as she involuntarily picked it up. Staggering beneath its weight, she brought it back to the table. "Does anyone know where I can find a chisel?"

Sandy pointed at a cabinet next to the kiln and winked. "I've been meaning to get out of modeling because I really want to direct, but I suppose I can pose for you this one last time," she teased, sucking in her cheeks for effect.

Jana managed a tiny smile. "Only if you smoke one Spiree's

funny cigarettes first."

Sandy, Amy and Spiree burst into peals of laughter. Jana watched passively as her hands maneuvered a hammer and chisel. Marble dust collected at her feet.

"Who died?" Sandy asked.

The women stopped what they were doing and stared at the Celtic headstone in Jana's workspace.

"No one!" Her tone was surprisingly defensive.

"Alright, I'm sorry!" Sandy raised her hands above her head in fake surrender and resumed focus on her painting: a lemony blond, Huntington Beach Jesus surfing boardless across the Sea of Galilee. She hesitated, set down her palette, and turned back to admire Jana's monument.

"But when somebody does," Sandy continued, "they'll have the best-dressed grave this side of the Mississippi."

Jana wrapped her arms around her shoulders defensively but softened when she saw that Sandy's eyes reflected a genuine admiration. Brushing dust from her hands and tucking her hair behind her ears, she pulled herself together as the group continued to work.

Calvin

While most boys his age were going to summer camp, planning fishing trips, and discovering untapped areas of interest around their neighborhoods, Calvin preferred standing underneath the antique silver and crystal chandelier in the mansion's kitchen and spinning for hours on end. His behavior alarmed Jana, and she immediately brought it to Russell's attention. They agreed that Calvin would benefit greatly from the structure and discipline of a more privileged education, and decided that boarding school was in order.

Scores of independent school catalogs for the upcoming academic year littered the kitchen island. Calvin spun with arms outstretched, lost in the horn section of his favorite Earth Wind and Fire album.

He was pulled out of his trance by the sound of Aunt Alice's bell ringing. He stopped spinning, turned down the music and ran to the foot of the stairs.

"What?"

"Don't make me yell down these steps! Come up here and see what I want!"

He trudged up the stairs reluctantly. Aunt Alice was sitting up at the edge of her bed. She wore a salmon pink nightgown with a

white lace yoke. Her hair was neatly sectioned into four braids. "What?" he repeated.

"Get your grumpy tail over here and give me a hug," she snarled. Calvin noticed that she wasn't wearing her dentures. He settled into her arms. She smelled like floral dusting powder. She squeezed him, hard, and gave him a kiss.

"I'm hungry," she complained. "Run down to the kitchen and bring me the rest of the greens and a sliced tomato."

"There aren't any left," Calvin proceeded to dash from the room, but Aunt Alice's quick grasp caught him by the shirttail.

"Stop telling tales, Calvin!" Aunt Alice accused. "I know we didn't eat up five pounds of greens in two days!"

"Dad took the rest of 'em to work." Calvin explained.

"I see," Aunt Alice said, the wheels of her mind silently turning. Calvin freed himself from her grasp and started down the stairs.

"Calvin," she sang.

Calvin rolled his eyes and returned to her side.

"How would you like some barbeque?"

Calvin grew excited despite himself.

"I'll get some barbeque for that baby," she grinned. "But first, reach up here in my nightstand and get an Efferdent tablet and change my denture water."

Calvin changed her denture water, vacuumed her bedroom carpet and dusted her television screen before she called Russell at work and asked him to stop in Germantown on his way home for Speed Queen Barbeque takeout.

"What do you mean you can't because you're working late?" she bellowed in response to Russell's protesting. "Isn't that what that flunky junior partner's for? Well, what am I supposed to do? That gal's out of town and you ate up...oh, Lord, you know I don't mean any...Jana's out of town, and you ate up five pounds a' greens for lunch...done broke your plate. I guess this is the thanks I get. I never let your rusty butt sit up in my house hungry…let you wrap your lips around all my food. That baby's hungry, too. Well, I'll let you tell him then. Calvin! Pick up the phone. Your daddy has something to tell you."

———————◆———————

"The Schuylkill was backed up all the way from the city, sorry I'm late," Russell mumbled sheepishly. He handed Aunt Alice three large brown paper bags stained with grease spots. She opened the bag and pulled out a Styrofoam container filled with macaroni and cheese. "Hey, Russell," she began.

"What? Did I forget something?" Russell looked ashen. "Oh, no! They didn't forget to put the lemonade in again, did they?"

"You didn't forget anything at all, baby," Aunt Alice stuck a plastic fork into the macaroni and cheese and sampled it. "I'm the one who forgot to say thank you."

Russell sat at the kitchen island nibbling barbequed ribs, studying independent school catalogues, and writing himself a reminder note to contact the Dean of Students at Phillips Academy to set up an interview for Calvin. Six months later, Calvin was accepted and the family planned for his move to Massachusetts.

He was met with admonishment when he arrived at the dormitory. A group of boys in polo shirts and madras shorts eyed him up and down as he passed the campus lawn, whispering in hushed giggles about how their tax dollars were hard at work contributing to the educational enrichment of welfare niggers. Calvin met their smirks with confusion and stalked ahead in search of his resident advisor.

The resident advisor was a lanky upperclassman with very fair skin and painful looking cystic acne. He handed Calvin a key and told him that his assigned roommate had decided to study abroad at the last minute, and that he would be rooming alone for a semester. Calvin walked down the corridor and unlocked his door. He set down his suitcase, sat on one of creaky twin beds and stared at the light fixture dangling from the ceiling.

At the initiation assembly, the varsity basketball coach saw Calvin's tall, slender figure standing a few rows to his left and asked him if he was interested in playing basketball. Calvin explained that he was only a freshman and didn't know how to play. The coach put his arm around Calvin's shoulder and told him that he had his eye on the regional championships and would be willing to make an exception to the upperclassman requirement in recognition of Calvin's talent. "You'll knock it out of the park," he said.

At basketball practice, the coach buried his head in his hands when all of Calvin's shots missed the backboard of the hoop entirely and sailed out of bounds. He threw his towel down angrily when the bell rang at the end of the period, scowled at Calvin and stormed off of the court and out of the gymnasium.

After practice, Calvin was showering in the locker room when he felt eyes upon him and turned around. One of the boys who had whispered behind his back was staring at him inquisitively, face flushed with embarrassment. Calvin turned his back to him and turned off the water, reaching for his towel as the boy spoke.

"I didn't mean to stare, but I can't figure out where it is." The boy looked nervous.

"What are you talking about?" Calvin answered, equally embarrassed.

"Your tail," the boy mumbled.

Calvin's throat fell into his stomach as he wrapped a towel around his waist defensively.

"My grandma said that all black people have them, but I don't see one." His voice trailed off. He started again. "Did you have it docked?" Sensing Calvin's alarm and apparent discomfort, he excused himself hastily and retreated to the lockers ahead.

Meals were served family-style at the school, with the formal dining room divided into rectangular tables with settings for twelve students, each headed by a faculty proctor.

The professor at the head of Calvin's table scratched his greying, chest length beard and entertained his students with a dramatic account of living in a haunted castle while researching his doctoral thesis in Scotland. A cherubic boy with a shock of red hair told the professor that the haunted castle experience was trite, so his family vacationed in the south of France and stomped on grapes at their favorite vineyard. A polished girl with sleek blonde hair and braces told the boy that the entire European experience was provincial, so her family was planning an upcoming trip to China. A girl with mousy brown curls and a green Fair Isle sweater rolled her eyes in disgust at the blonde girl and balked at the insensitivity of a privileged American family that would indirectly support the true inspiration behind Pol Pot and the Khmer Rouge regime.

Calvin scanned the room for something of interest. His eyes rested briefly upon a gingerbread girl with freshly oiled black braids and carmine flushed lips and cheeks at a table across the room. She wore a blue monogrammed sweater that was bunched up at the sleeves. He watched as her doelike eyes followed the course of discussion around her.

The voices around him melded as the meal slowly dragged to an end. He remained silent and wondered if he would someday get close enough to find out if she smelled like molasses and cloves.

Odette

In the spirit of campus homecoming, banners were hung, plans were set into motion, and student romances began to sprout. Girls feigned cries of protest as football players swung them over their shoulders and carried them, potato sack style, down the hallways between classes. Their damp, Prell-scented tresses lightly misted the faces of peripheral passersby. Odette breathed in the heady fragrance and put a hand to her freshly oiled braids.

Mollie, her roommate, had bragged to anyone who would listen about going to the dance. "Do you think anyone is going to ask you?" she had asked Odette in a saccharine voice, pirouetting spontaneously in her deck shoes, red-ink hearts drawn randomly about the white soles, arms and feet landing deftly in third position. Odette stared at the hearts and tried to appear undaunted despite the rising flames of embarrassment lapping at her cheeks.

She had secretly hoped that Calvin North would ask her. There was a kindness about his eyes and he was inclined to give her a shy smile from time to time, but when the morning of the dance arrived without an invitation she reminded herself that she had little commonality with the privileged boy from Philadelphia who knew nothing of the real world.

Mollie left for the dance early that Friday evening, giving

Odette ample time to put her plan into motion: the girl would eat those hurtful words, whether she was aware of it or not.

"Do you think anyone is going to ask you?" Odette mimicked in a babyish voice, sprinkling salt into the corners of the room with the shaker she'd stolen from the dining hall earlier that evening.

"Do you think anyone is going to ask you?" she wrote carefully onto a scrap of paper in perfect, copperplate lettering before rolling it up into a tight scroll.

"Do you think anyone is going to ask you?" she repeated, fighting angry tears as she routed through Mollie's desk in search of a hairbrush. Finding one, she removed the loose strands of hairs and twisted them fastidiously around the paper scroll.

She entertained the abstract notion of a last minute invite but quickly let it go. Not likely, she told herself, for a girl from the wrong side of New Orleans who had narrowly secured her scholarship through amateur magic.

"Do you think anyone is going to ask you?" she repeated one last time. She held a match to the bundle and watched as it burned to a crisp.

She spent the rest of the evening hand washing her sweaters, polishing her shoes, and arranging boxes of granola bars, bags of corn chips and bottles of soda around her bed. Later on that evening when the resident advisor knocked on her door to inform her that Mollie had broken her ankle at the dance and would be spending the night in the infirmary, she moved the snacks to her roommate's desk. *Get Well Soon, Mollie* was written on an accompanying note in perfect copperplate letters. Red ink hearts were drawn randomly in the margins.

Someone would understand someday but not in her present circumstances. She brushed her teeth and changed into pajamas. Perhaps she would travel north, or west; who knew what the future held? She thought about it as she turned off her bedside lamp and nestled snugly beneath her cotton blanket, shutting her eyes to the coldness of the world until sleep removed her burdens.

ANDOVER, MASSACHUSSETTS
1990
Calvin

He was fueled by a compulsion to know what went on inside the ears of musicians since the beginning of time. Before he could know this, he needed to understand the history and evolution of musical trends. In order to understand these trends, he needed to understand the inner workings of government and economic systems throughout the span of history. Additionally, he yearned to understand the relationship between math and music and hoped to uncover hidden frequencies that would lead him deep within the inner ears of unsung artists. Regrettably, math was not his strongest subject.

His teachers didn't like him very much. He didn't make them feel important, nor was he relatable. He never contributed to class, and hated being mentored. In short, they found him odd and annoying.

He refused to participate in extracurricular activities or socialize with his classmates. He preferred to be left alone. When he wasn't studying, he spent time alone watching music documentaries or teaching himself to play the guitar by listening to cassette tapes and mimicking the chords.

Towards the middle of his senior year, the dean of students contacted his parents and told them that Calvin seemed unusually despondent and mumbled under his breath consistently. A school physician examined him and recommended medication for a chemical imbalance.

Russell and Jana arranged a school visit immediately. They were alarmed by his skinny appearance and horrified when he told them that he wasn't going to college and planned on becoming a musician instead. He finished the rest of the semester, graduated with little fanfare and flew back home for the summer.

When his taxi stopped in front of the house, Calvin hopped out of the backseat and tightened the grip on his guitar strap. As he cowered in his tracks, he wondered why he never noticed that the leaded windows looked like prison bars.

Aunt Alice rolled her wheelchair to the front door to greet him. When she saw him, her eyes widened to saucers and she reached for the crucifix above her bosom. "Christ have mercy," she gasped. He kissed her cheek and disappeared up the stairs to the shelter of his attic bedroom.

It was a small room with an adjoining bathroom. It was sparsely furnished with twin bunk beds, a record player and a walnut dresser that housed a collection of antique Hungarian puppets that Jana found at yard sale.

At the record player, he placed the stylus at the edge of a record and curled into fetal position on the bottom bunk. Roy Ayer's *The Memory* washed his anxieties away and lulled him to the outermost edges of consciousness.

"I'm a vegetarian," he announced as Aunt Alice dangled a slice of pot roast over his plate. "And no potatoes. They're swimming in meat juice."

"Can you eat the turnip greens?" Aunt Alice snapped.

"Did you cook them in pork?

Aunt Alice scowled and set the bowl of greens on the table. She opened her mouth to reply. Jana interrupted.

"Aunt Alice made some macaroni salad this morning."

"I made macaroni and cheese." She pointed a fork at Jana. "You people make macaroni salad."

Jana threw down her napkin and stood up abruptly, eyes blazing in Russell's direction. Russell glared at Aunt Alice.

"Will you cut that out?"

"That old grown gal knows I don't mean any harm."

Aunt Alice shut her mouth and heaped her plate with second helpings. Jana sat back down and refilled her wine glass. Russell focused his attention on Calvin.

"You remember my buddy, Tony? He wants to meet with you."

"Oh?" Calvin sniffed.

"I told him you were deferring college for a year and he offered you an internship. Wasn't that generous?" Russell dunked a biscuit into his gravy.

Calvin's eyes narrowed. "What about my music?"

"I told him you already said yes, and that you'd meet him for lunch on Tuesday." Russell dabbed his lips with his napkin. "So I strongly advise you call him on Monday to confirm."

He froze in the icy triumph of his father and glanced at his mother in desperation. She held Russell's hand and finished her wine.

On Tuesday morning, Calvin stood in front of the mirror wearing his father's old Kuppenheimer suit. It had since been altered to fit him but was still too boxy in the shoulders. He pulled back his hair with his left hand, turned to his side and practiced smiling.

He took the R1 to City Hall to the Blue Line and casually glanced at the people on the subway. An old man sat across from him in a corner seat. He appeared to be a nonagenarian and wore a pinstriped zoot suit with a floor-length chain and a silver crown with red plastic gemstones. He wore open-toed sandals, and his nails were polished with a glittery shade of blue. His ebony cheeks were enhanced by a touch of fuchsia blusher. A trombone lay at his feet.

He pointed to Calvin and giggled. Jewels sparkled on one side of his mouth.

"Hey. Hey, wanderer!" the man shouted. "Didn't I just see you on Titan?"

Calvin pulled his suit jacket closed. The man squinted and leaned in closer.

"Yeah, it was you. So when you going back? When you coming home?"

He fought hard to keep his voice from breaking. "Do I know you?"

"Aww, now! You're not gonna sit up here with your uptown self and diss H.B., are you?"

The train stopped at Girard Station. The old man picked up his trombone and stood up to leave.

"You know me! I'm H.B! And you need to come home!" He stepped off the train as the subway doors opened and disappeared into a sea of faceless bodies.

He got off the train at Spring Garden and walked to Liberties Restaurant. He ordered a peppermint tea and played with the top of the French press. A few minutes later, Tony walked in. The host recognized him and pumped his hand vigorously. They exchanged a few words before turning in Calvin's direction. Calvin nodded numbly and rose to his feet.

"Hi, Calvin!" he smiled. "It's good to see you."

"My pleasure, sir."

"You look just like your Dad did when he was younger, except for the hair," he said. He nodded at Calvin's locs approvingly.

"Dad hates them."

"What does he know? But don't tell him I said that."

They sat at a booth and talked over veggie burgers for the next hour. Tony told Calvin about his experiences growing up in West Virginia. Calvin told Tony about his experiences at Andover.

"The key to overcoming adversity," Tony explained, dipping a fry into ketchup, "is bouncing back. How you gonna tell a boy from West Virginia about some assholes at boarding school?"

"But they hated me."

"They hated you. Oh, no." Tony appeared bemused. He swallowed a fry and sipped his Pepsi.

"They did."

"Doesn't matter. Change your priorities."

Calvin put his elbow on the table and rested his head on his hand.

"You're smart," Tony urged. "You're a vegetarian, right? Help people make better choices."

Calvin cleared his throat. "I like music. I was thinking about doing something with it, but I don't know what yet."

"You'll figure it out."

Calvin straightened up as a server cleared their plates from the table. "Maybe like a program to show people how music can enrich their lives?"

"Pitch. I'm listening." Calvin's voice took on a subtle trace of authority as he outlined a plan for an instrument drive for underprivileged children. He spoke of contacting music majors from Temple, Penn and LaSalle, and asking them to volunteer their services. He chattered excitedly about gymnasiums and community centers. Tony listened and smiled.

At dinner, Calvin told his father that the meeting went well.

"I'm proud of you," Russell said. "You be sure to follow through and get to his studio this week."

The following morning, Calvin took the Orange Line to Village Thrift and purchased three guitars, two tambourines and a few wooden recorders. The cashier packed them up in a cardboard box and thanked him as he left the store.

When he arrived at Tony's studio, the woman at the reception booth raised a curious eyebrow at the box of instruments and informed him that interns checked in on the second floor.

He rode the elevator to the second floor. The space was divided into cubicles, and the fluorescent lighting was harsh. Dusty rubber trees littered the corners. Stale coffee perfumed the air.

A young woman in a cubicle near the door pointed to a pad of yellow notepaper. "Just sign in your hours here." She glanced at the box of instruments. "What's that for?"

He smiled proudly. "It's for the youth music program I'm in charge of."

"Oh?" She handed him a stack of papers bearing Tony's logo. "Here's the intern schedule. Take whatever vacant seat you find." She stared at the box.

He stepped inside a cubicle, set the box down in the corner and glanced at the stack of papers.

Call clients to confirm appointments.
Deliver envelope to the tax accountant.
Fax notes to affiliate station in Los Angeles.
Clean the espresso machine.
Vacuum the carpet.

He sank into the chair and took one last look at the box of instruments that would remain untouched in the corner forever. He confirmed the client appointments, delivered the tax documents, faxed the notes to the affiliate channel, cleaned the espresso machine, and vacuumed the carpet. Twice. A few weeks passed before he began to hear the voices. Russell and Jana took Calvin back to the doctor. The doctor prescribed an antipsychotic medication.

Bela

Clutching a Goodwill bag in his hand and humming gallantly, he exited the Broad Street train at South Street and headed towards the dilapidated apartment atop the defunct dry cleaners at 13th. He walked up the steps to the front door, unlocked the four deadbolts and stepped inside, instantly greeted by the dank smell of settled dust and unwashed laundry. He locked the four deadbolts again and set down his backpack, beaming with grandeur as he carried the Goodwill bag to his bedroom. He set it down momentarily and sat on his bed to unlace the red canvas high top sneakers.

Minutes later, he was in the shower scrubbing with Ivory soap and humming along to the Royal London Opera Company's recording of *Madama Butterfly*. He was careful not to nick himself as he shaved. He put on his bathrobe, turned his body sideways and examined his silhouette.

He opened the Goodwill bag and removed the dark blue brocade smoking jacket that he had purchased. Peeling off the price tag, he slipped it on and studied his reflection. He rolled up the length of the too-long sleeves and brushed undecidedly at the too broad shoulders. He walked over to the overcoat that he had strewn haphazardly on the bed and retrieved his pocket watch.

The night air lingered with the scent promise as he thrust his hands into the pockets of his faded grey corduroy slacks and walked the five blocks to the Academy of Music. Gaslights set in cast-iron posts flickered along the length of Broad Street and illuminated the silhouettes of evening passersby. Brakes screeched, drivers cursed and horns blared belligerently as the last leg of rush hour traffic snaked its way around City Hall's facade.

The sound of hoofbeats trotting atop cobblestone approached in the distance. Ester smiled with gratitude as the driver of the stagecoach walked over to the passenger side and offered his hand in assistance.

Bloodstones and onyx flew into the night as she extended her lace clad hand, stepped carefully from the horse drawn carriage and smoothed down the boning of her dress. The Shire flushed with pride when she stroked its velvet nose.

Her eyes reflected the gaslight flames and caught ablaze in amber fire. Bela was overwhelmed by the brilliance and blindly felt for the hollow of her waist. The driver tipped the brim of his top hat cordially and raised his reins as the Shire trotted away into the mist.

Corinthian columns entwined with ivy curls looked onward as Ester and Bela glided in three quarter time beneath the sixteen foot chandelier in the lobby. Poetry and Music flirted at opposite sides of the proscenium, charging the air with lyrics.

"The Grand Old Lady of Locust Street," Bela bragged as they took their seats in the balcony. He proudly wrapped an arm around her shoulder. "Built in 1857. Feast your eyes on the oldest opera house in the United States."

Ester sipped from a glass of champagne and politely ignored the mothball odor that emanated from Bela's jacket. She adjusted the bridge of her rose gold opera glasses and leaned in for a closer look.

"Why are you using those?" Bela baited.

Ester smoothed down the length of her dress, straightened her spine and continued to press the glasses to her face. "I'd like to see the details."

"Well, you know that we're here to listen to the symphony, not to see an opera," he remarked, swelling with superiority. "It's gauche to use opera glasses when listening to the symphony," he said, huffing with self-importance. He regarded Ester pitifully and shook his head with exasperation. "When listening to the symphony," he overemphasized, "one closes his eyes and allows the vocal and instrumental constituents to meld together into a unified voice. Silly nilly," he sighed. "Whatever will I do with you? I can't take you anywhere!"

Ester lowered the glasses, raised an eyebrow and peered in closer to get a better look at the curiously horrid man seated beside her. Bela clasped his hands over his knee. He sighed deeply, smiled broadly at an elderly couple who took the vacant seats to his left.

Annoyed eyes with feather lashes narrowed with irritation. The ceiling cherubs looked at Bela and laughed out loud, flying down from the ceiling to rest at Ester's side, play with her hair, and trace the outline of her earlobes with gentle words of assuagement.

"I bet you don't even know who painted the ceiling, do you?" he prattled. Ester clasped her hands in her lap and cocked an eyebrow to feign attention. "Karl Herman Schmolze," he bubbled conceitedly. "Napoleon LeBrun and Gustavus Runge designed the layout of the building, and they commissioned him to paint it, did you know that? Huh? Don't you read, Ester? Don't you know anything?" He sighed again and shook his head.

She felt a polite, yet firm tap at her shoulder and turned in the direction of its source. Two men in their early thirties wearing jeans and leather jackets smiled at her and nodded politely at Bela in acknowledgment.

"Girlfriend," the first one began, "I just had to compliment your outfit. Is that a vintage whalebone bodice?" he asked, taking in the double stitching of the lace inserts at the eye hooks. "It's so beautiful! Are you a fashion major?"

"Thank you," Ester's smile was gracious. "You are so kind." Bela rolled his eyes, visibly upset that he was being upstaged.

The second man looked at Bela and smiled respectfully. "You must be very proud to be with this beautiful lady. Is she your girlfriend?"

Bela inhaled curtly and eyed him up and down, turning his nose up the meticulously polished finish of the man's expensive Italian loafers. "I'm her probation officer," he scoffed. The men took the cue to walk away as Bela turned abruptly in his seat, ignored Ester and fixated on the orchestra pit. The musicians took their places behind the instruments as the stage lights lowered.

A solitary violin wept in the darkness. Two violas joined in sympathy. The bass stood tall and rich. Subtle. Supportive.

"*The Adagio for Strings* is one of the most popular classical pieces of all time," Bela whispered furiously, intent on not being outdone. "Bet you don't know what Samuel Barber's inspiration was, do you?"

Her eyes grew heavy with the weight of the strings. "Kaspare River," she whispered with a distant voice. Bela recoiled at the stupidity of her response and turned away in his seat to roll his eyes in mockery.

She closed her eyes. Bows of crisp, fluted reed curved along the bass clef, rousing sleepy-eyed quarter notes from hibernation. Testing the vibrations, she wrapped herself around the gleaming wood of the viola, and sailed along the crescendo waves. She was soaked to the bone by the outpouring of music. Her nostrils reverberated with the sharp-scaled odor of amber resin.

Ripples of arpeggio cast the viola into a tailspin. She tensed her muscles and clutched her hands tightly around its neck. They bottomed out as the viola picked up speed and distance. It barreled through an expanse of sky and funneled towards a vortex of light.

Electric blue sparklers surged and crackled, filling the expanse with an acrid, burning scent. The sound of a wire coil sprung back upon itself. The viola chortled through a quark-induced chasm of time and space, its speed reducing into audible, half-life increment pops. The funnel narrowed significantly and the space grew tighter and blacker.

Charred trees embowering the smoking lining of the funnel sneered derisively at Ester. They snatched at the delicate boning of her bodice and reduced it to tattered shreds. Bela screamed out in fright from the flat note recesses in the distance and lamely shielded his face with his hands. The trees whisked the watch from the folds of his pocket and scratched bloody welts into his cheeks.

Full speed resumed and the trees crumbled to ash and scattered away. She gripped the burnt neck of the viola, wild eyes glued upon the fast approaching, white hot spectacle of light. Calves tensed, biceps curled and the sky cleaved into folds, revealing unseen lengths as she soared through the heart of the center.

Cascading waterfalls and bluebell voices marked the sides of the most startling structure that she had ever imagined. Cast completely from ice, it coiled upwards beyond her range of vision. Spires clustered with glass marbles marked the leaded tower windows.

An obelisk marked the entrance, surrounded on all sides by a moat. Ester stood agape, clutching at the tattered rags where her beautiful dress had once been.

The drawbridge lowered slowly. She dropped the viola at her feet and proceeded. Hot tears falling with terror and the realization that he had gone too far, Bela clung desperately to the remnants of the flat note and slid backwards through the cracks of the chasm.

Enchantment clasped Ester's hand and escorted her through a mirrored gallery to a tower parlor heaped with spools of thread, multicolored beads and a spinning wheel. Ester sat before the wheel and spun with determined persistence until her fingers were stiff and blistered and a handsomely beaded gown lay finished in her lap.

Peeling off the rags and slipping on the gown, she discovered a staircase in the corner. At the top was a room with a panorama of floor length windows and a lavishly set table heaped with fish, olives, figs, cheese, and gold and garnet wines.

She wiped her mouth with a crisp linen napkin and saw that the staircase continued. At the top was an exquisitely furnished parlor covered from floor to infinity with hardbound books.

Ester nestled herself against a downy pile of feather pillows and touched the surface of the gold leafed vellum binding, breathing in the subtle leather fragrance.

Patterns of light fused the edge of the pages and illuminated the passages, showing her the light inside darkness. The laughter inside bitterness. The beauty inside hideousness. The love inside hatred.

She closed her eyes and allowed the vision to comfort her. When she opened her eyes, the furnishings had melted away, leaving behind a clear perspective and a lumbering blanket of knowledge that wrapped its warmth around her.

———————

Bela opened his eyes to the dilapidated apartment atop the defunct dry cleaners at 13th Street, sat upright in bed and watched as his vision trailed forty-five degrees behind his body. The ceiling was in front of his face, the bathroom door was below his feet, and the floor, still wavering with the pulse of his altered reality, had somehow shifted behind his upright head.

Cold sweat rolled down his temples and pooled in the folds of his ears. When the nausea came, he stood up quickly and inched across the ceiling for support, tentatively stepping through the open bathroom door in the center of the floor.

The toilet jutted out like a panhandle in the wall in front of him as stood on top of the window panes. He wiped his mouth with the sleeve of his tattered smoking jacket and coughed as layers of soot dredged up from the surface and wafted into the air. He crawled back inside the bed laying flush to the front wall and curled up in fetal position until everything shifted back to its rightful place.

The diverse perfumes of South Philadelphia seasoned the air with the lot of their myriad spices as he walked outside and passed the pretzel and hot dog vending trucks. He screwed his eyes shut, pulled his scarf over his nose and tried in vain to ignore his sour stomach.

He headed north on Broad Street past the pumpkin vendors outside of Green's Market and the carriage drivers heading into Olde City. He passed a homeless man rocking back and forth on top of the steam grates at Lombard Street. Transgender prostitutes whistled at him as he continued on to Locust Street and arrived back at the Academy of Music.

A mouse scampered by as he gazed up at the imposing brownstone façade. He pulled the door handles, but they were locked. He turned up his collar and placed his hand into his pocket, feeling the cold, glass surface of his pocket watch. He pulled it out and ran a finger over the crack that cleaved the crystal into halves, hands stuck at midnight.

Sinking down onto the urine scented steps, he stared into the cold, soulless recesses where the gaslights once glowed and tried to figure out what had happened. He wondered if she made it back out and if she would come ever out again.

"I need to see some ID," the bartender at the North Philadelphia tavern said as Bela laid down his scarf and gloves and removed his overcoat. She scratched her scaly elbows and belched quietly. Bela slapped his driver's license onto the bar and hunkered down onto a stool.

The bartender picked up the license, extended her right arm and widened her eyes to make out the birthdate. Satisfied, she slapped a napkin down in front of Bela. "What'll it be?" she asked with a twinge of impatience.

"A Yuengling Black & Tan, please." Bela smiled like an annoying gnat. He paused as the bartender scratched her red, greasy ponytail and turned her back to retrieve a glass from the wall.

"History in the making," Bela baited hopefully.

She filled the glass from the draft and placed it in front of Bela. "Huh?" she grunted.

"What do you think is the beer capital of the United States?" Bela continued, bolstered by the nibble.

"I don't know, Milwaukee?" the bartender said. Her eyes settled on a group of new customers walking through the door. Bela exhaled incredulously.

"Pottsville, Pennsylvania," he spat. "The Yuengling Brewery of Pottsville, Pennsylvania is the oldest brewery in the United States!" He shook his head. "And you didn't know that! You call yourself a Pennsylvanian?"

The bartender ignored Bela, scratched at the elastic waistband of her pants and slapped napkins down in front of the new customers.

———————————◆———————————

He stroked the wool of his scarf and watched the snow falling from the view of the open doorway. A group of middle school girls waited for the bus across the street. They screeched and hollered as they scooped their mittened hands into the accumulating drifts and threw snowballs at each other, being careful to avoid their smoothly straightened, freshly oiled braids out of respect for each other.

He fixated on a serene one in a red dress coat. Three braids fastened with white barrettes poked out from beneath her matching acrylic hat. He stood up from the barstool and walked out the door.

Lurking at the edge of the bus stop, he fished in his pockets for a dollar bill before approaching the group. "Pick a number between one and one hundred!" he called out cheerfully, holding the bill above his head with both hands.

"Five! Sixteen! Forty-three!" the girls screamed gaily, rubbing their runny noses with their mittens and jumping up and down with excitement. A tall, spindly girl with a gapped overbite jumped up and nearly grasped the bill from Bela's fingers. A shorter, cornrowed girl with wide hips and stout legs punched her in the stomach. The tall girl drew back, whimpering.

"Sixty-six?" the serene one inquired, pausing briefly to wipe her nose. She sniffed and listened while the other girls continued to guess.

"Seventy-two! Ninety-four! A hundred and twelve!" the girls shrieked, whooping with laughter.

"That ain't no number between one and a hundred, you dumb ass," the cornrowed girl snorted. He approached the serene one carefully. "What's your name?" he asked, smiling casually.

"Hazel," she responded. Her voice was barely audible over the shrieking of her friends.

Bela traced the bill across her eyes, around her head and down the bridge of her nose before dropping it firmly into the palm of her mittened hand.

"What were you guys playing just now?" Bela asked her when he visited the bus stop the following week.

"*Cleopatra Jones,*" she said, fingering the champagne pearl that he had given her.

"Oh?" He clasped his fingers. "How do you play that?"

"We wear capes and drive to crime scenes in a silver Corvette and have phones in our cars and mow the bad guys down with karate chops and laser guns. Then when they're dead we dress up in flower jeans and go to the skating rink," she explained politely.

"Fascinating. Who are the bad guys, the principal? The landlord?"

Hazel shrugged her shoulders and continued to look at the pearl.

"Which skating rink do you go to?" he pressed.

"It's pretend." She glanced distractedly at her boots.

"Do you wear your uniform skirt when you play?" he inquired.

"Mostly jeans," she said, playing with the pearl.

Bela glanced at the three braids poking out from beneath her red acrylic hat. "What does your hair look unbraided?"

Hazel was bored. "I dunno."

Bela pulled out his cracked pocket watch, looked at it briefly and thrust it back into his overcoat. "Maybe you can wear it down sometime so I can see it," he said, tightening his scarf around his neck.

Taken off guard, Hazel looked up from the pearl, pulled her red hat down over her ears and clutched the neck of her dress coat defensively. The bus clattered in the distance and snaked its way up the street.

"Definitely," Bela grinned, rising to his feet. He fingered one of her plastic yellow barrettes and took a few steps backward before he turned around, covered his nose with his scarf and continued on foot down the street, growing smaller and smaller in the late-day sun.

———————————

"You sure do look nice today," he gurgled the following afternoon, taking a seat next to the girl as she waited for the bus.

She winced and dangled her raffia bookbag between her knees.

He put his hands in his pockets and smiled. "Hazel. Do you know who your namesake is?"

"My what?"

"Your namesake," he repeated, a bit louder and slower. "Don't you know what a namesake is?"

"No."

Bela feigned exasperation. "A namesake," he continued with bloated authority, "is the name of the historically important figure or family member you were named for. "Are there any other Hazels in your family?"

"No."

"Yes! Just as I suspected! Your namesake," he announced triumphantly, "is Hazel Scott."

Visibly unimpressed, Hazel stared at the tip of her shoe while Bela reeled in the catch. "Do you know who Hazel Scott was?"

"No." Unfazed, Hazel shifted her weight against the bench, reached into the bookbag and took out a textbook.

Bela's eyes blazed. "She was only one of the most prolific black actresses and musicians of the McCarthy Era. She was blacklisted by Hollywood for her political beliefs. Silly nilly, you must be sleeping during history class." He wrapped his knuckles against his forehead and sighed audibly.

Hazel saw that Bela was misguided about the origin of her name and looked up from her textbook to set the matter straight. "My Gramma named me Hazel because she liked that TV show about the maid."

Bela scoffed. "Unbelievable," he puffed dismissively. "Your Gramma named you after a fictitious, white Hollywood old maid whose historical significance is next to nothing and trivial at best."

The insult rolled off Hazel like an ocean wave. Bela's smile disappeared as she stood up and scowled in his face. "Unbelievable," she muttered, striding hurriedly towards the bus. "Your Momma named you after Dracula."

"You know I was just teasing the other day about your name, right?" He dug his hands into a bag of Fritos and urged it towards her.

Hazel ignored the bag and continued to stare at the perfect blue diamond he had given her, holding it up to the sunlight.

"Let's go to the Animation Film Festival today," he said. "I sure do owe you one."

"I don't think so," Hazel replied. "I'd have to ask my Gramma first, and she's not home," She rotated the gemstone in her fingers and stared at the prisms it cast over the snow.

"Where is she?" Bela asked.

"Work." She scratched her scalp.

"Oh? Where's that?" he asked, curiosity piqued.

"Hospital." She stretched out her legs and watched as the prisms extended to her socks.

"Well, what time does she come home?" he pressed.

"Nine thirty." She polished the diamond with the hem of her red dress coat and held it out again towards the sun.

"Who watches you until nine thirty?" Bela held his breath.

"I take care of myself."

He paused. "Of course you do," he crowed, "an able-bodied, competent, intelligent girl like yourself. What do you do for dinner?" Hazel sniffed. "She leaves it in the freezer. I put it in the microwave."

"Let's go out to eat instead. Do you like Moroccan food?"

"Like I said," Hazel repeated, "I'd have to ask my Gramma first and she'd say no, unless it was a field trip with the church or something."

"It's settled, then. You go home and I'll bring the Moroccan food to you, then maybe we could play *Cleopatra Jones* at your house until eight forty-five or so."

Realization clasped a fist around the pit of Hazel's stomach.

Bela placed his hands in his pockets and stared at her braids. "You know, like you were telling me before. The principal, the landlord?"

She did not take her eyes off of Bela as she felt around for the leather straps of the raffia bookbag that dangled under the bench. "You want to play Cleopatra Jones at my house?"

"So it's a date?" He waited, baring his grey teeth.

"So you can be one of the bad guys, right?" she added carefully, maintaining her steady gaze.

"If that's what you want me to be," Bela advanced, long fingers reaching towards her neck.

Hazel ran.

"Wait!" Bela leapt to his feet, "What about the bus? You forgot your...fuck!" he screamed as she hurled the diamond at his face and took off sprinting down Broad Street. It grazed his forehead as he reached out to catch. He watched in horror as it fumbled through his fingers, rolled into the street, and bounced off of the curb and into the gutter. He fell to his hands and knees and crouched down in the street, pressing an eye against the grate.

The horn of the oncoming bus blared menacingly and the driver yelled expletives. Bela scrambled to his feet to jump out of the way, brushing dirt from his overcoat in humiliation. Several yards ahead a wild-eyed Hazel was approaching the bus slowly, her right hand clasped tightly in the palm of a humorless looking police officer and her left with index finger pointed directly at Bela.

He squinted in the afternoon sun and tried to figure out what happened. Casting a final glance towards the gutter, he turned on his heels, jumped out of the line of traffic, and ran.

Calvin

He glared at his mother as she struggled to unload multiple SuperFresh grocery bags onto the kitchen island with one arm and push her falling sunglasses back on top of her head with the other.

"You promised to stop at Essene when you went into the city today!"

"I was running late, Cal. I wanted to beat traffic so I stopped up the road instead."

"But you promised!" he whined.

She grabbed a plastic gallon of milk and put it in the refrigerator. "I'll go later this week."

He rooted through the bags she had already deposited onto the kitchen table and pulled out a box of tea bags. "That's Lipton," he sniffed disdainfully.

"You told me to get tea."

"I told you to get white tea."

"What's wrong with Lipton?"

"Lipton tea is fermented. White tea has more antioxidants because it's closer to its natural state. I need my antioxidants!"

Jana placed a twelve pack of Diet Coke into the refrigerator. "There's a bottle of Centrum vitamins in the medicine chest," she offered. "They have antioxidants."

Calvin pushed the voices into the back of his head and spoke loudly through the din of their persistence. "Those are synthetic. I need biologically-active, food-state vitamins cultivated from organic yeast."

Jana folded up the grocery bags and placed them in a drawer next to the kitchen sink. "I don't know what you've done with my son," she joked, "but when you see him next, could you ask him to please take out the garbage?" She reached into her pocket for a cigarette, lit it and left the room.

After giving him an earful about the hypocrisy of formers doctor who took synthetic vitamins and smoked cigarettes, they ordered him to cleanse himself immediately. So he ran upstairs to his room immediately and carefully dipped the soles of his shoes into a diluted bleach bath that he kept outside the door.

He stood at his stereo and placed the stylus at the edge of a record. Brian Eno's *Sky Saw* billowed through the small attic bedroom. In the adjoining bathroom, he sprinkled rosemary and fir essential oils into the tub, turned the hot showerhead to full blast and closed the door. Steam filled the air as he sat on the edge of the tub and scrubbed his skin fastidiously with Jana's hairbrush. When it was quite raw, he set the brush aside and alternately pinched his nostrils with his thumb and pinky finger while breathing in counts of twenty. Then he wrapped himself in a towel and laid down on his bed to listen to the music.

Thorns rooted at the needle of the record player and sprouted vines in his impressionable mind. They disappeared temporarily behind the rosemary fir mist and reappeared around his wrists and ankles. They bored into his ear and down the side of his neck. He bucked his head, but it jerked back down against the stronghold. He whimpered.

The scratchiness gave way to cold silk handkerchiefs that slid down from his torso until only a sensation of flesh remained. It breathed in as he breathed out, supported his back with unseen fingertips and eased him into an upright position.

In the corners of the room, bonfire embers glowed with dusky, amber light. They knelt in front of each other with palms stretched outward in mirrored, kindred equilibrium. A hint of singed violets mingled with the vestiges of pine. A spotted owl swiveled his head toward the open window and watched.

The threads that fastened the hummingbird pendant around her neck had loosened. He reached for them, but she pushed his wrist away and tightened them herself. He took in the faceted beads that sparkled in her hair and the knowledge that poured from her eyes.

Walking away from her, he looked up to the ceiling and spun. Faster and faster, arms stretched out to his sides, into a funnel that he had never seen before but somehow knew had been there all along. He kicked his toes up as he spun and swallowed the air, thirsty for dizziness.

"I'll come back," she whispered. She repeated herself into the funnel amplifier, dismayed by the reverberations of the myriad entities competing within him for her attention. "Not you. Not you. Not you. Not you. Not you."

"Me?" Calvin's watery, yet sober response caught the voices off guard. "Me?" he whispered.

"Yes." Then she was gone.

They tried to distract him with indignant buzzing as he searched the room for evidence of her visit. He found nothing, which didn't surprise him. Toxins were in the way.

He crept slowly down both staircases as quietly as he could and minced through the kitchen's back entrance.

"What's that noise?" Aunt Alice called out from her bedroom.

"Nothing, ma'am, go back to sleep."

He found a box of senna leaves in one of the cupboards and set it on the counter. Kneeling down on the floor, he opened the storage drawer next to the stove and sifted through a collection of metal cookware until he came across a forgotten glass saucepan that hid at the very bottom.

Using a paper towel, he brushed away the dead gnats that had collected inside before filling it with distilled water, a generous pinch of leaves, and a splash of apple cider vinegar. As it boiled, he grabbed a bolt of Saran Wrap from the drawer next to the refrigerator and tucked it under his armpit, then waited for the pan to cool slightly before carrying everything back to his room.

In the adjoining bathroom, he sprinkled rosemary and fir oils into the tub, turned the hot showerhead to full blast, and closed the door behind him. Steam filled the air as he sat on the edge of the tub, drank part of the concoction and gave himself an enema with the rest.

Swathed in Saran Wrap, he stood at his stereo and placed the stylus at the edge of a record. Miles Davis' *Bitches Brew* filled the small attic room. He closed his eyes and asked the forces of nature to cleanse his body and mind. When they responded, he bumped into his dresser as he lurched towards the bathroom, knocking Jana's hairbrush, an assortment of snack wrappers, and the bottle of antipsychotic medication that had remained untouched for nine days onto the floor.

Screeching eighth notes mocked the stars that lined up outside his window to watch the unveiling. And if he had the slightest doubt that his eyes were truly seeing the message spelled out in the sky before him, the buzzing in his ears soon took it away.

*COME*HOME*

Hans

Despite the irony of his side gig, Lasse and his wife, Lynda, tried to conceive for years. Lynda carried babies to term on two occasions, but complications related to double-dominant syndrome caused the infants to die within hours of birth. She was devastated, but still determined to become a mother.

The Eriksens had been on the waiting list of a California adoption agency for over two years when they were notified that the newborn son of a sixteen-year-old unwed mother had been put up for adoption and would be available the following afternoon. Lynda and Lasse completed the necessary paperwork and brought him home. They named him Hans.

Lynda did her best to create a comfortable home environment, but Hans was irreparably cold and sterile. He rubbed his hands together vigorously in an attempt to generate heat. He obsessively motioned to his fingers and mouth until Lynda wiped them with Wet Naps.

Hans continued to focus on this behavior throughout the remainder of his infancy. Lynda longed for him to focus on speech. She constantly repeated the words *mama* and *daddy*. In lieu of crying, Hans expressed feelings of discontent through controlled, staccato shrieks that ceased invariably when Lynda wiped down his face and feeding tray with Wet Naps.

On the morning that Hans turned thirteen months old, Lynda continued the attempts to make him speak. She waved a stuffed bear in front of his face. "Are you Mama's baby boy?" she cooed. "Can you say Mama? Say Mama!" Hans resumed his litany of clipped, controlled shrieks, his arms outstretched for Wet Naps.

Lynda lost her temper and slammed the bear down on the table. She grabbed a crumpled paper napkin and wiped Hans' mouth abrasively. "Why do you always do that? Why can't you say, Mama?"

Hans stared back with unblinking icebergs and removed the napkin from his mother's hands with tiny, exacting fingers. "Because I have a busy head," he answered. Licking the napkin carefully, he dabbed at his own lips. This sent Lynda into a screaming, frantic tailspin to the kitchen telephone.

Lasse left his office immediately, stopping on the way to pick up his blind mother at her home in Norwalk. When they arrived at the house in Anaheim, he took her arm and led her through the front door.

In the den, a crazed Lynda was crawling on her hands and knees, and Hans was trying to escape her. "Say it again! Say it again!" she bellowed.

"How's my big talker?" Lasse began a playful round of shadow boxing with his son.

"Grandma's little smarty pants!" Lasse's mother folded up her guidance cane and carefully made her way to an overstuffed chair in the corner. "Who's my little Great Dane?"

"He's not a dog!" Lynda spat.

"Well, he's a Dane, isn't he? And Danes are..."

"Don't even think about starting that race bullshit with me," Lynda threatened, shaking a finger in the blind woman's direction. "Not today. And besides, you don't know if he's Danish or not. He's adopted!"

"Lynda! Ma! Please!" Lasse scolded. "Lyn! Go grab the tape

recorder upstairs!" Lynda rolled her eyes and did as she was told. When she arrived downstairs with the tape recorder and microphone, Lasse and his mother were arguing.

"No, *you* shut up, Lasse! He likes it! Listen!" She rolled her eyes in her daughter-in-law's direction. "Lynda! Give me your hand! Quickly!"

Lynda made a nasty face and grasped her mother-in-law's hand. The blind woman's eyes rolled obliviously. Lasse glared at his wife and extended his hand. When the circle was complete, Lasse's mother began singing *Thanks for the Memory* in a scratchy voice. Lynda and Lasse joined in. A few moments later, the trio was laughing and singing loudly. Hans stared on in bewilderment.

"Lynda! Ma! Be quiet! I think he's trying to say something!" Lynda broke the circle and scurried to put the microphone under Hans' mouth. They waited.

The moment had come and gone, and Hans remained silent. Lasse tapped his foot impatiently and sighed with condescension. "What, so now you won't talk at all?" Lasse's mother waved the stuffed bear. Lynda continued to hold the microphone.

Hans shifted his attention from Lasse's body, to Lynda's helium shrill, to Lasse's mother's rolling eyes and back again. "What have you done with my mother?" he asked. A deafening silence ensued.

When Hans was in the fourth grade, his teacher phoned Lynda in hysterical tears and informed her that he killed the classroom's pet gerbil, tarantula, and hermit crab during recess by saturating them with Clorox bleach. He was asked to explain his actions during a meeting with the elementary school psychiatrist. He told her that the lives of classroom vermin were insignificant to the greater functioning of the Earth because their tiny brains were intellectually irrelevant.

The psychiatrist wrote in a spiral notebook and focused her gaze on Hans' unblinking iceberg eyes. "So what you're saying is, not all life forms are relevant?"

"Yes." Hans answered without shifting his gaze.

"Does this theory apply to humans as well? Let's say your classmates, for example."

"All life forms include humans. Humans include classmates." His voice was monotone.

"Do you feel the need to hurt any of your classmates?" she pressed.

Hans ignored the question and focused on the pattern of her yellow and burgundy Kente Cloth shift. "Why do you wear that?"

The psychiatrist glanced down at her shift. "Because I like it."

"Why do you like it?" he pressed.

The psychiatrist took a deep breath and held her gaze. "It's a cloth from Africa. It aligns with my cultural identity, and the colors make me happy."

His eyes were sterile. "You're worried about my sociopathic tendencies because I'm not sorry about having a little fun with the stupid rodents."

"So you found it fun to kill them?"

His lips curled into the slightest of smiles. "I meant my classmates. Watching their faces when they saw what I did to their pets." He glanced at her breasts. "Why does it align with your cultural identity? You don't have a West African accent or any African accent at all, for that matter."

The psychiatrist cleared her throat. "Because I'm African American. Surely you understand the relevance of ancestral connection."

He winced but never blinked. "Then you're the sociopath."

"And how's that?"

"Kente Cloth is a commodity like everything else. The merchants who own it reap status and class. The laborers who produce it rot in sweatshops. It aligns with your cultural identity, but you perpetuate the same ethnocidal cycle that was supposed to end in America with Lincoln." He picked at a scab on his elbow. "I'll bet an impoverished, underage West African girl was paid ten cents an hour to work in a factory to make your dress. Then she spent a third of it taking a bus home at three am and got raped by an HIV positive vagrant that was hiding in the bushes. I don't feel the need to hurt any of my classmates if you want the truth, and I guess you do, because you asked."

Hans knew full well the fallacy of this argument, but, like everything else, facts and truth were pliable like clay and easily molded to suit his purpose at any given moment. It didn't matter, anyway; he could tell by the look on the psychiatrist's face that she believed everything he had said.

———————————

He spent the remainder of his elementary school career devoid of incident, but staff and students alike were wary of him and kept a comfortable distance. In high school, he never spoke unless an opportunity arose to challenge his teachers. He didn't participate in sports or academic teams. His sole extracurricular activity was rebuilding the engine of a crumbling Volkswagen Beetle that he purchased on his sixteenth birthday.

One evening during his senior year, while his parents were out on a dinner and movie date, he sat in his bedroom reading his acceptance letter to MIT. He had just turned on the television to watch the ten o'clock news when the telephone rang. It was his grandmother. Her home health aide never showed up for work, so she needed Lasse to come over immediately because she felt ill. Hans explained that his parents were out for the evening, but he would stop by to see her instead.

At ten twenty, he pulled his ancient Volkswagen Beetle into the driveway of his grandmother's two-story Norwalk home. He opened the front door and called for her. When she didn't respond, he walked up the stairs and found her bedroom empty. He started to check the bathroom but heard a faint whimpering coming from the first floor. He followed it down the second floor landing and across the kitchen to the basement door, where his grandmother was lying at the bottom of the concrete steps with two broken legs and a dislocated shoulder. She turned her neck slightly in his direction and whispered for help.

He ran down the steps as fast as she could and glanced at the items around the room: an old side-by-side refrigerator. Rows and rows of canning jars. A washer and dryer.

A laundry basket filled with sheets, blankets, and a pillow rested on top of the dryer. Hans removed a blanket from the basket and held it to his nose. It smelled like fabric softener. He put it back into the basket, carried it to his grandmother and placed it by her side.

He knelt down and cradled her neck gently. Her eyes rolled back and forth. Taking her hand, he guided her fingertips to his mouth and curled his lips into a deliberate smile. She shivered. Tears streamed down her face and saturated the dry, cottony hair at her temples. He brushed them away, reached into the laundry basket and covered her with the blanket. She continued to shake uncontrollably.

He hummed as he held her, rocking her back and forth in his arms like an infant. Moments later, he was singing *Thanks for the Memory* in a loud, earnest voice. He took her hands in his own and moved them along in tempo, inviting her to join him in song. She didn't sing but opened her mouth and reluctantly produced a succession of guttural noises similar to the ones a rodent might make while being saturated with Clorox bleach. The noises gradually gave way to a coughing fit, followed by more shivers and the release of her bowels. Hans removed the pillow from the laundry basket, held it over his grandmother's face and relieved her of her misery.

LOS ANGELES, CALIFORNIA
1991

Peggy

Stranded alone on the shoulder of the Imperial Freeway in a stalled car, Peggy Hope decided it was much too dark out to walk alone in search of a call box. She popped the hood of her Mercury Tracer, got back inside, locked the doors and waited for help to arrive.

She slapped her palms against the faded dashboard and cursed. She was used to car trouble, but the timing could not have been worse. She always made it a point to be on time; it was her first week on the job and she couldn't afford to lose it.

Her calf muscles were cramping and she needed to stretch her legs. She fiddled with the lever to pull back the driver's seat, but it remained as irreparably stuck as it had been the day her neighbor's cousin drove the cash-sucking lemon to her family's home in exchange for the three thousand dollars she had saved in high school.

She turned her body sideways and draped her long legs diagonally into the backseat. Forever and a Day Legs, her parents and brother often teased. All of her friends at CSU Fullerton were in the habit of telling her that her wholesome looks and five feet eleven inch frame could bring her more success as a model than her job as a home health aide ever could, but she ignored them. She enjoyed her work. Looking after Mrs. Eriksen was relevant to her goal of becoming a registered nurse, and she managed to sneak in a good deal of studying during her shifts.

When Officer Bob Murano showed up an hour and a half later, his handsome face and broad shoulders put her instantly at ease. He told her not to worry; he would arrange for a tow and drive her to work. As they headed to Norwalk in the police vehicle, she relaxed and put a plan into place. Once she got to Mrs. Eriksen's house, she would, with the moral support of the handsome young policeman, explain the situation to the elderly woman and apologize profusely. Then she would call the staffing agency and attempt to clean up the gaffe.

When they arrived at Mrs. Eriksen's house at ten thirty, the front door was wide open and a suspicious vehicle was parked in the driveway. Bob insisted on escorting her inside to make sure that everything was okay. Peggy did not protest. He did his very best to be as respectful as possible and not get distracted by her wholesome looks and Forever and a Day Legs. He failed miserably at the latter.

Raising a finger to his lips, he led the way as they entered the house cautiously and quietly looked around. Peggy stayed a few paces behind him, squeezing his bicep with her forearm and losing herself momentarily in the intoxicating scent of his neck. He turned to her momentarily and stopped. He stared longingly at her wholesome face, took her hand gently in his own, kissed it and motioned for her to stand back. As they minced across the living room and headed towards the kitchen, the distinct sound of a male voice singing emanated from the direction of the basement. He raised his gun and stepped into the doorway at the top of the basement steps. At the bottom of the staircase, Hans was crouched over Mrs. Eriksen's lifeless body with a pillow pressed firmly over her face.

Bob ordered Hans to freeze and screamed for Peggy to get out of the house. Crying, she ran out of the open door and towards a neighboring house for help. Hans looked down the barrel of the gun and did as he was told. The deliberate smile never left his lips.

Calvin

The voices informed Calvin that he was not allowed, under any circumstances, to continue polluting his body with insidious medical substances. He flushed the pills down the toilet and replaced them with identical looking tablets of alpha lipoic acid.

He made an effort to appear normal in front of his family. At dinnertime, he laughed freely at Jana's jokes and was overly helpful towards Aunt Alice. He complimented the foods that the voices allowed him to consume and gushed about his new job when questioned about the internship. Despite his thespian sensibilities, Jana remained suspicious.

"He's looking awfully slight and pale, don't you think?" Jana confided to Russell one evening while Calvin was washing the dinner dishes out of earshot.

"That vegan diet is bound to shave a few pounds off of him," Russell reasoned, "but he eats more vegetables than we do. Besides, you watch him take his medication every morning."

"Didn't you notice how he keeps batting at his ear?" Jana pointed out. "I think we should take him back to the doctor."

"He's due back for a physical in three months," Russell said.

"He's eating regularly and holding down a job. I think you're overreacting."

Later on that evening, Russell and Jana were watching a movie in the projection room and sharing a bowl of popcorn. Calvin walked in with his hands clasped behind his back and calmly inquired about seeing a doctor for procaine shots.

"Procaine?" Jana repeated in disbelief. "Cal, procaine shots have never been approved by the FDA. Why do you want them anyway?"

"They make your joints more flexible," Calvin explained. "They stimulate the production of new cells in the body and fortify the old ones. If I become more flexible, I'll reap more benefits from practicing yoga."

"Even if you found a doctor who would agree to it, and I don't think you would, it's not a good idea for someone your age to be messing around with that crap," Jana remarked. "It really isn't."

"Not on your salary, anyway," Russell added, munching. He squeezed Jana's hand. They laughed. Defeated, Calvin turned around to escape to the privacy of his bedroom.

"Aww, come on, Cal! Don't you want to finish watching *Whatever Happened to Aunt Alice?* It's one of your favorites," Russell called out, "and Miss Tinsley's about to become a pine tree."

Atonal glass scratched across musty violin strings and bored greedily into Calvin's left ear. "I believe I'll be off to bed now."

"Aren't you going to give your mother a kiss?" Jana pouted.

"You'll have to wash your face first," Calvin challenged.

"Wash my face? Why?"

"Your face is caked with talc-based powder and I'm not breathing that poison into my lungs!" He turned on his heels and ran up the stairs.

Russell put his arm around Jana and kissed her forehead exaggeratedly. "I'll take that kiss," he teased. "I'll take the chance."

They set aside the bowl of popcorn and embraced, only to jerk apart upon hearing the sound of a heavy crash and Calvin shouting. Seconds later, Calvin reappeared in the doorway with his shirt off and fire blazing in his eyes. He held a tube of toothpaste.

"What's that noise? What is it? What's happened?" Jana and Russell were alarmed as they rose to their feet and stared at their son, waiting for him to explain himself. Calvin shook the tube of toothpaste in Jana's direction. He stuttered with anger.

"I just asked you to do me one simple favor, Mom," he shouted. "I just asked for the toothpaste!" he bellowed.

"I got what you told me to!" Jana was shocked and defensive. "You told me to get Tom's of Maine."

"Spearmint fluoride-free!" he screamed at the top of his lungs. "Spearmint fluoride-free! Spearmint fluoride-free! I asked you to get the spearmint fluoride-free with propolis and myrrh and you got me Cinnamon fluoride! Cinnamon fluoride! Cinnamon fluoride!"

"What's all that noise?" Aunt Alice called out from her bedroom. Who in the hell is carrying on like that? Russell? Russell? Why won't you answer me?" A second passed before the bell began to ring with persistence. "Russell? I know you hear me calling! Russell!"

Visibly agitated, Russell stormed off in the direction of Aunt Alice's bedroom. Jana's attempts to assuage her sobbing son were futile.

"...because it's gonna give me bone cancer. No, it isn't safe. No, that's a myth about it making your teeth strong, and it's cinnamon. Because spearmint grows wild around here. Mom, when have you ever seen cinnamon growing in Philadelphia? Then how do you know if it's indigenous to the northeast?"

Jana was worn out by the exchange. She turned off the projector and tearfully went to bed. Russell went into the kitchen to fix Aunt Alice a plate of cheddar cheese, graham crackers and a glass of warm milk before following his wife upstairs. Aunt Alice snacked voraciously, occasionally looking up from her plate to wipe crumbs away from her nightgown, grab the remote control and adjust the volume of her television set. Calvin disappeared into the shelter of his bedroom tower and mercilessly scrubbed his teeth with table salt until his gums were raw and bloody.

He had been asleep in bed for nearly three hours when he was abruptly awakened by the lucid realization that the voices were carnivorous locusts fighting to gain control of his bloodstream. Hopping out of bed, he positioned his body into the plough posture and placed his nose squarely onto his chest. Using his chest as an x-ray, he found that he could see them quite clearly.

They swam through the winding canals of his veins and sipped from blood-filled highballs. They built a bonfire over his pancreas and drank blood from earthenware steins. They dusted their noses with talcum powder and toasted to future prosperity with overpoured Riedel balloons. They waved sheets of aluminum along his mercury-filled molars and revealed a purple path to Titan's orange surface.

Calvin ran to the toilet, vomited, and decided to stay awake until he knew what to do. He curled up on the couch in the projection room with a bag of ice chips and an old army blanket and flipped through channels, crunching.

An infomercial about the Rejuvenique facelift mask caught his attention. Calvin watched, enrapt, as a panel of women in tailored suits donned expressionless phantom masks lined with metal probes and discussed how wonderful the electric currents made them feel. In that instant, he decided that the voices and the mercurial path would not stand a chance against the power of the metal probes. He wandered back downstairs, found Jana's open purse on top of the kitchen island, and rooted through the contents until he found her Visa card. He held the telephone line quietly for half an hour until a representative became available to take his order.

He hid the mask from Jana and Russell and used it within the confines of his locked bathroom. Stunned by the power of the electric currents, the locusts grew bewildered and began to doze for lengthy periods. However hopeful, Calvin was plagued by lightheadedness and headaches.

One afternoon, while having a lunch of short grain brown rice, lotus root and daikon sprouts at Essene, he found a pamphlet article on the dangers of mercury dental fillings. He was excited to share the article with his parents. Reading further, however, divulged that removing the fillings could potentially be more harmful than keeping them intact. Conflicted, he continued to read. Contact information for the National Dental Amalgam Mercurial Syndrome Support Group was listed on the last page. He tore the page out of the pamphlet and folded it into his pocket.

The following week, he attended his first support meeting and took solace in the knowledge that he wasn't alone. To celebrate, he returned to Essene and purchased a velvety bouquet of purple-tinted integrifolia. He put the bouquet into an empty coffee can and displayed it on his dresser near the collection of antique, handmade Hungarian puppets.

At dinner, Jana and Russell noticed the shift in his personality and inquired about his whereabouts that afternoon. Calvin smiled and told them about his lightheadedness and headaches, that he had Dental Amalgam Mercurial Syndrome, and that the support meeting had really helped.

"I don't think your headaches have anything to do with your fillings." Jana passed a platter of crabcakes to Russell. "You're not getting enough protein, and the dosage of your medication needs to be adjusted."

"Your mother's right." Russell grasped an artichoke with tongs and held it out towards Calvin's plate. "Aunt Alice?"

"No, Lordy." Aunt Alice rolled her eyes. "You know I don't eat artichokes."

"We discussed moving up your routine physical to make sure everything's okay." Russell continued. "I'll make an appointment for early next week."

"In my day, we were so grateful to have dental care we would've been happy with cement fillings," Aunt Alice remarked, eyeing the crabcakes.

"Have a crabcake, Cal." Jana reasoned. "It's shellfish, not meat. It wouldn't hurt you to eat a little shellfish every once in a while, would it?"

"I don't need it." Calvin was stubborn. "I had a sun chlorella, spirulina and blue green algae shake this morning."

"Spira who?" Aunt Alice asked.

"Spirulina," Calvin continued. "Algae have just as much protein as flesh foods." He paused. "They counteract the symptoms of mercurial poisoning, too."

Jana sighed with false brightness and emptied the contents of her wine glass in one gulp.

"Are there any more greens in the Frigidaire?" Aunt Alice wanted to know.

"You ate the last of them with your lunch." Jana reminded her.

"What other vegetable did you make?" Aunt Alice stared aghast at the platter of artichokes.

"I didn't." Jana sighed with a note of exasperation. She uncorked the bottle of Chardonnay and deftly refilled her glass.

"That's a damn shame," Aunt Alice glared. "You know I don't eat artichokes. Black folks don't eat artichokes. You can't cook worth a damn, and you always make these damned foreign foods!"

"Aunt Alice," Russell warned.

"Well it's true!" Aunt Alice whined. "And you're a fool for not telling her. No wonder that baby's eating spiro, spuru, what you call it, Calvin?"

"Spirulina," Calvin replied soberly.

"That's right. Spirubina," Aunt Alice growled. No one bothered to correct her.

Jana folded her napkin and stood up to leave the table. Russell glared at Aunt Alice. "Was that really necessary?"

Aunt Alice spat out a piece of crab shell. "That old grown gal knows I don't mean any harm," she mumbled to her plate.

Russell put his hand out and touched his wife's arm. "Sit down," he reasoned. "She didn't mean it." "No, I'm done," Jana choked, walking away from the table. Russell started after her but sank back into his chair. Aunt Alice's eyes widened as they traveled from Russell to Calvin to the half-eaten crabcake on Jana's plate. "Is she gonna eat that?" she inquired, dabbing her lips with her napkin. Russell plopped it onto her plate and shook his head.

After dinner, Calvin stood in the privacy of his bathroom and regarded himself in the mirror. Huge, hungry eyes stood out from his chiseled features, shaded by a mahogany sprouting of locs. He removed his shirt. Lanugo grew on his arms, stomach and the concave area that shielded his heart.

Kneeling down on the tile, he wrapped his arms around himself in a comforting embrace, riding feelings of dizziness as the floor shifted gently beneath him. He rested his head on his knees. His x-ray vision had extended beyond his chest, and the locust colonization was proceeding in full force.

He pulled his shirt back on and yanked back the blankets of his bed in search of the Rejuvenique mask. Finding it, he sat at the foot of his bed and coated its probes with conductor gel. A whippoorwill called at the ledge of the bay window and tapped politely on the pane. A spotted owl hooted softly in acknowledgment.

Calvin opened the window and sat on the ledge. Ester waited gloriously below, holding a star in each of her outstretched palms. The starfire reflected from her eyes and cast prisms onto the surface of the glass. Calvin watched as she blew onto the surface of her palms. The stars rose to the surface of the window and left metallic trails in the evening sky.

He lunged forward to touch them. The spotted owl was startled by his abruptness and hastily retreated to an oak tree. Calvin stared wistfully as the first star danced onward and disappeared into the black horizon. The spotted owl caught the second one in its beak.

"Let it down," Ester challenged playfully.

"What?" Calvin widened his eyes and looked around nervously.

"Let it down!" she repeated with a toss of her head and a playful laugh.

Calvin turned around and let his head fall back with the weight of his hair. Ester buried her nose into the roots and breathed deeply of their fragrant earthiness. With certainty of footing, she climbed up the length until she was safely inside the ledge. Calvin lifted her into his arms and guided her safely to the floor.

Trembling knuckles brushed against the contour of her neck. A whirlwind of violet seized his nostrils. It reverberated through his hollow stomach, causing him to levitate towards the sky. Silken fingers endowed with a deceptively subtle strength grasped his shoulders and kept him grounded.

He gasped with joy and fear. Leaping to his feet, he stumbled to the dresser and removed the bouquet of purple integrifolia from the coffee can, urging it towards her in offering. Ester smiled, kissed his cheek in gratitude and disappeared into the bathroom with the bouquet. Calvin looked on in confusion.

She emerged ten seconds later with a spool of dental floss and a small pair of scissors. Sprawling onto the floor, she divided the bouquet in half and twisted the stems together with dental floss, forming two separate crowns. Calvin's eyes trailed downward from the moonstone hummingbird at her throat, the translucent sheath of gauze draping her shoulders and torso, the fringe of leather and coral at her waist, the faded denim draping her legs and the glass platforms encasing her feet. Smiling with the weight of her accomplishment, she stood up, placed one of the crowns onto her head, and adorned Calvin with the other.

"I hereby crown you Prince of Purple Velvet with Dental Floss," she mused as Calvin admired her handiwork in the mirror. The harpsichord chimed in gently as she reached into her back pocket and handed Calvin an envelope.

He opened it and pulled out two concert tickets for George Clinton and the P-Funk All Stars. "Did you drive here?" he asked.

Ester kissed him on the forehead and carefully swung her feet out of the open bay window. "Onward, soldier," she teased. "Adventure awaits."

He looked past the open window to the sight of a floating, crushed purple velvet tapestry with the words, MIND FOLLOWING ASSES emblazoned in copperplate letters. Yards of dental floss streamed behind it in the wind.

Calvin panicked and instinctively felt for his Rejuvenique mask. Ester slid gracefully onto the tapestry. She held out her arms. Calvin closed his eyes and blindly dove in.

They watched the house grow smaller and smaller as the tapestry glided in the sky. The spotted owl hooted as they floated over the horizon and out of sight, a trail of silver behind them.

They floated to the corner of 10th and Arch Street and hovered in front of the Trocadero Theater. Ester stepped carefully onto the pavement, brushing silver tendrils from her blouse and jeans. Ignoring the stares of passersby, she ran ahead inside of the venue. Calvin handed the bouncer the tickets and waited to have his hand stamped.

The venue was packed. Bodies flocked en masse to the shelter of the bar where servers clad in sleeveless black shirts and chain link belts slid glasses filled with rainbow-colored liquor to anyone who would catch them.

The stage was lit with red, blue and yellow. A blonde girl

holding a Rolling Rock bottle and a lit cigarette screamed in Ester's direction, enveloped her in a series of hugs and urged her into her coterie on the dance floor. Calvin watched as the women laughed and danced, their asses following the beat of their freed minds.

Calvin approached the closest bar and watched the bartender pour Kamikazes into shot glasses. He slapped a twenty onto the bar and downed two of them within seconds.

A warm, sultry, unconquerable feeling overcame him. He looped the hem of the t-shirt into its neckline and fingered the rim of his boxers with his index fingers. Women paused to stare at the gentle contours of his abdominal muscles.

Calvin floated out to the dance floor, cast his arms out to his sides, and spun. He spun because he was talented, sexy, and a roguish drinker to boot. He spun because he was clean and unpolluted by meat, dairy, and other unmentionable contaminants. He spun because he wanted to be back on the tapestry gliding into the darkness with Ester. He spun because he was going to take care of her, regardless of the fact that he had not bothered to call the studio when he had ditched work in order to attend the Dental Amalgam Mercurial Syndrome Support Group, and that his job was potentially in jeopardy. He spun because it was fun to spin, he had the energy and grace of a frolicking gazelle, and because his medication was presently hard at work in the septic tank alleviating the Schuylkill River's paranoia.

Enlightenment had come to its full realization, and Calvin followed it back to the bar. A flaming Dr. Pepper here, a Yuengling there and Calvin had reached Nirvana. He was standing in line for a urinal when the voices returned in earnest and openly laughed at his bravado. They sent a signal to the other concertgoers to alert them of Calvin's absurdity. Soon everyone in the theater was laughing mercilessly at him, despite valiant attempts to hold themselves together.

The laughter began as a low, barely audible buzz. Calvin

batted his left ear with his hand. He pushed his way against the crowd and up the staircase to the balcony bathroom. He splashed his face with cold water and proceeded with alternate nostril breaths.

H.B. appeared in the attendant's chair and smiled. Diamonds sparkled from the left side of his mouth.

"Back home," he began as he handed Calvin a paper towel, "everything sparkles like diamonds. Back home, everybody grooves and the moons have no dark side. Back home, you can see in front of your eyes and behind your head at the same time. When are you coming home, baby?"

Smoke from a medley of cigarettes rose from the air and into Calvin's face and lungs. He instinctively reached into his back pocket for the surgical mask that he sometimes wore on the subway but remembered that he had left it in the pocket of the jeans that were balled up on the floor next to his bed. He saturated a paper towel under the running faucet and placed it over his nose and mouth.

"Back home," H.B. continued, "the air is so pure it's like walking around in a hyperbaric chamber. Happy lungs! When you coming home, baby?"

The voices grew tails and dispersed themselves evenly into the seminal smoke. They competed aggressively for entrance into Calvin's nasal cavity, intent on being the first to fertilize his brain.

Crawling on his hands and knees, Calvin held the wet paper towel over his nose and mouth and began to descend the staircase, much to the curiosity and bewilderment of the people surrounding him. Comments and giggles were heightened as if broadcast over a loudspeaker. His cried out fearfully as he searched among the motorcycle boots, Birkenstocks and Doc Martens for a glimpse of Ester's glass platform slippers.

He called out her name until his voice was hoarse and bleeding. He crawled past the bar to the edge of the dance floor, tears falling freely. A young bartender with a low-slung ammo belt and a large, fluffy afro saw him crawling towards the dance floor. "Are you okay?" she screamed above the music. Her forehead wrinkled with concern. "Are you sick? Do you need a doctor?"

He curled his knees into his chest and lay in fetal position at the edge of the dance floor. A barrage of people stepped over his body as he piteously clutched the paper rag to his face. A man with his hands full of drinks lost his footing as he tripped over Calvin's purple velvet crown. He kicked it angrily across the floor before kicking Calvin squarely in the back. The bartender picked up the in-house phone to alert security.

At the opposite end of the bar, Ester waved to the blonde girl, who was being tugged away by a tall man with a concise haircut and a camouflage jacket. She finished her glass of club soda and started across the room in search of Calvin.

Securing her purple velvet crown, she walked past the coat check and up the front staircase to the balcony. She forced her way through the crowd at the upper-level bar and down through the lines for the bathrooms.

A security guard tried to hoist Calvin off of the floor. He lashed out at them with balled fists, crying bitterly despite himself. Vomit stained the front of his t-shirt. "I don't wanna go home! I'm not going home! Not my home!" he shrieked.

"Let's just get you some air. Okay, man?"

A crowd surrounded the edge of the dance floor, backlit by the rapturous thunder of George Clinton and the P-Funk All Stars and the frenetic oblivion of concertgoers dancing a few yards ahead. Ester spotted the security guard and weaved her way through the crowd to kneel down beside Calvin's head. The bartender took a damp rag and blotted away the majority of vomit from Calvin's lips and shirt. Ester draped her arms around his shoulders and gently urged him to an upright position.

Calvin's surroundings vanished into a blanket of white clouds. When the blanket parted, the stage was lit up with blue. George

Clinton and Bootsy Collins stood on either side of the stage, dressed in diapers. Ester sat center stage next to a harpsichord, strumming with a delicate precision. She threw her head back and closed her eyes, backlit by the simulated moons of tech lighting. Buds poked their way through the wooden floorboards of the stage as she played and sprouted into vines clustered with fragrant, white blossoms. Mesmerized by the subtle rhythm, they wavered back and forth and filled the theater with an ethereal scent of lily and jasmine.

Ester stepped forward and paused Calvin's heartbeat with the intensity of her gaze. The vines throbbed in a stylized, rhythmic trance, and the white blossoms shriveled up and withered to the ground. The moonstone hummingbird glowed with an unearthly, lurid light. Clutching it in her fingers, she spun, disappearing into a silver funnel that disappeared in a clap of earth-shattering thunder, cleaving the stage in two.

An incarnation from Calvin's deepest nightmares emerged as lava flowed from the chasm. She twisted her shoulders to the beat of the vines, rocking from side to side in rhythm. She rested her hands on her knees, shook her dimpled buttocks in his direction, and blew kisses at him between cloven hooves.

H.B's diamond grin sparkled as he watched from the balcony with outstretched fists, arthritic hips wriggling to the drum beat. "Get it, Erzuli," he preached. Calvin urinated.

Calvin could smell her warm, acrid breath as she winked at him and smiled, lava dripping from the corners of her mouth, down her jowls and onto the floor, burning holes into the wood. She licked his left ear teasingly, forked tongue lagging provocatively, stinging what she chose to caress.

Calvin defecated.

The dimensions shifted, transforming her teeth into the bars of a prison cell. Ester gripped the brown, calculus-pasted bars and banged against them with her fists, crying futilely. Calvin sprang up to rescue his beloved, but unseen hands clenched his shoulders.

White clouds reappeared and blanketed the crimson panorama as the security guard and bartender cleared the area. The paramedics came and lifted Calvin onto a stretcher. He resisted.

"Can we get some water over here?" the paramedic asked the bartender. "I'm really thirsty."

Ester placed a cool hand against Calvin's cheek and kissed his forehead repeatedly, comforting him as the paramedics picked up the stretcher and loaded him into an ambulance.

It was nearly four a.m. when Russell and Jana hurried through the lobby decorated with modern art and plastic green plants and approached the nurses' station at Hahnemann University Hospital. Jana wore sweatpants, slippers and a pair of oversized sunglasses that hid her tearstained face. Russell wore a scowl.

Russell shook his fists at the nurses when they told him that visiting hours began promptly at eight. He proceeded to remind them who he was, threatened to bring down the entire establishment if he was not permitted to see his son immediately and clutched his Motorola 3200 cellular phone, cursing. The head nurse called the hospital staff director, who apologized profusely to Russell and granted an exception. Russell stormed ahead to the elevator while Jana trailed behind and extended her gratitude to the head nurse on her husband's behalf.

When they entered the hospital room Calvin was awake, albeit stunned by the stomach pump and other treatments administered for his blood alcohol poisoning and paranoia-induced delusions. He weakly acknowledged his parents and managed a slight smile.

Jana kissed him fervently and praised God for keeping him alive and safe. Russell paced back and forth in front of the window and was not quite as understanding.

"He can't make any constructive decisions on his own!" Russell raged when he and Jana left the room to stop at the cafeteria for coffee. "I've been far too lenient with him! All of his freedoms are what got him here in the first place. When I was his age I didn't have any choice *but* to do the right thing. And what's so bad about listening to me? I came from dirt floors, and I still make a high six figure salary. You're missing the point. This is not about some goddamned medication withdrawal. He's hiding behind that. Boy just wants to be sick. I guess this is the thanks I get, putting my name and reputation on the line to get him a position with one of the most powerful brothers on the planet. Gonna turn his nose up to the meat when we had to struggle to put square meals on the table. Gonna throw some mess about fluoride and not seeing a dentist but drink enough liquor to fill up a goddamn steed. Gonna throw away his Andover diploma, skip college and focus on his music. Jimi Hendrix, my ass!"

Calvin was released from the hospital the following afternoon. Jana offered a few brave attempts at conversation during the car ride home. Calvin stared out the window at a gaggle of geese flying in V formation. Russell kept his eyes on the road and maintained a steely silence.

At dinnertime, Calvin took his medication from Jana's fingers and swallowed it as she watched him closely. He thanked her in earnest for the barbequed seitan and macaroni and soy cheese dishes she had prepared and forced down as much as his weakened stomach would allow. Aunt Alice chatted obliviously and ravenously attacked a platter of turnip greens. Russell picked at his food and avoided eye contact with everyone.

"I found *Whoever Slew Auntie Roo?* and *Dear Dead Delilah* on VHS the other day, Cal." Jana broke the silence. "I remembered that they were two of your old favorites. Why don't you head to the projection room, and I'll make some organic popcorn with soy margarine and sea salt? Everybody game? Russell? Aunt Alice?"

"Count me in," Aunt Alice said. She shifted her body upwards in her wheelchair. "Calvin, roll me in there, would you? And Jana thanks for the turnip greens. They were delicious."

Jana kissed Aunt Alice on the cheek and wrapped her in a tight hug before Calvin rolled her away from the table and towards the projection room. Breathing a sigh of relief, she finished her glass of wine. She proceeded to clear the dishes from the table. "Russell?" she began, "Why don't you go ahead and join them? I can manage these dishes by myself."

"I've got work to do," Russell answered curtly. He stood up from the table and disappeared into the library.

Calvin and Jana carefully lifted Aunt Alice from her wheelchair, placed her onto the couch, and wrapped her in a blanket. Calvin smiled a bit too broadly and forced himself to eat some of the popcorn that Jana had prepared. Jana emptied the remainder of the bottle of Chardonnay into her wine glass and excused herself to go back down to the wine cellar. Aunt Alice thrust handful after handful of popcorn into her mouth and gleefully outlined her favorite scenes of the movie.

"Ooh, she's a crook!" she giggled. "Shelley Winters gonna tell that lie to the orphanage that Katy and Christopher are hiding when she kidnapped those babies. That Katy's a dumb assed child, gonna send her brother back in the fire to risk his life to get that ole stuffed bear William. Just get a new bear! Shit."

He returned to his room after the movies, got into bed and closed his eyes. Stars twinkled in the distance. Chopin's *Nocturnes* wrapped an arm around his waist and rested its head on his chest. Calvin basked in the warmth of the rare and peaceful moment.

He had almost drifted off to sleep when a locust rapped at his eardrum to inform him that his medication was useless and the infiltration process was still in full effect.

His x-ray vision extended vertically from his cerebrum down his spinal column and branched outward. He was shocked and amazed by what he saw.

They frolicked about in tree-lined parks and sipped from bottles between frisbee games. A son fell off his bicycle and twitched as his knee began to ooze. His father crawled to his side and told him to keep going. His sister admired her bias cut dress and twirled in the grass, beaming with pride.

Calvin peered beyond the banner of aluminum reflecting the surface of his mercury fillings and studied the path to Titan for future infiltrators. To his horror, the glowing substance had replaced the blood in his feet and ankles, and inched slowly up the length of his legs.

Tiptoeing down to the kitchen, he scooped up a bowl of ice chips from the freezer and chewed furiously until his throat felt quite frozen. "What do you want?" he moaned. His hair bristled at the back of his head. He had not really expected an answer.

A locust crawled to the base of his eardrum. "Your blood," it answered, sending reverberations along the length of Calvin's spinal column. Calvin picked up the Rejuvenique mask, strapped it to his face, and turned it up to the highest setting.

He resolved that he would replace the blood and started by turning to Jesus. He wandered from church to church, listening to services and hanging around for communion, eagerly awaiting the consecration of wine. When the day was over, he returned to his room with a cheap bottle of red and dutifully continued with consecrations of his own.

He felt confident that his blood levels were stabilizing and began to feel a bit better, but when his x-ray vision revealed that the purple mercurial matter had nearly extended itself to his knees, he sat in the projection room in the middle of the night, armed with a bowl of ice chips and the Rejuvenique mask, and reassessed his strategy.

The following afternoon, he walked to SuperFresh and purchased a small steak. He placed it raw onto the makeshift altar in his bedroom that he had constructed from cinderblocks, plywood, and an ancient white bed sheet. Hoisting a steak knife in his right hand and uttering a prayer for the soul of the cow, he cut off a small piece and chewed furiously. Overwhelmed by both the intensity of the flavor and the moment, he followed the bite with a large drink of wine and genuflected with fervor. "I'm sorry," he apologized to the steak atop the altar. "It's about survival."

Nausea occurred in rolling waves. He finished the rest of the steak and the entire bottle of wine. He passed out and slept dreamlessly, a consistent stream of drool saturating his pillow. The midnight air teased his chest. The dryness of his throat woke him up.

He took a long drink from the bottle of distilled water on his nightstand. He wiped his nose with his fingers, and they came away spotted with blood. He swung his legs to the edge of the bed. His x-ray vision had extended to 365 degrees. The purple mercurial substance had completely replaced the blood in his knees and inched towards the base of his navel.

He felt at the side of his bed for the mask and coated its probes with gel, ignoring the violent shaking of his hands and the irritated, amphibious quality that his skin had assumed from chronic overuse. Curling into fetal position, he wept, floating in and out of consciousness.

He awoke to the sound of an album skipping, followed by screams.

The spotted owl clutched a star in its beak, screaming as a shard of glass held by an invisible hand stabbed its bloodstained feathers. It dropped the star at its feet. The star burst into flames that enveloped its body.

Calvin lurched forward to rescue it, but he was locked in a state of catalepsy. "No! No! Stop it! You'll kill it! You're killing it! Please!"

A frenzy of panic was met with a smothering of violet hugs. Ester held him close and fought to gain control of the forces competing within him for her attention. "It's okay... It's okay...

It's okay," she repeated. Tears mingled with the sweat at his temples until her voice had been sufficiently amplified.

A sober, watery response caught the voices off guard, leaking a stream of tentative drool. "Okay?" he whispered.

"I've got him, see? He's with me."

Ester was framed in the window, and the spotted owl perched unharmed on her shoulder. Calvin watched as she straddled the ledge and disappeared into the night, owl on shoulder, silver trailing behind them. "Hey, wanderer," a male voice called from the distance, "You ever seen the dark side of the moon?"

Calvin watched as the moon turned on its axis and the surface began to ripple with facets as if pounded by an unseen mallet. The facets sparkled like diamonds and illuminated the room. Soft colored, icy rings began to take shape around the sphere.

There was a knock at the window. Still in a cataleptic state, he watched as H.B. climbed over the ledge escorted by two women, one blonde and the other brunette. They were dressed in half shirts with Saturn's Disco emblazoned across the front in glittery letters, midriffs exposed. They had large breasts and wore layers of garish makeup. Suntan colored nylon stockings peeked out from underneath their denim hot pants. Feathered, hot-rollered hairstyles framed their faces. Fluffy pink pom-poms adorned their white leather roller skates. Wah-wah pedals resonated through the air as they flanked H.B. and formed a conga line. H.B. laughed from his place in the middle and flashed his diamond teeth.

"On Titan," H.B. began dramatically, "we all have mind-following asses." The brunette woman withdrew a comb from the back pocket of her hot pants and carefully feathered her hair.

"Who are you?" Calvin managed.

"You're still trying to pretend like you don't know me?" H.B. frowned in jest. "I'm in you all the time; why you trying to fight it, baby?"

"Come aboard baby," the blonde woman bared her teeth.

"Why you trying to fight it, baby?" H.B. repeated. He grabbed the buttocks of the brunette as she wriggled in front of him suggestively. "Room enough for you," he sang, "Room enough for you, indeed."

The women laughed and spun on their skates. "Hey, Emmaretta, go fix me a martini, please," H.B. ordered. The blonde nodded and skated off to the bar that appeared in the north corner of the room.

"Shaken, honey?" she asked, behind in the air as she searched for a bottle of vodka.

"Apple." H.B. adjusted the brim of his feathered fedora and spun gracefully on his skates.

"Got some spirulina back there too, sugar." Emmaretta winked at Calvin as she skated to H.B.'s side and handed him the apple martini. "The oversized glasses!" the old man chimed approvingly as he swatted her behind and crossed over to the mirrored grand piano that appeared in the south corner of the room.

A contagious melody filled the room as H.B. tickled the ivories. Calvin glanced at his abandoned guitar collecting dust in the east corner of the room. He looked at H.B. and attempted to follow his head along the bends of the melody. H.B. met his gaze and nodded.

With the nod came an audible pop. Calvin felt his body unlock from the catatonia. He slowly moved his fingertips in front of his eyes and stared at his hands. An electric current rooting at the base of his abdomen and emanated towards his heart as he walked over to his guitar, plugged it into his amplifier, and allowed the song to unfold. Back at the bar, Emmaretta lit candles with a long taper while her brunette partner rattled a martini shaker and strained the contents over a glass before holding it out to Calvin.

He set his guitar down to accept the glass from her neatly manicured fingers and sipped gratefully at its icy sweetness. H.B. walked over to Calvin and offered his hand. Calvin grasped it. They levitated.

"Look up, baby," H.B. said softly. The ceiling wall had disappeared and they were surrounded by constellations. The tip of Copernicus wriggled. Pluto's heart beat quietly. Andromeda swayed playfully in the distance, high on gas and laughing.

"Phooey, Octavia, you're getting that all over me," Emmaretta whined as the brunette sloshed the contents of her glass before setting her empty glass on the bar.

"Sorry, Em!" Octavia offered. The two women grasped hands and floated upwards to join Calvin. He sucked in his breath as Octavia snuck behind him and wrapped her arms around his chest.

"This will never come out," Emmaretta stared in dismay at the large, green stain spreading down the front of her chest.

"Oh, well. Guess you'll just have to take it off," Octavia sighed. She nestled her bare stomach against the small of Calvin's back and slid her fingers downward to circle around his navel.

Emmaretta pulled the half shirt over her head and softly shook her hair out of her eyes. She grasped Calvin's hands and cupped them onto her swollen breasts. Octavia slid her fingers down lower, stroking the length of his erection. H.B. observed from a distance and chuckled.

A bittersweet tidal wave laced with bloody undertones flooded Calvin's nose, mouth and stomach, causing him to lose his footing and sink helplessly into the arms of Octavia. The buoyancy of Emmaretta's cream dollop breasts rocked him gently up and squarely back down into the harbor of Octavia's hot velvet wetness. An intense procession of spasms ensued as Calvin shuddered violently with release.

Martini glasses laced with traces of syrup and half eaten apple slices littered the bar. The sun peeked voyeuristically from the depths of the eastern horizon, intent upon stealing a glance of adventure.

Floating, H.B. placed his arm around Calvin's shoulder. Calvin stood in peaceful silence and watched as Emmaretta and Octavia glided through the air in synchronized unison.

Cartwheels melded into splits as they rolled from their backs onto the soft pads of their stomachs. Peacocks merged into somersaults, breaststrokes into scorpions, and ultimately, swan dives into flights of freedom.

Octavia dove first, swept onward out of the open window by cottony pillows of wind. True realization of wingspan unveiled itself as she shed her skin, metamorphosed into a butterfly and gracefully fluttered away in the direction of the fast approaching dawn.

Emmaretta was next, lingering at the base of the window to lightly caress Calvin's cheek and kiss him softly on the mouth. The clouds graciously deferred as she closed her eyes, outstretched her arms and fell backward into the trusting arms of the sky. Disappearing momentarily beneath the boughs of the oak trees bordering the side of the mansion, she reappeared as a silken, black and yellow bumblebee. She paused at the morning glories in Jana's garden before flying away, happy and drunk.

Crystal tears fell from Calvin's eyes and spilled onto the windowsill. H.B.'s arm patted his shoulder reassuringly. "No time for tears, baby," he said soothingly. "Home is where the love is. It's all about love, baby. It's all about love."

He placed his fedora onto Calvin's head before diving and emerged as a stately blue heron soaring evenly through the air, eager to start its morning with a hearty catfish breakfast along the river. Calvin removed the feather from the fedora's velvet band and traced the outline of the fading stars before hurling it into the blanket of sky and quietly diving in.

Russell

He picked up a photo from the edge of his desk and tapped it softly with his fingers, laughing out loud at the memory of his horrified, seven-year-old son attempting to remove the hook from the bleeding sunfish he caught during their boating trip at Lake Superior.

Another photo captured a wild-eyed Calvin clutching Jana's arm in terror atop the American Eagle rollercoaster at Six Flags. His image was a direct contrast to that of the other children, arms thrust boldly into the air, gaping mouths distorted with laughter.

"What's really scary," a stocky, badly sunburned boy holding an enormous cone of blue cotton candy had said to Calvin and Jana as they waited for their turn in an hour-long line on that sticky August afternoon, "isn't the descent at all but the way the stray chunks of wood and cotter pins pop out of the foundation and fly up into the air and the seats go rickety rickety rickety right up to the very end." The boy gnashed his teeth, extended his elbows and curled his fingers into claws to accentuate his point, causing Calvin to recoil and drop his double dip strawberry cone on the asphalt.

When the tears came, he buried his head in his hands and sobbed at his desk for what seemed like an eternity. When his throat was too hoarse to make any more sounds and his body too dehydrated to produce any more tears, a hummingbird fluttered to the edge of the desk and came to rest upon the edge of a silver frame. His eyes trailed to the opposite end of the room, where Paul sat on top of the window seat.

"This can't be real."

Paul brushed off his suit. "It only seems that way because the ceremony was closed casket."

"I meant you. I must be hallucinating."

Paul gazed at his luminously buffed fingernails before clasping his fingers together. "That's up to you. As stated before, I am a beacon of clarity to be revealed at various crossroads in the life of you and yours." He paused. "Sometimes I am available for counsel."

The hummingbird fluttered from the picture frame and flew out of the open window. "What counsel are you here to give me?"

"He's free. That's all."

He closed his eyes and bowed his head against the desk. When he lifted it up, Paul was gone.

TRANSIT
1991

Calvin

Calvin lost track of the butterfly, bee and heron after diving out of the window, but he didn't care. He was too busy enjoying the rolling waves of the wind carrying him forward. He closed his eyes and lost himself in the feeling. The more he surrendered to the sensation, the faster the locusts that had plagued him for so long began to fly away, one by one, until he was finally alone with the clarity of his thoughts for the first time in as long as he could remember.

His senses heightened, the layers of the atmosphere were visibly distinct. A thin metallic taste formed at the base of his tongue and coated his throat and lungs. Corporeal sensation ceased there; the rest of his body seemed weightless. He shouted into the sky. His voice was as sharp as a razor and as deliberate as a foghorn. He continued to shout with pride, piercing the morning with candor as he sailed into the sun and gently drifted to a landing, swathed in pillows of blinding light.

When the light diminished, he was standing in front of a house. It was small with a thatched roof and brown crossbeams that reminded him of a countryside European villa. Honeysuckle blossoms lined the path to the blue painted front door. The welcome mat was made out of flower petals and bird feathers.

Calvin knelt down and popped a honeysuckle blossom into his mouth. The flavor exploded with the scent of something baking in the oven inside that wafted from an open window. An attractive young woman stood at the window waving.

She was skinny with joyful brown eyes and brown hair arranged in a neat updo. The sleeves of her white blouse were pushed up at the elbows. She opened the door and beckoned Calvin inside. Her calf length skirt gracefully swished around her legs in a way that reminded Calvin of the actress from the movie *Roman Holiday*. She wrapped her arms around Calvin and squeezed him with all of her might, breathing a small sigh of relief.

"There you are, Calvin," she exclaimed, with a hint of Mississippi drawl. "We've been waiting for you all night! I thought you'd be here a bit sooner, but better late than never. Come on in!" She stepped out of the way and beckoned him inside.

Calvin wiped his feet on the mat and shyly ducked into the low doorway. He found himself standing in an open, breezy kitchen space with a red brick hearth at the center. Wooden crossbeams lined the white walls. Bunches of flowers were hung from the crossbeams to dry. Baskets heaped with heirloom tomatoes, sausages, an assortment of olives and pungent hard cheeses wrapped with string surrounded a rustic oak table. A variety of floral seedlings were spread out on the table. The aroma of something baking grew stronger.

Birds sunned themselves on various perches throughout the room. Some of them whistled at Calvin in greeting. Others ignored him and greedily munched on a snack of shelled walnuts and millet. Calvin identified a cockatoo, a parrot, two parakeets, a robin, an owl, and a jackdaw. He glanced at the hearth. His stomach rumbled.

"Let me get a good look at you," the woman said. She looked at Calvin's hair wistfully. "May I?" she asked. Calvin nodded and stooped down a bit.

She stroked his hair, tentatively at first, timid in discovering a new dimension of texture and softness. "Beautiful," she whispered, "absolutely beautiful." A tear rolled down her face as she rubbed her cheek against his hair. "A first kiss," she murmured. "It feels just like a first kiss."

"A first kiss, a first kiss," the cockatoo mocked. It squawked at Calvin and cocked its head to the side. Gladys continued to hold Calvin. He started to respond, but she brought her soft fingers to his mouth.

She wiped back a sudden spill of tears and fought to take control of her trembling voice. "You know I never wanted it to turn out this way. I wanted to get to know you before, but what I wanted didn't matter. My husband's fate was to deny the truth, and I couldn't compete with it because I was a part of it, you know?"

She looked away in pain for a few moments and then brightened up considerably. "Look at you. You're here now." She fingered his locs. "And you're so beautiful! We've got so much catching up to do!" She snuggled in closer to Calvin and wiped her runny nose against her sleeve.

Calvin continued to hold the woman, patting her on the back in politeness. "Ma'am," he said gently, "I'm sorry. What did you say your name was, again?"

Surprised flooded the woman's face as she straightened up to look at him and saw the confusion in Calvin's eyes. "Oh, honey, I'm sorry. I thought you knew. It's Grandma! I'm your grandmother, Gladys!"

"My grandmother?" Calvin snorted in disbelief at the young woman standing before him. "No, you're not! First of all, you're not old enough. Second of all, my grandmother is dead! Mom said that her last letter to Mississippi was returned unopened and postmarked deceased."

Calvin's voice trailed off as he remembered the events that led up to his diving from the third-story attic bedroom window. Trembling, he sat down at the kitchen table, covered his mouth with his hands and stared at the floral seedlings spread out in front of him. Gladys looked away graciously, leaving him alone to solve the puzzle. Even the birds quieted down in an apparent display of politeness.

"You must be hungry," Gladys' voice was uneasy as she broke the silence. "There's sheep's milk cheese, heirloom tomatoes and fresh bread. Sausage, too. Do you eat meat?"

"Sometimes," Calvin answered truthfully. Relief washed over Gladys' face as she busied herself by preparing a plate. "I've been meaning to get to the vegetarian books, but I'm still getting the hang of the basics." She laughed. "Audrey Hepburn I never was, but my peach pie is divine."

She hummed as she sliced up tomatoes, cheese, sausage, bread and olives. She loaded up a plate for Calvin and set it down in front of him. He brought a piece of cheese to his lips and nibbled. Gladys smiled as Calvin took a big bite of tomato and licked his lips. "Aren't you going to eat?" he asked.

She opened the refrigerator and took out a martini glass and a pitcher. "I'm not hungry, sweetheart," she said, pouring herself a drink. She stole an olive from Calvin's plate, dropped it into her glass, and took a large swallow. She waited until he had finished eating before standing up and removing a peach pie from the oven. Cutting a generous slice, she placed it on a fresh plate and set it down in front of him.

Calvin raised his fork and slowly took a bite. An explosion of peaches and spices spread through his mouth like brushfire. Calvin closed his eyes. "This is the best pie I've ever tasted," he remarked.

"Audrey Hepburn I never was," the parrot squawked.

Gladys gave the bird a dirty look. "Thank you, Calvin," she blushed, holding up her glass in salutation.

The sound of the doorknob turning diverted their conversation.

"Did someone mention peach pie?" a gentle voice asked. "You know it was your peach pie that made me fall in love with you all those years ago, Gladys."

A square-jawed man with tightly curled, shoulder length blond hair and blue eyes walked in, carrying a birdcage that housed two doves in one hand and a large bunch of purple flowers in the other. He wore jeans and sandals. He looked at Calvin and smiled in welcome. "Hey there," he said, eyes smiling. "We were just beginning to worry."

"Who are you?" Calvin was puzzled as he watched the man's brawny hand set the birdcage down at the edge of the table. He stared at the man's casual attire.

"Grandson!" The man's youthful voice rang out with love.

"What's going on?"

Gladys stood up suddenly, wobbling a bit from the martini. "Out of the mouth of babes," she giggled nervously. Changing the subject, she eyed the purple flowers at the edge of the table. "Those are pretty. What are they?"

"*Eichornia Crassipes*," the blond man recited proudly, "More commonly known as hyacinth."

"Isn't it amazing?" Gladys purred with admiration. "Ask him about any flower, Calvin. He knows everything there is to know about every type of flower or bird that you can think of!"

A confused Calvin attempted to piece the situation together. "Harlan?" he asked.

"Linden," the blond man chuckled, holding the bouquet towards Gladys in offering. Mildly agitated, she held it for a few moments and set it down on the table.

Calvin looked to Gladys for an answer. "Grandma?"

Gladys threw her head back, downed the contents of her martini glass and smiled brightly. "I'll explain later," she said, plopping a second helping in front of Calvin before he could refuse. "Just eat the pie," she hissed.

He raised his fork obediently and watched as Linden unhinged the cage door and encouraged the doves to roam about the house. A hummingbird hovered in the open kitchen window. Calvin pushed his empty plate away and walked over to the window to get a closer look. "Hey, hummingbird," he greeted her shyly. He cupped his palms and held them out to her.

She was timid as she approached his open palms, but his heartbeat won her over. She glowed as Calvin stroked her iridescent feathers and tenderly kissed her miniature beak. She would stay with him, he thought to himself. He would never let her out of his sight again. He had never stopped loving her and would take care of her for the rest of her life. He would do anything he could to protect her.

Giddy with the buzz of the martini and a nerve pill, Gladys sat down next to Calvin. She kicked off her shoes and propped up her bare legs on the table. Picking up the bouquet of hyacinth, she twisted away until a purple crown rested in her hands. Linden sat down, placed the crown atop his head and stretched out his arms towards his lover. Gladys tumbled into them and eyed the peach pie.

She reached into the pie tin with her fingers and scooped up a bit, holding it out to his lips. Linden licked the pie slowly from her fingers, lingering there even after they were quite clean. He tickled her. She shrieked. The hairpins slid out of her tidy hairdo, sending her pin-straight brown hair cascading down her shoulders. She placed her hands inside of Linden's shirt. They kissed passionately while Calvin looked on, mesmerized by their infectious energy. Soon he was scooping up pie with his fingers and cramming it into his mouth. The three of them laughed and scooped up pie until the pie tin was empty and their fingers were sticky.

The hummingbird watched the exchange from the windowsill. When she was ready, she flew away and never came back. A chill crept into the space where she had lingered and spread through the windowsill. Calvin's breath was frosty as he watched as the silver threads at the window fade into crystal dust. The rejection stung like a wasp.

Linden put his hand on Calvin's shoulder. "Some birds keep flying. It used to make me sad, but now I just enjoy the company of the ones that hang around. You know what I mean?" He blew a kiss to his lover. "Gladys?"

"Let's go upstairs," Gladys answered wickedly. Linden raised a lascivious eyebrow. He stood up and held out his hand as Gladys clasped it and stood up. They walked towards the edge of the room to the base of the staircase leading to the second floor. Linden scooped up his lover over his shoulders like a sack of potatoes. Gladys laughed and held her arms out towards Calvin. Her hair was in her face. She looked like a naughty child. "Come on, Cal!" she squealed. Calvin walked to the base of the stairway. He hesitated.

Gladys' eyes grew sober when she sensed his fear. "Put me down." Linden nodded and gently lowered Gladys to the floor. "Go on ahead. I'll be up in a little while." Calvin watched as Linden turned and started up the steps. The blond man's figure grew transparent as it ascended and eventually vanished into the frosty clouds.

Calvin twirled the stem of the martini glass with his fingers. "It's perfectly fine to take your martini upstairs with you if you want." Gladys motioned towards the drink reassuringly.

"Stay away!" Calvin warned. "You're trying to rush me! I'm starting a music center with Tony for the kids! I finally got rid of the voices! I have to bring Aunt Alice her snacks! I have to be there for Mom and Dad!" He downed the contents of the martini glass and threw it against the wall. Shards scattered in the air like fireworks.

Gladys was patient. "I can't rush you. Your time is when you want it to be; it's not my decision to make." She tucked her blouse back into her waistband. "But you've been through so much I figured you'd be ready to rest by now. I'm going up now.

Linden's waiting."

Calvin let go of the big picture and allowed himself to focus on the surrounding negative spaces, where clarity is often overlooked. "Linden." He shook a finger accusingly at Gladys. "You had an affair with him."

"Linden is your real grandfather, the man I should have married, the man I've always loved." She reached out to touch Calvin. He flinched.

"How did you find me?"

Gladys remained patient. "Blood instinct leaves a trail. I smelled it the moment I held you. You smell like Jana. Jana smells like me. Did you smell it, too? Maybe that's what led you here."

Calvin's fingers gripped the icy banister. His feet were planted firmly on the ground. His eyes blazed.

"Your husband was a murderer! He was in the Klan! You abandoned Mom! You abandoned me!"

The chill spread down from the windowsill and permeated the kitchen space. Gladys turned her body to face it directly.

"I live with the course of sorrow I've set. I can't erase it. But pain doesn't have to be a part of our reality anymore. We can be the source of each other's happiness, if you allow it. Or you don't ever have to see me again."

Calvin refused to budge and looked away.

Gladys burst into tears. "I hope it doesn't come to that, Calvin, because I love you. I always have. I'm going upstairs. And when you're ready, if you're ever ready, I'll be waiting for you." She turned away and started to climb the stairs.

She hesitated and lingered at the base of the stairs, hugging her elbows as she suddenly remembered her manners. "Do you feel a chill? There are blankets in the cedar chest. You know where the food is. Help yourself to anything you need." She shivered and ascended the staircase. Her silhouette grew transparent and gradually faded away.

Calvin held onto his stubbornness for as long as he could, but the tears still came. He was angry with himself for being vulnerable and weak. He stalked to the cedar chest and angrily snapped open the latch. As his fingers explored the piles of wool and cotton blankets, they came across something furry at the very bottom.

He pulled out an old-fashioned, fur lined parka and held it up to his cheek. The softness was comforting. He pressed it to his nose and was instantly reminded of his mother.

He was three years old, and they had shared a hug. He knew he felt love for her in that moment. He was too young have to have collective memories. No one taught him how to love her. He was too young to understand the profundity of dependence, so his love wasn't contingent upon necessity or desperation. It was inherent, a genetic truth. A gift from Jana, or perhaps from her mother. It did have a scent. Gladys was right.

He put on the parka and looked towards the top of the staircase. Woodwinds, triangles, wind chimes and bells melded into a harmonious wave and cascaded down the icicle steps. He took a step forward to listen, and in doing so he felt more assured.

He climbed to the top and found himself alone in a ceilingless room with four walls. Three of the walls were filled with books from the floor to as far as his eyes could see. He was certain that they piled onwards towards infinity. The fourth wall was bare except for a pair of ice skates tied together by the laces, hanging from a white door in the center. Calvin swung the ice skates over his shoulder and opened the door.

He was standing amid a mountain range lined with snow-capped evergreen trees. A frozen blue pond curved along the length of the range where Linden and Gladys sported furry parkas and ice skates.

For the most part they were graceful. Gladys skated forward and Linden skated backwards. His hands occasionally gripped her waist for balance. They remained upright despite a few stumbles, laughing. The sun beat down on their bodies and illuminated their hair. The wind flushed their cheeks to a rebellious shade of red.

"I can do an axel jump!" Gladys' breath was frosty as she playfully pushed Linden aside. He fought to keep his balance and watched as she skated ahead. She was focused on her goal and determined to gain her momentum.

A pack of six wolves strutted purposefully past Calvin toward the shelter of the evergreen trees. The Alpha proudly carried a fresh kill of antelope in its mouth, trailing blood on the white carpet of snow. The members of the pack followed closely behind their leader. They had survived throughout the winter with barely a scrap of food. Now they smelled the blood of bounty and were anxious to have a taste.

The baby of the pack tried hard to bring up the rear but was sidetracked by the scent of the air and the excitement of being wild and free. His eyes squinted in the sun and turned towards the shade. Then he saw Calvin. He stiffened, pointed its ears and locked eyes with him.

Something in Calvin's gaze compelled the wolf to abandon the pack for a moment. Calvin was perfectly still as the baby wolf walked towards him, circled him and cocked his snout in appraisal. Without warning, it charged at Calvin and knocked him to the ground. Calvin screamed for help. His heart seized as he brought his hands up to protect his face. The wolf, however, was relentless. It wagged its tail and mercilessly attacked Calvin with a barrage of licks and kisses.

The wolf's mother noticed that her baby was missing. She looked over from her place behind the leader of the pack and saw it frolicking with Calvin. She gave her baby a menacing growl of warning. The baby wolf brought its tail between its legs, feeling the sting of its mother's reproval. He gave Calvin one final kiss and trotted back, slightly embarrassed, to his rightful place before the pack disappeared into the shelter of the trees.

Gladys spun into a perfect axel and landed gracefully on her feet. She held up her hands in triumph and skated back to Linden. He scooped her up and whirled her around. They kissed.

Calvin laced up his skates and carefully skated towards the middle of the ice. His grandparents backed up a few paces in order to give him space.

He charged the ice to gain momentum and speed, then lengthened his stride and shifted gears to skate backwards. Blind spots were irrelevant, as were vestiges of fear. Eyes fixed on the highest peak of the mountain, he leapt into the air at the precise moment and spun. Icicles lit up his peripheral vision like jewels in a tiara as he landed smoothly on the ice.

"Bravo!" Gladys brought her fingers to her mouth and blew him a kiss. Linden whistled and threw a red rose at his feet. "*Rosa Hispida!*" he called out.

Calvin skated to the rose and picked it up. It was deep and dark with luscious drops of dew. Bowing deeply, he pressed his nose into the tender bud and breathed in its perfect aroma.

Hans

He was tried as a minor and released from prison eleven years later. To celebrate his newfound freedom, he took himself out to dinner. When he arrived at the upscale Anaheim restaurant, he felt bombarded by the penetrating stares of onlookers. At first, he thought it was paranoia. Then he glanced across the dining room and saw his elementary school psychiatrist, dressed in full Kente garb, dining with her husband.

He removed the steak knife from the table and slipped it quietly into the pocket of his pants before standing up to leave. In line at the coat check, his fourth grade teacher wriggled into a full-length ermine coat. Hans abandoned his jacket, made a beeline for the door and fled to the safety of the valet stand outside.

Forever and a Day Legs emerged from the passenger door of a white BMW. Hans watched in horror as Officer Murano linked his arm protectively around the waist of his grandmother's home health aide and handed his keys to the parking attendant.

He fled to the shelter of a hole-in-the-wall corner pub. A female bartender on the shy side of forty slapped a napkin down in front of him. He ordered a bourbon Manhattan and watched her prepare the cocktail on the metal bar top. He told her she was beautiful. She smiled and refreshed his drink. He fingered the knife in his pocket.

He disposed of her mutilated body at the side of a lonely road an hour later and wiped the knife blade clean. His eyes rolled back with the euphoria of the moment. Consumed by a bloodlust he had never truly realized, he continued to drive around until he found himself in Los Angeles outside another dive bar.

Recoiling at the sight of an overweight male bartender with rubber bands in his beard, Hans stood up to leave. At that moment, a young woman opened the door and stepped inside. Hans sat back down as she approached the bar. The bartender slapped napkins down in front of them.

Unblinking icebergs stared at the young woman. "What's your name?"

"Odette."

"Bourbon Manhattan, straight up, and whatever Odette would like."

Odette ordered a drink. Hans tried hard to look charming and fingered the knife in his pocket.

TRANSIT
2002

Ester

She couldn't see through the cloud of ash swirling around her. Her fingertips were nearly frozen, but she could feel fragments of life beneath them. Some of them pulsed slightly. Others were necrotic, reeking and still. Her hair was heavy with ice. Her throat was raw. Her clothing was wet and tangled.

Everything shifted abruptly, as if suddenly moved by an unseen lever. The temperature warmed slightly and the darkness subsided a little bit. With the slight increase in temperature came the exposure of random vignettes in tiny windows. A fairy princess in a nylon nightgown waved an aluminum foil wand over an audience of dolls. Giant toads lurked in the distance. Scorpions mated in the corners.

When the motion stopped, the enclosure opened like an unsealed tomb. She leveraged her palms against it and hoisted herself upwards. When she had crawled away, she found herself lying she found herself on top of a carpet of moss at the edge a freshwater pond. It was surrounded by patches of blackberries. A wintry mansion loomed in the distance.

She checked for broken bones, stood up and shook frozen twigs from the folds of her gown. The hummingbird was secured at the base of her throat. The spotted owl was perched firmly on her right shoulder, holding a bright star in its beak.

The fresh water sparkled between her fingers as she cupped it into her hands and drank. She plucked blackberries from the vines and cried with relief as their sweetness moistened her tongue. Illuminated by the owl's lantern star, she made her way carefully ahead.

Toadstools and moths littered her hair as she abandoned her pumps in the brambles and walked barefoot towards the stone facade. Gargoyles snarled menacingly from the spired roof and guarded the turrets. An oversized jackdaw supervised the weathervane but offered nothing in the way of welcome.

She hunched in the frame of the heavy, wooden door and slowly pushed it open. Barren stone walls flickered in a dimly-lit corridor flanked with iron torches. Her bare feet were cold against the stone floor. The air was thick with dust.

Her breath was visible as she walked down a long corridor into a slightly warmer room. The cobwebbed wainscoting was dressed with massive oil portraits of veiny gooseberries and orange pomegranates arranged among folds of dark velvet.

A canopied, black wood bed was dressed with ivory sheets. Fragrant white blossoms floated in a bowl of water on top of an old table. Black grapes and blood red apples attached to clusters of dried green leaves rested on a tray. A panorama of mirrored wardrobes and steamer trunks lined the perimeter.

The spotted owl rested at the base of the massive bed as she opened one of the wardrobes. Hooked inside the door was a silk nightgown that smelled of the white blossoms in the glass bowl. She peeled off her dress and slipped her arms into the loose bell sleeves. Then she nestled among the sheets and bit eagerly into an apple from the tray of fruit.

A large grey spider in the corner of the ceiling paused from her handiwork to acknowledge her. Ester nodded in greeting and admired her flaxen web.

She felt her eyes clouding over with opiate sands. Unseen hands stroked the length of her body and pinned her against the mattress. She struggled to leverage herself against the bed.

Above her head, the ectoplasmic canopy quivered to the edges of the square ceiling and shrouded it in black tar. The tar cleaved into quarters and melted down the sides of the four walls, exposing crumbling mortar and rats.

The tar spread to the center of the floor, where it coagulated and rose upwards into a gooey mass. It seized the bed with powerful fingers and held it, suspended in the air. The walls curled down into petals and shook the room furiously, hurling the portraits, table, steamer trunks, and mirrored wardrobes into the mouth of the calyx.

She wrapped her legs around one of the posters and climbed towards the canopy. She could see that the calyx was using shards of wardrobe mirror for teeth, and that it was hungry. Very hungry.

The owl flew to Ester's shoulder and buried its face in her hair. Her body waved like a pennant as she gripped the canopy and clung for her life. The jagged teeth came closer.

The spider waved frantically from a large web fastened securely to the remnant of the ceiling. *Up Here Ester* was spelled out across the length, its flaxen threads contrasting sharply with the tar. The spider crawled above her head and lowered a silk rope. She grabbed it and climbed, taking her place in the web between the spider and the spotted owl beyond the reach of the petals.

The calyx was using a pair of black grapes for eyes. It smiled at her lasciviously, revealing its jagged teeth. She screwed her eyes shut and nestled deeper into the web.

It chuckled softly, causing the web to rock back and forth.

"Join me."

She stayed where she was.

"Pity." The calyx pouted. "Guess I'll have to find someone else."

She loves me."

A petal detached itself from the stone flower with a dramatic crack, causing pieces of the remnant ceiling to crumble and fall in slow motion towards the gooey mass of tar.

"She loves me not." The left corner of the web loosened from the ceiling as a second petal detached. The trio scrambled to the right.

"She loves me." Black grape eyes glinted contemptuously as the third petal crumbled away.

"She loves me not." The web detached completely as the last petal fell, sending Ester, the owl and the spider directly into the jaws of the calyx.

She screamed with rage as she lost sight of the owl and the spider. The bloodied fingers of her left hand clung desperately to a mirror shard tooth as the open palm of her right battled the advances of the calyx's spiny tongue. She eventually succumbed to the violent shaking.

Everything went white.

"The woodcutter's wife sent them into the blizzard for four-sided snowflakes and waited until they were deep in the woods before she got the munchies and ate the sourdough breadcrumb trail they made to find their way back home. Then they found a goose skating on the ice with a submarine sandwich in its beak. They started skating with it. They laughed and sang and danced and shook their booties and the goose quacked and sang and danced and shook its tail feathers and had a good time. It shared its submarine sandwich with them. When the sun set and they couldn't find the trail of breadcrumbs leading back to the house the goose wrapped its wings around them and they slept in the warmth of soft down. When the sun rose they walked and walked and walked and walked and the goose waddled and waddled and waddled and waddled until finally they found their way back home. The woodcutter's wife looked pissed because she thought she would never see them again, but then she saw the goose. She looked at the goose and the goose looked back at her and her mouth watered because she was really, really greedy and she praised the children for bringing such a fine goose home for dinner and told them to start the fire and the goose looked back at the children, so they did. The woodcutter's wife hung a cauldron on top of the fire and told the children to hand her the goose and the goose looked back at the children and the children yelled, 'No way, lady!' and pushed her into the cauldron instead. They boarded up the doors and windows with the pile of cut wood at the side of the cottage. She tried to step out of the cauldron but she couldn't because it was too narrow and she was too fat because, like I said, she was really, really greedy, so she burnt up in the fire and they smiled and the goose smiled and spread out her wings and they climbed onto them and flew off into the clouds to the McDonalds fly thru and they ordered Happy Meals with extra fries and they were really, really, really, really happy and they said, 'Goose, will you be our mother?' and she said, 'Of course, my darlings,' and that's how Mother Goose got her name."

"Lies."

"It's true."

"Then what kind of submarine sandwich was it?"

"Why does it matter?"

"'Cause it does. So what kind of submarine sandwich was it?"

"Ham."

"Cousin's?"

"Who cares?"

"I still don't believe you."

"I'm just trying to make you feel better. It's not my fault your mama's never home."

"Go away. I'm tired of your dumb old stories. They make me want to punch through glass."

"Did I make you mad? Do what makes you feel better. I'll carry your rage."

———————————

Her cheek shifted against something cold. When she opened her eyes, she was sprawled on top of a glass sphere. Murky green smoke shifted inside.

She plastered her eye to the surface. A woman emerged as the smoke cleared. Her caramel brown skin was illuminated with touches of bronze and flushed with hints of carmine. Her spiraling coils sprang defiantly at her shoulders. She was crying out for help and struggling to free herself from the restraints that bound her ankles and wrists to a steel table work table. A man held a knife to her throat.

"I promise it won't hurt. For long."

His lips curved into a smile. His eyes were unblinking icebergs as he unfastened his pants.

She pounded away at the surface until she smashed it with her wrists. Ignoring the pain and throbbing, she pried her way through chunk by chunk. The owl flew to her side, flinging dust and droplets of tar from his feathers, and immediately started to peck at the glass in assistance. The man looked up in lurid rage when he saw them. Water seeped slowly through the opening.

They continued to pry and peck until the globe cracked in half and the man was swept off of his feet. Enraged, he swam towards Ester as water poured through the crevice. The owl flew to the woman's side and pecked at the restraints. The woman fainted with relief.

Waving her legs, the spider led them to a raft with the words, THIS WAY GUYS woven in block letters along the length. Working quickly, she crawled to the edge of the raft and weaved a silk rope across the water.

The owl broke through the restraints, lifted the woman in its beak and flew to the safety of the raft. Ester lunged for the silk rope, but the man was faster. He clasped his hands around her neck and squeezed until the moonstone hummingbird left an imprint on her bruised neck as the silk rope swung back around and stuck to the side of the raft.

He continued to grip her throat in his hands but lost his footing in the rising water. He fell back against the floating steel, causing them both to slide backwards through the flooded house out of the front door and into the electric fence.

Everything went flat green.

Lilith

Screams rose from the trails of Jemez, New Mexico, prompting Helen Winters, Nina Baldwin and Spiree Roundtree to find the source. They abandoned the bonfire at the base of their campsite and stumbled through cacti, sagebrush and trees.

"Up here!"

Helen saw her first. She threw aside her walking stick, tucked her bobbed hair behind her ears and brushed burrs away from her shorts. "I found her! Hurry up!"

Huddled against a boulder was an emaciated, naked woman in her late thirties with blazing red hair and wild, emerald eyes. Her arms and legs were covered with bruises.

Nina plucked a stray twig from her afro before kneeling down next to the woman. She gently examined her head. Blood seeped from a gash at the base of her skull. Her companions piped in with a barrage of unanswered questions.

"What's your name?"

"Do you know where you are?"

"Who did this to you?"

Nina looked up at her friends. "Do you think she was running from an animal?"

Helen looked at Nina as if she had two heads. "You flashed your tits to UCLA's Board of Regents, didn't you?"

"Excuse you?"

"I said, with logic skills like that, who did you bribe for a PhD? A person did this. I wonder if she can identify him."

"Tit meet nipple. Because women almost never know their attackers personally, right?"

"Well I guess we'll never know since he got away, huh?"

"Unless they're in cahoots. Felons on the lam living off cactus pears and snake meat."

"Bullshit. That's a bottle job if ever I saw one. A salon one, at that."

"And the stylist chose twigs and dirt over a round brush and product because?"

"Because her hair, her choice. And if her accomplice shows up he can't hurt all four of us."

"Well at least you're right about that. Because we have this."

Nina reached into her pocket and pulled out a small, black Glock 33 handgun.

"Are you kidding me?" Helen pulled her bobbed hair back with her fist and looked aghast. "She has a goddamn gun!" She glared at Spiree. "Did you know about this?"

"We need the protection."

"Oh, that's right. How could I forget? I'm always the problem." She narrowed her eyes.

"Hey, Helen?"

She folded her arms in front of her chest. "Spiree?"

"Have I told you lately how white you are?"

Helen thrust her arm out dramatically and pointed to her watch. "Not since, oh, ten this morning, but I was just about to remind you."

Spiree knelt down next to the woman. "Can you stand up?"

She stared at an odd necklace of feathers and bones that loomed a few inches away from her face. A stray lock of Spiree's hair tickled her nose. She swatted it away with her fingers.

"All the time I've spent lobbying for gun control…"

"Look, we can argue about this when we get back to camp."

"Spiree, can you get reception out here? Maybe we shouldn't move her. We should call an…"

"No!" The woman's voice was surprisingly strong. Her eyes darted back and forth between the women as she grew increasingly agitated.

"But…"

"Please!"

Nina sighed. "Let's just get her to the tent, okay?"

They eased her into standing position. Spiree untied a sweatshirt from her waist. She placed it over the woman's head and guided her arms into the sleeves. The woman traced the UCLA logo with her fingers and tried to pull it off.

"No!"

"Let us help you," Helen said.

"I have clothes. Where's my coat?"

"What coat?"

"My coat! It's green. It's full-length cashmere."

The three women briefly scanned the area.

"Look," Helen said. "I don't see it right now, but we'll keep our eyes peeled for it on the way back to camp, okay?"

"Okay."

"Lean on us."

She pulled up one of her knees in pain after trying to put weight on her soles. Nina knelt down and noticed that the bottom of her feet were raw and scabbed. Her biceps rippled as she scooped the woman up and over her shoulders like a sack of potatoes.

"I'll give you a pair of flip flops when we get back to the tent. But until then…"

"Lead the way, Cleo Jones!" Helen cheered.

"You got it, Mommy."

She fell asleep watching the upside-down sunset as Nina carefully led the way down the incline. Spiree and Helen followed closely behind.

She bolted awake to the sound of laughter and guitar playing two hours later. She was inside a tent and lying on top of an inflatable mattress. She was covered in unwashed blankets and wearing a t-shirt, boy shorts and flip flops. Her head was wrapped in gauze. And she was thirsty. Terribly thirsty.

She unzipped the opening and peeked through. Three women surrounded a bonfire. One was playing a classical guitar. A second rested on her back and watched the stars. The third was pulverizing burdock and ginger root against a rock and trying to read the label of a bottle in the starlight.

Spiree's voice rose over the din of the guitar. "Burdock and ginger warm and descend. Use glycerin."

Helen loved a good performance.

"Just because you're indigenous doesn't mean you know everything. You think I don't understand the fundamental properties of herbs, but I aced my continuing ed herbal studies class."

Spiree, too, had thespian chops of her own.

"I've only been wildcrafting since I was four years old, but do what you want. As you said, you aced your continuing education herbal studies class. All one of them."

"As usual, my life experience is sorely lacking compared to yours. But isn't it a bit ironic, seeing that Wyoming's a billion times whiter than New Jersey, and New Jersey's the fucking Garden State?" She snatched up a nearby bottle of glycerin and dumped its contents into a bowl.

Spiree threw her head back with laughter. Nina applauded. Helen stepped away from the bowl, gathered the edges of an imaginary skirt in her fingertips and curtsied.

She stepped out of the tent opening and stood outside of it. New Mexico's big sky was a gestalt of stars. A hot spring glimmered in the distance.

"Welcome back. Did you have a nice nap?"

She stayed where she was and shifted her gaze to the guitar.

"Do you play?" Spiree asked.

She watched them for a few more seconds and glanced down at the too-large flip flops on her feet. Turning carefully, she minced in the direction of the hot spring. She removed the t-shirt and flip flops, placed them on a rock and tested the temperature with her toe before stepping in. She waded until the water was chest high, unwrapped the bandage from her head and disappeared briefly under the bubbles.

Nina sniffed her armpits. "She's got the right idea."

Spiree scrambled to her feet. "I'll grab the salt scrub. Coming, Helen?"

Helen felt upstaged. "You go ahead. I'll finish making dinner." She swigged from a bottle of red wine and turned her attention back to the pile of burdock root.

A doe peeking through the nearby trees bolted away as they immersed themselves in the water. Nina massaged her scalp with a blend of sesame oil, sea salt, and helichrysum attar. Spiree poised for monologue.

"All the elements play nicely in the spirit realm," she baited. "The fairies in the forest. The nymphs in the water. The angels in the air. Except for one, that is. Always to my exclusion, of course."

Nina bit but only out of boredom. "What are you talking about?"

"It's never about the fire!"

"So?"

"So? Aren't *all* elements vital? Why is *fire* excluded from positive spirit ascription? Why does *fire's* association with hell preclude its collective value? Why is *fire* solely associated with hell when all the other elements are spared? Aren't they equally cataclysmic?"

"Oh, no. You're serious!"

"And offended! I want a damn fire fairy."

A loud fart erupted from beneath Helen, who was passed out on her back on top of the air mattress at the edge of the bonfire. The bottle of wine was still in her hand.

They squealed with laughter. Spiree resumed her ranting.

"So I'm supposed to just let that bias go?"

"Nope. Not without weed you don't. Hold up."

Nina reached into the pile of clothing on the rock behind them and grabbed a joint and lighter from her jeans pockets. She lit the joint and passed it to Spiree.

Spiree inhaled. "That shit's what caused me to question Christianity in the first place. And I was all in, back in the day."

"Since when are you Miss Literal Minded?"

"Says Nina the Christian girl."

Nina coughed. "I'm not being an apologist. I mean, isn't dealing with the etymological and cultural differences of translating Japanese into English tricky enough? Why should we expect to do any better when tackling the divine? And it's supposed to be mystic. It's not a Linux manual."

"Step away from the semantics and focus on the patriarchy. Eve was the spawn of Adam's rib. Scroll back to the Gnostics. Lilith was purported to be a destroyer, demonized, and reduced from Adam's equal to an owl."

She turned her head at the sound of her name and waded towards the women. Nina prayed for God to interrupt Spiree by making Helen fart again.

"Why are white women so obsessed with Lilith?"

"Excuse me?"

"Sorry. Why are white women and you so obsessed with Lilith?"

They laughed.

"You don't see her undoing as a patriarchal blow?"

"I don't know. Being an owl sounds pretty cool to me."

"Maybe you're right. The whole thing's a blur, anyway. Forest fairies. Water nymphs. Air angels. Lilith."

She cleared her throat and answered.

"Yes?"

They turned to face her. Her wet hair was slicked back from her face, and her cold emerald eyes sliced through the night sky like lasers.

"You know the myth of Lilith?" Spiree asked.

"I am the myth of Lilith," she sneered. A drop of blood trickled from her forehead and splashed into the water. Nina and Spiree opened their eyes wide, turned to face each other and exploded into a fit of laughter.

Bristling, she stepped out of the water, pulled on the t-shirt and flip flops and disappeared into the trees.

"Hey, Fire Fairy! Wait! Come back!" Nina yelled after her.

Nina and Spiree continued to giggle as they wrapped themselves in towels, gathered up their belongings and headed back to the tent.

The smell of food led her back to the bonfire a half hour later. Spiree was the first to greet her.

"So you're the myth of Lilith."

"It's silly, actually," Lilith almost smiled. "Idolizing the cult of my celebrity."

Spiree cocked an eyebrow. "I'm Spiree. You remember Nina. And this is Helen."

She nodded and glanced at a large pot resting at the edge of the fire.

Helen stood up. "I made tempeh chili. I'll get you some."

She ignored Helen and made a beeline for a bag of apples in the open cooler. Selecting the largest, reddest one, she raised it to her mouth with both hands and bit into it, grunting. Her eyes closed. Juice dripped down her chin as she devoured its flesh down to the core. Nina, Helen and Spiree were speechless as they watched.

When she became aware of the women staring at her, she froze defensively.

"What? Like it's an Eve thing?"

"Try this, too." Helen filled a bowl with tempeh chili and handed it to her. Lilith devoured it ravenously and accepted a second.

She appeared serenely disturbed as the women huddled around the bonfire and passed a bottle of mead back and forth.

Nina broke the silence. "So where are you from?"

"Glaivelind. But I was born in Phialind."

"Where's that?"

"North."

"Scandinavia?"

"Way north of that."

"What's north of Scandinavia?"

They waited for her to respond. She stared up at the stars and said nothing.

"Where did you come from just now?"

"The Adam Case."

"How did I know that? Did he give you those cuts and bruises?"

"Things got crazy sometimes."

"Did he come here with you?"

"I fly solo."

Nina stared at Lilith's hair. "Some oil might work some of those knots out. I could help you."

Lilith glanced down at her red, waist length hair. It was embedded with branches, twigs and some kind of berries at the very ends.

"Okay. Thanks."

Nina rubbed sesame oil into Lilith's hair and tried to work the knots out with her fingers. Helen attempted to fill the space with conversation.

"It's a good thing we were here. It could've been weeks before anyone found you. It's a pretty desolate spot. And it's getting colder."

"I've endured much colder weather than this," Lilith shrugged. "I have a full length cashmere coat and nine hundred dollar boots."

Helen smiled in a gesture of fake adulation and wondered if Lilith's delusions were potentially dangerous. She glanced down at Nina's pocket and hoped the gun was still inside.

"More chili?" she offered disarmingly.

Nina worked as carefully as she could, but the knots wouldn't budge. She finally gave up.

"I can't get through all the knots and twigs without causing you serious pain because you have scabs all over your scalp. Why don't you let me cut it? Then we could wash the scabs with peroxide and they'll heal easier."

Lilith's voice held the slightest air of condescension. "I get my hair done at a salon in Barterlind. It takes weeks to get an appointment."

"That's a long time to wait. Tell you what. I'll just cut where it's matted the worst and your stylist can shape it up later. Okay?"

"Okay."

Nina raised scissors to Lilith's hair and started cutting. Spiree took a large swig from the bottle of mead and looked at Lilith. Her eyes misted over.

"I just want to tell you that I stand in complete solidarity with you."

"Why?"

"I was appalled when I read about you in the texts. You're not a destroyer. They destroyed you. And now you're the weak one needing care. But don't give up. You'll get stronger."

"You took that shit literally?"

"You're lucky, really. It could be worse. You could be a disembodied rib bone." She passed the bottle to Lilith.

"What?"

She waited briefly for a punchline that never came before

raising the bottle to her lips and taking a generous swig. "Oh, I get it. The Eve thing again." She pointed to Spiree's necklace. "Is that heavy?"

Spiree touched it proudly. "It's my talisman. Want to hear the story?"

"Sure."

"Back in Wyoming when I was young, my grandfather shot a pheasant and brought it to the house. I remember him holding it by its feet. It was bleeding through the heart and everything."

Lilith nodded.

"I didn't want to eat it for dinner, but my parents made me. When I went to bed that night, a sharp pain in my chest nearly bowled me over. It was like the bird was showing me its wound and saying, 'It's too late to save my life in the literal sense. I will nourish you, but be aware that it comes at the cost of my pain and sacrifice. Please be grateful.' So I rooted through the garbage to rescue the feathers and bones and made this necklace to honor its memory."

"That *is* heavy."

Nina continued to snip and shape until Lilith's hair was closely shorn with a few long tendrils that framed her face and curled down her shoulders and back.

"Holy smokes, Nina!" Spiree said admiringly. "Gorgeous work! You could actually turn pro at this."

Helen applauded briefly, then opened a compact mirror and held it out to Lilith. She gazed at herself and brought her fingertips to the top of her head.

"It feels so freeing. I love it. Thank you so much!"

"I surprise myself sometimes," Nina said. "And you do look stunning."

When the bottle of mead was finished, Helen and Nina nodded off on the air mattress. Spiree picked up the guitar and began playing again. Lilith listened quietly.

The ground around her was covered in a nest of fiery plumage interspersed with twigs and berries. She picked up a shorn lock of hair, dangled it over the fire and watched it burn away. Then she scooped up a large handful and cast it into the flames.

"No! Stop!" Spiree stopped playing and recoiled at the sight of Lilith hovering over the fire with her hands filled with hair. "What are you doing? We can wrap it with threads and make a necklace!"

"Or I could just buy one. The boutiques I shop at have amazing jewelers."

Spiree persisted. "Why don't you make a talisman and wear it around your neck to remember what you endured? To protect yourself from a reoccurrence?"

"I won't forget. And it's never going to happen again."

"The imagery would symbolize your progress."

"Then would it be for me, or for the people looking at my neck?"

Spiree reflected. "I never thought about it like that before."

She picked up another lock of hair and handed it to Spiree. Spiree gazed at it wistfully before setting it down on the fire. Together, they continued to feed pieces into the flames until the pile of hair was gone.

"My God. The air feels so much cleaner now."

Lilith exhaled. "Holy smokes, indeed."

"I have an idea."

"What?"

"Come back to LA with us. Sort things out while Adam drops off the radar."

"And do what?"

"Become a Fire Fairy."

"However does one attain such a great distinction?"

"I don't know, but I'm sure you'd figure it out. You're a natural. And I like having you around."

"You're a bigger sucker than I thought. I say that respectfully."

"You'd light UCLA on fire. I say that respectfully, too."

"I'll think about it."

"And if it doesn't work out you can always go back to Glaivelind. But it will. Work out."

"You're sure about that?"

"Yes. I can feel it."

"In your feathers and bones?"

"Good night, Lilith."

"Sleep well, Spiree."

SCEPTRELIND, HJULDER
2002

Lilith

"Seriously?"

She stared in disbelief as the hem of her maxi dress caught on a jagged patch of cobblestones a few yards away from the Myling family residence in Sceptrelind and shredded the hem in a full circumference tear that ended abruptly above her left knee.

As she bent down to free herself, a gust of wind, the only one that dared to appear in a month, rudely claimed her straw hat for itself and promptly ran away with it, leaving her shoulders to burn defenselessly under the sun's lurid wrath.

So much for my overhyped sunblock.

Her fragrance was reminiscent of a bulb of week-old garlic as she held the torn hem of her yellow dress. Butter, the salesclerk had called the color. The bodice clung to her body like a wrecking ball despite its featherweight linen fabric. Glorified burlap, really. Garlic butter burlap.

There had been a time not so long before when Barterlind's skyline was abuzz with the activity of hover cars. These days, the cars were largely replaced by tiny, solitary residence bubbles that flooded the sky with an unprecedented emptiness.

Having remained unmarred by technological advancements, Sceptrelind was empty in a different way. The overgrown grasses whispered a dirgelike chorus as she reached into her dress pocket for a granola bar. She tore the wrapper open and devoured it, but what she really craved was water.

As long as it didn't come from the Kaspare River that surrounded her home. Her former home, anyway.

What's black, white and red and goes a hundred miles an hour? A bird elf in a blender. Two if you're lucky. Creepy fucks.

It was a trade off, and an unfair one at that. All the castles, butter burlap dresses and overhyped skincare products in the cosmos had never been sufficient compensation. A few days prior, she decided to quit her job, abandon her castle, and try her hand at creating a new life.

She met with her accountant earlier in the week to work through the financial ends. She had even been magnanimous enough to grant Clyde Briberis one last interview. This was it. She was ready to bid adieu to Hjulder for good. Almost. But she had one more thing to wrap up.

No one would guess that she was paying Ester Myling's parents a visit. The last time they had been interviewed together, Ester had described an unfinished series of Earth cases. If she hadn't been ripped to shreds by now she would be soon enough, much like her worthless dress.

Her leather sandals crunched wearily through the oat colored grass. She knew she was the walking embodiment of a savior complex. And that was cringeworthy. Had it really come to this? Ester's fate was Ester's business. But that business didn't have to be a shapeshifting, mindfucking carnival. Was it really so bad to remind her?

She scrolled through the contacts in her phone and looked up at the house. 7 Storyville Lane seemed more distant than memory had served.

Time ceased as she approached the unadorned front door, which was still the color of sunbleached bones. She cursed, knowing it would be damn near impossible to make a good impression in sliced garlic butter burlap. Not to mention shoulders rivaling the hue of her overpriced bottle job. She hesitated then knocked, gathering up what remained of her dignity and courage.

She waited nearly thirty seconds without a response. "Hello?" She cupped a hand to a window just to the right of the door. The pane was newly chipped and resembled a skull's eye socket. "Mrs. Myling?" She waited a few seconds and knocked again, but again nobody came. She tentatively turned the knob and was surprised to find that the door yielded and slowly creaked open.

A shadow crossed in front of the sun as Lilith stepped into the doorway. "Hello?" Holding the torn dress hem in her hand to avoid tripping, she stepped out of her sandals and waited for a response. "Mrs. Myling?"

The house was dark except for the flickering light from a blaring television in a room off the hallway. She brushed her fingertips against the coat rack next to the door. They came away dusty. Holding her elbows in apprehension, she took a few steps forward and peered into the room. She was suddenly face to face with herself.

"In tonight's broadcast, I have the rare and precious treat of welcoming a very special guest and old friend into my home. She's an extraordinary beauty and talent. Please help me welcome the one, the only Lilith Brisbane!"

Lilith paused to watch the image flickering inside the Myling family's archaic television. It opened with a mysteriously lit, wide angle shot of the living room inside Clyde Briberis' high rise apartment. Lilith and Clyde were seated six feet apart in oversized wing chairs and sipping cocktails from fancy double old fashioned glasses. Between them, a burl wood platform table stacked with a white rose and orchid centerpiece and a pile of coffee table books rested atop an ivory hairhide rug. Behind them, Barterlind's evening skyline of skyscrapers and hoverpods illuminated a floor-to-ceiling panorama of windows.

In the light of the television screen, Lilith could make out the kitchen from the hallway. The cold tile felt good beneath her feet. She groped around the wall until she found a light switch. There was a note on the counter.

Back in two weeks, Lumen. Please water the plants and fetch the mail.

Lilith touched the yellowing paper with her fingers. They came away dusty. She opened the pantry and looked inside. A scent not entirely dissimilar to one of a used book store wafted from the neatly arranged boxes and cans that lined the shelves.

A radiant Lilith waved from her chair inside the television. Her bright red hair was closely cropped into a fashionably piecey style that framed her face and betrayed a sprouting of grey at her temples. She was barefoot and wore an ecru linen kimono and matching slim cropped pants. Her glowing skin was sunkissed and bronzed. Her smiling lips were glossed with a lustrous shade of pinky gold.

She chewed the insides of her mouth and opened the refrigerator. A lucite pitcher filled with violet liquid sparkled amid nondescript food storage containers. *Lumen's Butterfly Pea Tea* was handwritten in cursive letters on a strip of masking tape. She set the pitcher on the counter. Inside the freezer was an aluminum tray of ice. "Oh, bless," she mumbled, trailing an ice cube over her forehead, eyelids, cheeks and lips. She selected the tallest drinking glass from the rack by the sink, threw in a handful of ice and filled it to the top with the violet liquid.

The kitschy décor of the Myling family room rivaled a movie set in its own right. She brushed dust away from the couch and sat down. Its wooden lattice frame and ornate armrests were ostentatious yet unimpressive. The low-sinking cushions had no interest in supporting her body. The fabric was oppressively warm against her skin in the summer heat.

You had one job, couch.

She sipped her tea, balanced the icy glass between her knees and turned her attention back to the television. Clyde's veneers shone like laser beams on the dimly lit stage. "I'm so glad you made it tonight, Lilith. It's been a minute."

"A ha ha ha ha." Onscreen Lilith indulged Clyde in her throatiest voice. She rested the cocktail in her lap, batted her eyelashes coyly and quickly did the math in her head. He had to be sixty-five. At least.

"Stop it. Stop it, Clyde, I can't stand it! You're the one who made the time to see me with your busy schedule. You're as tight as a drum these days."

He squared his face to the camera and attempted to look as natural as possible. Just three weeks before, he had undergone a deep plane facelift and liposuction on his abdomen and flanks. He had planned to lie low for another month, but his accountant called that morning and told him he'd spotted Lilith Brisbane in the city. Clyde called her immediately and asked her to do an interview in a month. She said she wouldn't be around but could tape that very evening if he was available. Desperate for ratings, he had agreed. Reluctantly.

When she had arrived at his apartment that afternoon, he was sitting in a makeup chair peeling off a black rubber compression mask. Maybe she had screamed, maybe not. She promised to guard his secret when the cameras started rolling but couldn't resist the opportunity to poke him in the ribs. Figuratively speaking, of course.

"It's been a minute, Lilith. Where has the time gone? What's going on in your life?"

"What's going on in your career, Clyde? You've had quite a stretch."

After establishing call time, he had contacted his hair, makeup and lighting team and offered them double pay to cancel their plans and report to his home immediately. Despite their professional acumen, they were feeling the heat. And then some.

"Lilith! The folks at home want to hear about you! Tell me all about your latest cases."

She smiled modestly. "No cases lately, but I'm sure you already knew that. Nothing gets past you, Clyde. Your eyes are wide open."

He gave her the side eye, a calculated move that proved doubly effective for throwing mock shade and concealing his stitches. "Hmm. I sense there's something."

Lilith took a deep breath. "Well, there is. I don't know how else to approach it except to just come out and say it. I'm retiring."

Clyde opened his eyes wide to feign shock at her announcement. Lilith wondered if his stitches would start oozing at that very moment. That would suck, because it could sabotage her ecru linen ensemble. Or she could flag down the makeup artists. Surely they'd had the good sense to ask for double pay in light of the last minute notice.

"So when do you return from...oh, enough of this game already!" He squared his body to the camera, sucked in his cheeks and placed his hands on his hipbones, being careful to avoid his abdomen and flanks. "Reliable sources have confirmed your new romance."

Lilith straightened in her chair. "New romance?"

Clyde cheated out to the camera and gave her a knowing look. "Yes. Your new romance with a man in Phialind Valley. What isn't clear is whether you're relocating to Phialind to start a family in privacy, or if he's moving into your Glaivelind Forest castle. So? Anything you'd care to share with us?"

"Start a family." Lilith sipped from her glass thoughtfully. "You think I'm pregnant. That's what this is about."

Clyde raised his glass and lowered his chin. "Honey, your trunk is no junk by any standard, but you can't expect us not to notice that there's a little bit more of it these days. And believe you me, no one is complaining!"

He was too disciplined to miss a beat in front of the camera, but Lilith could see the exhaustion in his eyes. Despite the expert lighting, she thought she could just make out the tiniest area of his expertly applied concealer threatening to give up his secret under the strain of hot lights. She glanced in the direction of the makeup crew and wondered who would pay for the mishap later.

"Pregnant." She chuckled. "Your allegation is quite a browlifter."

Clyde raised his hands in an exaggerated gesture of inquiry and was instantly glad he had doubled his painkillers. "But the producers confirmed it! You're not?" Embarrassed, his hands fell to his sides.

"Samosas."

"What?"

"And good cheese. Stroopwafels."

"Yikes. Sorry, Lilith."

"Not me. Have you seen my wine cellar lately? And I meant what I said about retiring. There'll be no return. In fact, I'm leaving Hjulder. Permanently."

She thought she could see the color draining from his face before her very eyes, despite the layers of makeup. He ignored the cameras for a moment and turned fully in his seat to regard her questioningly. Squaring her chin to the camera, she discreetly traced the tip of her finger down the hollow of her temple to the front of her ear. Grateful for the cue, he lowered his chin in mimicry and cheated his eyes in her direction.

"Why?"

He surprised himself with his earnest tone but made no attempt to conceal or take it back. Shifting in his chair, he jerked his abdominal muscles a bit too suddenly. Lilith watched him swallow his pain and graze the compression garment underneath his shirt. Her softened gaze betrayed an air of compassion that lingered between them for three, four seconds tops. Then she narrowed her eyes, winked at the camera and seamlessly resumed her banter.

"Gut instinct, Clyde. But there's something I have to ask. However do you maintain those killer abs of yours?"

He tried valiantly but failed miserably to pass off his horror as sarcasm. Lilith was glad. It was payback time.

"I'll bet this junky trunk can still do more pushups than you! Up for a challenge?"

Jumping up from her chair, she pushed the sleeves of her kimono above her elbows, flexed her biceps jokingly, and knelt down on the ivory hairhide rug.

Clyde flashed his veneers for the camera and resisted the urge to touch his face. His painkillers were wearing off, and he hoped his sweat didn't appear as profuse under the lights as it felt. He lowered his chin, squared his eyes to the camera and took a large sip from his glass.

Still on the ground in pushup position, Lilith spotted a rectangular object perched amid the stack of coffee table books. She pushed her chest off the ground with her hands and leaned in for a closer look. It was a deck of Bicycle cards. She snatched it up and sat back down in her chair.

Clyde had regained his composure. "That's right! Bring that junky trunk right back here; we're still discussing this! You could easily extend your career. Easily. Why not go for it?"

Lilith placed her hand over her heart and threw her head back dramatically. "Such kind words, Clyde! You're always so uplifting."

The lighting and makeup crew assessed their work in the monitors and breathed sighs of relief. They were close to wrapping, and the production had been a success. Clyde's makeup was holding up, the lighting was spot on and the ambient skyline had elevated the stage to an unexpected level of artistry. They were almost out of the woods. Almost.

Clyde raised his glass. "You're the best and the brightest. You have the entire universe in the palm of your hand. Why not stay with us for a bit longer?"

She shifted in her chair and held tightly to the cards. "That's right, Clyde. I have the entire universe in the palm of my hand."

She carefully gathered up the pile of coffee table books and set them on the rug. Then she removed the deck from the packaging and promptly began shuffling the cards over the table. She held them out in Clyde's direction. "Cut it."

Clyde took the deck from Lilith and cut it. He had to give her credit. This level of spontaneity could never be achieved by the amateur ranks; she knew how to play an audience. It hadn't been that long ago, he thought to himself, when he himself had enjoyed a time of spontaneity, imagination and courage.

"Pick a card and show us," Lilith commanded. Clyde slid a card from the deck but held it to his chest.

His days as a third-rate actor had taught him a thing or two about living in the moment, like meeting Celia. They were twenty years old when she was hired as a last-minute understudy in his fledgling stage production. They fell in love at first sight and got married soon after the play had closed to minimal fanfare.

Their wedding attire, rings included, had come from wardrobe department castoffs. During the ceremony, their faces were adorned with the dregs of an abandoned makeup kit that lay unclaimed backstage. Before the reception, they draped the walls of their shabby walk up apartment with an ancient pair of cigarette-burned stage curtains (they barely noticed the mildew smell after a few weeks) and danced, barefoot and drunk, into the wee hours of morning with fifty of their closest friends, until the soles of their feet were blackened with dirt. Housekeeping had never been much of a priority for either of them.

Every aspect of loving Celia had been a euphoric study of living in the moment and relinquishing control until her death in a car accident two years later. After that, being onstage was practically unbearable because it required him to engage. He could barely make a living, either.

When the tabloid gigs started pouring in, they offered more security than he had ever imagined and an unexpected perk: any bad behavior or moral shortcomings exhibited on account of his inner demons was expected and encouraged. Engagement was unnecessary; he was paid to shift focus away from himself and onto the subjects at hand. And, speaking of hands, he was never, ever expected to reveal his own.

Fast forward to the present and Lilith stood before him, choosing to embrace an uncertain future in the middle of the road because she still had the will to engage. She was out-of-her-mind insane. And that was incredibly sexy. He wanted to stand up, grab her junky trunk and kiss every last bit of pinky gold gloss off of her lips until she clenched her toes and spilled her fancy glass all over his ivory hairhide rug. He wanted to, but he wouldn't. That'd be weird.

Lilith's held out her hand. "Show me your card."

The image inside the television rolled vertically a few times and flickered as Clyde held his card up to the camera. He lowered his chin and twisted his mouth wickedly. "The Joker! Folks at home, you saw it here first."

Where could the Mylings be?

Her hips were numb from the unsupportive cushions, and she had stayed longer than planned. She took another sip of tea and reached over to place the glass on the end table. A dusty caddy filled with plastic coasters was resting on top of a coffee table book. She picked up the caddy and glanced down at the book title: *Storyville Portraits* by E.J. Bellocq.

She set the caddy back down and continued to watch her screen persona.

"We all play the hand we're dealt in life, Clyde."

She balanced the glass of violet tea between her knees and picked up a dusty coaster by its edges with her fingertips.

Don't they believe in clocks?

She used the torn hem of her skirt to wipe off the dust. The Queen of Clubs emerged, looking elegant and composed.

"Not fair, Lilith! The Joker isn't a real card. Don't I get to pick again?"

Something isn't right.

She stared at the Queen in her hand for a while before slipping the coaster into her pocket. Slowly, she turned to face the screen again. Her onstage eyes narrowed into a provocative twinkle.

"Are you real, Clyde? Do you even know? What if you're a phantom? I have the entire universe in the palm of my hand. You said it yourself, remember?"

Stagnancy fused the atmosphere of the Myling family room like a fireplace bellows painted on a backdrop. The couch fabric was uncomfortably warm and sticky against her legs. She tried to stand up, but the cushions would not support that decision. All she could do was stare at the television and watch as the story unfolded.

Grogginess crept up in waves. Onscreen, the pixels wavered unctuously and distorted the image. She stared at the remaining bit of violet liquid in the bottom of the glass.

Lumen's Butterfly Pea Flower Tea.

Onscreen Lilith raised her fancy glass to the camera and puckered her glossy lips. Visibly disturbed by her words, Clyde squared his face to the camera and bared his veneers to conceal his rage. He squeezed his fists so tightly that the knuckles turned white. His hands grew translucent and vanished, then reappeared a few seconds later as if the moment had never happened.

That never happened. I was sitting right there!

The couch tightened possessively as her body melded deeper into the cushions. She forgot about the glass of violet tea in her hands and clenched her fist in terror. The glass folded into pieces under her grasp. A trickle of blood trickled leaked from her palm and seeped through the bodice of her dress.

Beneath the lights, Clyde's anger percolated. It rose up slowly through his translucent hands and into his arms, then spread like lava through his neck to the top of his head. As it reached the boiling point, pulsating dots of ooze illuminated his stitches. Amber oracles, free of hemoglobin or cells. Resinous amber, teeming with insects. Sand flies poked in and out of the tiny incisions like Morse code and crawled down the sides of his neck. Translucent larvae wriggled out of his eyes, ears and mouth. Then it all ceased abruptly, as if the moment had never happened.

What the fuck was in that drink?

Onscreen, Clyde and Lilith seemed frozen in time. His face was squared to the camera with veneers bared. Her twinkling eyes were narrowed in provocation. They held their positions and turned to face each other. The barbed silence lingered uncomfortably for a few seconds more before it was broken by a scene-stealing outburst of dueling laughter.

"She has the entire universe in the palm of her hand, folks! And she's leaving Hjulder behind. So tell us, Lilith. Where on Earth are you going next?"

She found the momentum to wrench herself up from the couch and into a standing position, but the torn hem of her skirt betrayed her. It weaved itself through the wooden lattice frame and bound her ankles together. She jerked backwards into the low-sinking cushions. Her head rolled from side as she rocked against the couch and tried to free herself.

MOTHER FUCKER!

"Southern California." Her screen ego sparkled. "I want to give back. I want to help women, and offer them support as they figure things out. It's a beautiful place. You'd love it there, Clyde. You'd fit right in, for sure."

"Thank you for joining us, Miss Lilith Brisbane!" Clyde extended his hand towards Lilith in a gesture of announcement. She placed her hand over her heart in an act of modesty and met his outstretched hand with her own. He kissed it.

LET ME GO! LET ME GO, GODDAMMIT!

They stood up together, faced the cameras, and bowed deeply. They rotated a quarter turn and bowed again. Rotating a quarter turn for a second time, they motioned to the crew and clapped freely in their direction. Joining hands one last time, they bowed again, and indulged the cameras with brilliant, tandem smiles that erupted the set lights into a prismatic display of fireworks.

Curls of black smoke leaked from the Myling television. The stagnant air was soon overpowered by the stench of electrical fire.

Lilith blew a kiss to the camera and exited stage left. Clyde gave the peace sign and one last wave before exiting stage right. The crew members exchanged high fives with each other and enveloped Lilith in a powerful group hug as she approached them offstage. It was a wrap.

WHAT IN THE ACTUAL FUCK?

She gathered her strength and determination together and willed herself up from the couch. A shard of glass crunched under her bare foot. She ignored the searing pain and scrambled into the hallway.

I'm never coming back here again.

Choking from the smoke, she leveraged herself against the door and fumbled into her sandals.

I tried to help you. I really did.

She extended a shaky hand to close the door, leaving a bloodied print behind. Then she set out, hem in hand, into the frying pan outside.

I'm sorry, Ester!

Ester

She wept as the silver thread weaved through the universe.

Mother Goose heard her exhausted sobs from the rear of the gaggle. Swooping up behind her, she nuzzled her neck and preened her hair until she fell asleep. When she woke up, she was surrounded by a desolate panorama of jagged rock cliffs and nestled inside a large crater filled with stardust and spare goose feathers. A basket of fresh eggs lay at her side in offering.

She spent the next few nights collecting bits of rock from the nooks of the cliffs and polishing them into tools. In this way, she replaced the eggs that she had eaten until the night she returned to the basket and discovered that the eggs were gone and the surrounding food supply was bleak.

She decided to climb the highest cliff in hopes of finding her bearings and reestablishing the direction of her course.

Using the tools, she crawled upward little by little and willfully maintained her tread until she came across a small brush of flowering trees. She picked the flowers and ate them. They were sweet. Then she nestled herself along the boughs and fell asleep to the subtle vibrations within the crater.

When she awoke, she sharpened her tools and set upon the path once more. She conquered a little bit more of the cliff and came across a smaller brush of flowering trees. She picked the flowers and ate them, despite their strange flavor. After she finished eating, she nestled herself along the boughs and rested, eyes open to the nuances surrounding her.

As she climbed the following evening, the foliage grew austere and sparse as she neared the top. The leaves were strange colors she had never seen before, and their odors were just as foreign. She didn't eat them. The cliff became sharper and abstracted as she grew hungrier.

The top was a barren plateau bathed in rays of curious colors. She rested for a while and absorbed the peculiar strand of beauty.

Pockets of oxygen encased in colorless spheres floated through the inky sky. She caught one in her hands, cracked it open with her fingers and inhaled the sweet breath from within.

Rock cliff forests expanded for miles beneath her feet. She rotated slowly and drank in the view.

Her breath grew shallow as she realized that she couldn't find Earth, or recognize any of the celestial bodies surrounding her. She scoured the edges of the rockscape looking for something familiar.

She caught another sphere in her hands, cracked it open and inhaled the contents. The empty shell floated away. She reached for another, and then another as she walked towards the opposite end of the plateau. The remaining spheres floated through the rockscape canyon far beyond her reach.

It was silent as stared at the brilliant, peculiar colors illuminating miles upon miles of jagged rock. Waves of panic subsided into futile gasps for breath and chortles of wry laughter. She curled up in the crater and nestled her hair around her body. All awareness faded quickly into densely leaded black.

"She pricked her finger on the spindle and fell asleep for a hundred years and one day a prince was riding through the neighborhood and came across the castle and he saw her with her hair fanned out on the pillow and thought she was the most beautiful thing that he had ever seen so he kissed her and she woke up and he was happy and she was happy and he swung her over the back of his horse and they rode off into the sunset and lived happily ever after."

"Really?"

"Yes, really."

"Lies. Let's play Stretch Armstrong meets Stretch Monster."

"Lies?"

"How could she sleep for a hundred years? Didn't she have to go to the bathroom?"

"Princesses don't do that in the stories."

"And he kissed her awake? She must've had some funky breath after a hundred years."

(Giggling)

"And her hair was fanned out on the pillow? When I wake up in the morning my hair's standing straight up to the sky like Don King's and that's only after one night."

(More giggling)

"I still don't believe you, especially about the prince waking her up. Princes don't wake up a hundred and fifteen year old princess. I don't care how neat her hair is. And Mama was only thirty-five. I miss her."

"Please don't cry. I'll protect you. I'll always hold your pain, anger and sorrow for you. I'll make them disappear. I promise. Then we can play with Stretch Armstrong and Stretch Monster."

(Reveling in icy triumph) "It's too late for that. I wanted to see what made them stretch, so I cut off their arms and buried them in the sandbox."

Odette

"Odette Ridley?"

She stood up from her chair in the reception area of UCLA Health and followed the office coordinator through a set of adjoining doors.

"Right this way, please." He led her down a hallway of offices and stopped at the last door on the left. He knocked softly before turning the doorknob.

"Odette?"

"Dr. Brisbane?"

"Hi! So nice to meet you! Come on in."

Odette stepped into the office. She wore light jeans and a high-necked shirt with long, thumb-holed sleeves that grazed her knuckles. A halo of black coils spiraled recklessly around her face and shoulders. Her gleaming bronze skin was accented with touches of carmine and gold. She turned her feathery lashes to Lilith.

Lilith stood up from her chair as her assistant approached her desk and handed her a manila folder. "Thank you, Finn."

He nodded, stepped out of the room and closed the door.

"Have a seat. I'll be with you in one moment." Lilith motioned across the room to a pair of green tufted sofas flanking a window.

"Okay." She briefly glanced at the inkjet label on the edge of the folder in Lilith's hands.

*UCLAHealth RIDLEY, ODETTE *new*

She stood in front of the window briefly. In the parking structure across the street, a Honda was trapped between the exit gate and a line of impatient vehicles. The driver reinserted his ticket, pressed the call button frantically, and cursed at the missing attendant.

She glanced at the reading materials pushed to the side of the coffee table before sitting down.

UCLA College Magazine
A Confederacy of Dunces
Your Own Personal New Orleans Tour

Lilith sat at the couch across from her. "Brilliant day, isn't it?"

Odette fidgeted inside her thumb-holed sleeves. "In Southern California, too!"

Lilith laughed. "We're so spoiled here. Is that why you moved here from New Orleans? The weather?"

"I'm from there originally, but I went to school back East."

Lilith looked at her files. "Ah, yes. I see it now. Andover and Penn. Moving to California from the East Coast is still a big change."

Odette adjusted the neckline of her shirt and glanced at the diplomas on the wall.

USC College of Letters, Arts & Sciences, Bachelor of Arts: Gender Studies

The University of California David Geffen School of Medicine: Doctor of Medicine

Lilith motioned to the coffee maker on the end table to her left. "Can I offer you some water or coffee? I just brewed a fresh pot."

"No, thanks."

She glanced at Odette's shirt. "Are you warm? I can turn up the air."

"That's okay. I'm fine."

"Do you have roommates?"

"I live alone."

Lilith rustled the chart in her fingers. "What was your major at Penn?"

Odette crossed her legs and shook her foot. "Astrophysics."

Lilith looked up from the chart and smiled. "Excellent. What do you do now?"

"I'm a research assistant at a lab."

"Are you thinking of going back to school?"

Odette exhaled slowly. "I'm not sure. I've been living with something for a long time."

"Okay. Would you like to talk about it?"

She stared at the file in Lilith's hands. "Is the suicide attempt mentioned anywhere in my records?"

"Yes."

"That's what I'm here to discuss. What if I told you that I never attempted suicide, and that it was all a misunderstanding?"

"A misunderstanding in what way? Are the hospital records wrong?"

"Not exactly, but things aren't always as they seem."

"Okay. What happened?"

Odette took a deep breath and slowly exhaled. "It's hard to explain. I guess you could say I'm talented."

"There's no doubt in my mind about that."

"I was surrounded by magic as a little girl living in New Orleans. I have a gift. I can look behind the eyes of other women."

Lilith took a breath and nodded simultaneously. "You mean

you're an empath?"

Odette reached into her pocket, removed a Queen of Clubs card and slapped it on the coffee table between them. "It started with this. It's been happening for almost as long as I can remember."

"What's been happening, Odette?"

Odette's patience began to wane. "I was looking behind her eyes for a long time. After a while, it was almost like she was a part of me. And I know who you are, Lilith. I've been looking for you. You know who I'm talking about. It's Ester. She saved my life. Ugh! This is awkward. I hooked up with the wrong guy. It wasn't my best judgment. It all went wrong."

She pulled her shirt over her head. A burn scar in the shape of a hummingbird covered the skin at the base of her clavicles and spread outward to her bra straps. "I didn't do this." She held out her arms to reveal the wounds on her wrists. "I didn't do this, either."

"So how did it happen?"

"I can't remember, but it was inside a glass sphere. Almost like a snow globe but a really thick one. There was water inside. He had a knife. He was going to rape and kill me. I was screaming for help.

After a few seconds, Ester heard me, and I was looking behind her eyes like I've done in the past. But it was different this time. She protected me. She took my fear, pain and danger into her mind and body and blocked them from me completely. She stood in front of me like a shield and fought my battle.

She smashed the glass with her bare hands and pried a hole to get me. That's how she cut her wrists. An owl and a spider helped her do it. I don't know how I got home. I was in my bathtub when they found me. My wrists were bleeding. The hummingbird was on my chest."

"Did you report the assault to the police?"

"And tell them what? I don't know where I was when it

happened. I came to at home in my bathtub. Any physical evidence had been washed away."

She reached for a tissue. "I'm terrified he's going to find me someday, after all this time. I barely leave my apartment. I know he's lurking out there."

Lilith pulled her hair away from her forehead with her fist. "Do you remember what he looked like? Would you still be able to identify him?"

"Just that crazy smile. I've tried to forget it, but I can't. It's stuck in my head like a disembodied Joker."

The two women stared at the Queen of Clubs on the coffee table. A long pause ensued.

"What about your family?"

"You mean my mama? She's dead."

"What was she like?"

Odette sighed. "Beautiful. Distant. Distracted."

"Were you close?"

"I never saw her while I was in boarding school. I had work study every summer. I spent my holiday breaks on the east coast with classmates."

"When did you last see her?"

"Right after my high school graduation. The ceremony was on Sunday. I hit the road Monday morning and arrived in New Orleans on Wednesday. We spent three days together."

"How was that?"

"It was fine. We didn't really do much, but I was happy to see her. She made lamb gumbo with okra and black eyed peas. And king cake, with a toy baby baked inside and everything. We basically just sat around and ate for three days. On Sunday morning I got up early and started the drive to Philadelphia. I had a full time job booking river cruises until the fall semester started."

"How does that make you feel?"

"Like our life collapsed into a house of cards. I knew she was trying to save me. But it felt like she abandoned me. After she was sentenced, I felt numb more than anything else because I was so busy with school. I took a long weekend and flew out to see her. When I got to Orleans Parish, the guard said that mama had declined my visit. She didn't want to see me. So I turned around, went back to school and tried to stay on track. I thought I would see her again. But they called me a few weeks later and told me she was gone."

Odette pulled her turtleneck back over her head and briefly closed her eyes. "I slather it with tepezcohuite cream and keep it covered from the sun, but it's irritated and scabbed. And my wrists have permanent nerve damage. I could stick my hands in fire and never feel a thing. But I get what I get. My mama sacrificed everything she had to get me out of Storyville. And I took it all. I took her dignity. I took her security. I even took her life."

Lilith stood up from her couch, sat down beside Odette and drew her close. They both cried freely.

"I needed her, Lilith! I still need her!"

"I'm so sorry. I am so very sorry!"

"I can't figure anything out anymore. I never get anything right!"

"That's not true, Odette. I'm glad you're allowing yourself to cry. For a long time I felt impervious to pain. It's not healthy because when you finally allow yourself to feel something everything crashes down at once. You have to let it go so you can find comfort. You have to let it go so you can heal."

Odette helped herself to a fresh tissue.

"Would you like my professional opinion?"

Odette nodded.

Lilith dabbed at her own face with a tissue and cleared her throat. "You're dealing with the collective trauma of your mother's death, an aggravated assault and a suicide attempt, respectively. It's a heavy load, and you've been carrying it around for a long time. You can't just whisk it under the rug like a dust bunny; it needs to be resolved. And until that happens, your brain is going to compensate in the only way it knows how."

Odette looked up. Lilith shook her head and kept talking.

"It's perfectly normal for our minds to manifest things to help us cope in the presence of unresolved trauma."

Odette took the comment like a slap. "But I came looking for you because I know you know I'm not making any of this up!"

"The manifestation of anthropomorphic delusions to the extreme you've described is quite unusual, but then again, so are you. In any case, they've served you well. They protected you from alienation when the truth of your circumstances became too isolating and polarizing to accept. No one can face that level of despair alone; it's inhumane. Everybody needs a network, Odette. Where there is community, we do better. All of us."

Outraged, Odette stared at Lilith in disbelief. "No! Stop it! Why are you treating me this way? There's no one else here. You know that I know who you really are. I know you're connected to all of this!"

Lilith's eyes were gentle. "I'm sorry, Odette. Any manifestations that your mind creates belong to you and you alone. I would never, could never stand in the way of your progress by indulging a folie à deux. I'm not willing to gamble with your mental health or destroy my professional reputation by following you down a rabbit hole. Not only is it unsafe, it runs contrary to the oath I swore to uphold at the start of my medical practice."

Odette's eyes blazed. "Your idea of professionalism is lying to my face and calling me delusional when I know you know I'm telling the truth?"

"Doing no harm is the first rule of healing. You're doing the opposite. That's the real truth, isn't it?"

"And how is that? I didn't harm myself or anyone else!"

"I might encourage you to examine that rationale a bit further.

If you hurt yourself, is it your responsibility to heal yourself? And if you hurt someone else, is it your responsibility to heal them?"

"I never said that."

"Maybe. But if it's what you meant, you're brilliant."

"Thanks."

"And that makes you a sadist."

"What?"

"To hear you tell it, you and Ester are old friends who go way back. You get in a bind and beg her for help. She drops everything and voluntarily takes your hits. In what parallel universe is it okay that you allow her to be your personal bellhop until you finally get around to sorting things through? If she's real, and you maintain that she is, don't you think she has better things to do with her time and energy?"

"I don't know."

"In reality, I can only do so much for you, Odette. My professional responsibility is to guide you, but the real work falls to you. So I'll ask you again."

Lilith pointed to the Queen of Clubs card. "What are you doing with this?"

"At this point, I'm out of ideas."

"I'm not. Up for a road trip?"

"Where?"

"Philadelphia."

"What for?"

"There's an opportunity at a university. The role is writing grants and proposals for program development, alumni and community outreach. You could also enroll in a Master's program if you're interested in resuming your studies. I would happily put in a good word for you. Your record is stellar. Pun intended. Would you think about it?"

"The responsibilities don't quite line up with my field of experience."

"They're an equal opportunity establishment. Trailblazers are encouraged to apply. My colleagues Spiree and Nina would help with details. Spiree's here at UCLA. Nina's at Lincoln University. That's where you'd be."

She passed a framed photo to Odette. "This is Spiree, Nina and me at a fundraiser last year."

Odette took the frame and studied the photo. "Nice." She handed it back to Lilith.

"And here's a photo of Spiree at a hippy dippy Christian retreat back in the seventies."

Odette studied the feather and bones around Spiree's neck. "Groovy necklace."

Lilith urged another frame in Odette's direction. Inside was a grainy photo of Spiree standing with a group of women inside a greenhouse. The film had degraded over time, and the casual image appeared to have been captured without their knowledge.

"You know who Gil Gentry is, right?"

"The country singer?"

"Yeah. The brunette woman standing to Spiree's left is his mother, Amy."

"She's lovely."

"And the blonde with the 4A hair standing to Spiree's right? That's Jana North."

"What do you know about 4A hair?"

"Here's a better shot of Jana with her family. That's her husband, Russell, and their son, Calvin. Russell was a big shot civil rights attorney. He died of brain cancer last month. The elderly woman in the wheelchair is Russell's Aunt Alice. She passed away about five years ago."

"Oh, no. I'm so sorry to hear it."

"Calvin passed away, too. He took his own life about fifteen years ago."

Odette examined the photo carefully. "Wait. The Norths? I remember them. I know Calvin. He was my classmate at Andover. He killed himself? That's awful! I'm so sorry to hear it. I never really got to know him, but I always liked him."

Lilith shook her head. "It's very sad."

"You knew I was an Andover grad. And you have photos of my classmate's mother."

"Odd coincidence, isn't it?"

"It is. Especially since I'm the one who came looking for you."

"Oh. Are you sure about that, Odette?"

"Like anything surprises me anymore."

Lilith held up the coffee carafe. "Are you sure you don't want any?"

"I'll take some. Thanks."

Lilith poured a cup of coffee for herself. "I've given you my professional opinion, Odette. In reality, I can only do so much. The real work falls to you."

"I understand."

"Would you like my off record one, too?"

"Of course."

Okay. But let me grab a coaster first."

Lilith removed the Myling family's Queen of Clubs coaster from its hiding place under the cushion. She placed it on the coffee table in front of Odette.

"Off record. In reality, the real work falls to you." She pointed to the inkjet label on Odette's file.

UCLAHealth RIDLEY, ODETTE *new*

"In reality and everywhere else."

Lilith pinched the label with her fingers and pulled it away to reveal a different label underneath.

*THE JANA CASE

She opened the folder and began to read.

"Jana North, age sixty-eight. Née Montgomery. Born in

Natchez, Mississippi. White daughter of a Pentecostal preacher and subservient mother. Wandered into the river looking for Jesus and was bitten by a poisonous snake. Stumbled across a gay black couple who saved her life. Her Klansman/Silver Dollar dad murdered one of the men to teach his daughter a lesson. But he wasn't her real father. Her mother had stepped out on him with a traveling flower man while he was away at a church revival and took the secret to her grave. Became a pediatrician in Orange County, California. Had a coat hanger abortion performed by a shady chiropractor. The procedure was done on Halloween, or Samhain, as it's called in some circles. Blackmailed by the chiropractor's business partner. Scandal erupted. Walked away from her career in shame. Married a prominent Black civil rights attorney. Had a son. Lost him to suicide. Cared for her husband and his aunt until their deaths. Since then, she has all but stepped away from the world."

Lilith looked serious. "Would you like to take this case, Odette?"

"What do you want me to do?"

"Get to know her."

"Why?"

"She's an undiscovered gem with a wealth of knowledge and experience, but she's never had the chance to express it. She doesn't know her own value. If it were up to me, she might resume her medical practice, or serve on the Board, or maybe go on the lecture circuit. Sixty-eight is the new thirty; there are endless possibilities. But it's up to her. If she wanted to become a world class cougar or organize a boxed wine tasting guild, I would fully support those decisions, too. I don't care about the details, really. I just want her to heal."

Lilith closed the file and placed it on the coffee table. She looked at the clock. "I guess we're out of time."

"Thanks."

"Oh. There's one more thing, Odette. After the scandal, Jana manifested an anthropomorphic delusion to cope with the trauma. She believes she set a course of sorrow into action when she displaced her daughter's spirit from her body. And she doesn't believe she's dead. She thinks her daughter visits her from time to time but primarily takes up residence inside the North Star. Something like that, anyway."

Lilith fanned herself with the file before setting it down on the coffee table. "Can you imagine what it would be like if someone came into her life and helped her find a sense of closure? I wonder who could do it. Do you know of anyone?"

Odette stood up from the couch. She held eyes with Lilith. She took the file, placed the Queen of Clubs card inside, and headed towards the door.

"So you can move to Philadelphia by the end of summer, right? Does that give you enough time to quit the lab rat job and pack? You'll stay safe out there, or at least try to, won't you? You'd better!"

Peggy

She sat in a chair next to the hospital bed holding a clipboard and skimming the patient's medical file.

Name:	*RIDLEY, ODETTE*
Age:	*29*
Sex:	*F*
Race:	*BLK*
Address:	*5110 FOUNTAIN AVE #7 LA CA 90029*
Notes:	*BIRTHMARK/SCAR CLAVICLE/STERNUM*
	RESUSCITATED WITH DEFIBRILLATOR
	SELF-INFLICTED WRIST LACERATIONS
	FOUND IN BATHTUB BY APARTMENT MANAGER

Her eyes shifted from the bandaged wrists to the red and white intravenous carafes hanging above her head. What on earth had triggered Odette...

the patient

What on earth had triggered *the patient* into doing something so desperate?

It almost didn't seem real.

They were the same age. They could have easily been friends. She could picture them spending a Saturday afternoon together shopping at the Beverly Center, or meeting up with a group in San Gabriel for a Chinese hot pot dinner.

Not that she was thinking about anything at the present moment except hitting the pillow. Yesterday was her ninth wedding anniversary, and she had celebrated her only night off in months by going out to dinner with her husband, Bob. She was paying for it now.

Bob always said she was too much of an empath; his twelve years with LAPD had taught him how to compartmentalize. Her transition from nursing to medical school to her current residency at Cedars Sinai demonstrated that she was capable of learning just about anything. Except how to toughen up. And it was getting out of hand.

She was glad that Odette...

the patient

She was glad that *the patient* was finally sleeping comfortably. Her unresponsive state had not appeared restful; Peggy would never forget the look of terror in her eyes as the paddles resuscitated her heart. Odette was such a pretty name, too.

Bob's right. You really need to cut it out.

She stretched her Forever and a Day legs out as far as the uncomfortable chair would allow and struggled to stay awake.

Did I really just see a shimmer hovering in the air for a split second?

She jolted upright and dismissed her mind's trickery. Sleep deprivation led to hallucinations. She really needed to check herself.

She couldn't sleep just yet, but maybe she would blink. But only for five minutes. Ten minutes max.

When she opened her eyes exactly eleven minutes later, the patient's bed was empty.

"Odette?"

On the right side of the room, the bathroom door was closed. She scrambled to her feet and rapped twice before opening it.

"Odette?"

She wasn't there.

A bird chirped outside the window. She hastily pulled the

curtains aside and slammed her palms against the glass. She peered down into the street below. A handful of pedestrians crossed between buildings at San Vicente Boulevard, but the patient wasn't among them.

She opened the door, stepped into the hallway and yelled.

"Odette!"

Two women behind the nurses' station stopped their chatter and looked up from their computers when they heard her. She approached them directly.

"Did you see where the patient from Room 7 went?"

The two nurses looked at each other and shook their heads. One spoke up.

"We didn't see anyone come out of the room, Dr. Murano."

Peggy was frantic. "It was in the last ten minutes."

"We've been here the entire time."

"That's crazy!"

"Do you want us to call someone?"

Panicking, she scoured the area in front of the station before taking off down the hallway. Dr. Sakaguchi, the attending physician, was standing by the elevator bank. She ran to him and explained the situation. Together, they hurried back towards the room. When they got there, the patient was in bed sleeping peacefully.

Dr. Sakaguchi was mildly amused. "There's no place like home," he quipped. "Looks like she missed you, Auntie Em."

Peggy crumbled. "I'm not crazy. I know what I saw."

"You fell asleep."

"I wasn't sleeping! I was blinking!"

"Our minds play tricks on us sometimes, Dr. Murano. It's okay."

"But she wasn't there. I saw it."

"Then her lungs are clear enough to walk. There's always a silver lining."

It wasn't a lining. It was a shimmer. I saw it with my own eyes.

Something isn't right.

"How did she manage to unhook the fluid bags before she slipped out and re-hook them before we got back?"

"Most obvious answer? It never happened. You said you were blinking. Moving forward, just remember to be careful. Excuse me."

He reached for his cell phone and raised it to his cheek. "Herman's downstairs at Starbucks. Want anything?" He turned away from her and walked towards the window for better reception.

Peggy continued to stare at the patient sleeping on the bed. Her lips appeared to be stained by pomegranates.

"Iced passion tea, right?"

She leaned into the hospital bed railing until her face was directly in line with the patient's. The sleeping face was framed by twisty, spiraling coils that reached out to her from the pillow.

Like antennae.

"One second." He fiddled with the curtains and turned his head to face her. "They're out of passion tea, but they can sub from the secret menu. One pump of sugar, right?"

That bed was empty. I saw it. Where did you go?

"I'll get you two pumps. You need a boost."

As she stood watching, the lips gradually curved into a smile. She thought she had seen it before, but she didn't know where. The back of her neck was prickling, but she didn't know why.

The lashes were long and feathery.

Like spiders.

They fluttered slightly as the eyes opened and stared up at her.

What troubled her most was that they almost looked the same. The size, shape and color were consistent. But they were worlds apart. She had seen the patient after resuscitation. Those eyes had a lucid quality that drew her from the outside in. These eyes emitted a light that effectively drove her out. Phosphorescence, maybe? And when the lips curved, these eyes didn't. Instead, they relaxed into a downward slackness that continued to evolve subtly, even after it should have ceased. Like antigravity.

Was it somewhat inhuman?

"Who are you?" Peggy's voice cracked.

The patient's curved lips parted slowly. Her clipboard slipped from her fingers and clattered to the floor.

"Did you say something?" Dr. Sakaguchi put his cell phone away and walked over to the bed.

She shook her head and dropped to her knees to retrieve the clipboard.

He turned his attention back to the patient and smiled warmly. "Welcome back, Ms. Ridley."

The patient's response was a hoarse splinter. He placed his hand on her shoulder reassuringly. "Don't talk." He set the earpieces of his stethoscope firmly into place. "Can you give me some deep breaths?"

The patient stared up at him and breathed. Peggy stood at his side, not quite knowing what to think.

"What just happened?"

"We've all blinked before, Dr. Murano."

Dr. Sakaguchi moved the chestpiece from the patient's chest to her back. A slight clinking noise rose from under the bedsheet.

He put down the earpiece and looked at the side of the bed. "What do we have here?"

The patient's eyes followed Dr. Sakaguchi as he pulled a handful of thermometers from under the sheet.

"Where did you get these, young lady?"

The prickling sensation at the back of Peggy's neck spread as the room grew unbearably hot. Sweat pooled in her armpits and dripped down the small of her back.

Dr. Sakaguchi wiped his brow. "Wow. Did someone adjust the thermostat? The mercury really is rising in here."

More like Bad Moon.

"Are you okay, Dr. Murano?"

"I think I'm going to be sick."

The slack eyes turned to stare at Peggy. "There's a bathroom on the right." The curved smile returned.

She had no words to offer as she slowly backed away from the patient's bed and headed for the door.

She nearly collided with Herman, the ward assistant, as he stepped into the doorway. He was holding two Starbucks drinks. The first was a hot beverage inside a paper cup labeled, *DR. S.* The second was an iced, kaleidoscopic-colored beverage inside a clear plastic tumbler labeled, *DRINK ME*. His blue fingernail polish glimmered as he urged the second drink in her direction.

She flinched in horror and shielded herself defensively with outstretched palms. "What on Earth is this?" Terrified, she wedged herself between the doorframe and Herman and fled down the hallway, crying.

From the doorway, Herman watched Dr. Murano's body grow smaller and smaller until it finally disappeared in the direction of the elevators.

"Earth? Is that what planet this is?" His laughter exposed the diamond teeth on the left side of his mouth. He shrugged, pursed his lips against the straw of the kaleidoscopic beverage, and drank.

Odette

After two months on the job, she was accustomed to her weekday morning routine of walking to City Hall and riding the Blue Line to Lincoln's University City campus. Today, however, was different. She was taking a long weekend and driving to Gladwyne to meet Jana North.

She walked the block to the monthly lot where she kept her car and took the elevator to her assigned parking space on the fourth floor. She unlocked it, placed her coffee into the cup holder, tossed her weekender bag into the backseat and started the engine.

She turned onto 18th Street from the structure's exit and headed towards JFK Boulevard. The cool morning breeze rustled her hair through the open driver side window. It felt good to be behind the wheel of her car. After two months of walking and taking the train to work, driving was a welcome reprieve.

From JFK Boulevard, she turned onto Arch Street. Pumpkins, cobwebs and skeletons adorned the city in celebration of Halloween. The entire month of October had been festive. The weekend prior, she had attended a haunted house at the Eastern State Penitentiary with her colleagues. They had gasped and shrieked like grade schoolers. Her weekend shopping excursions at the Reading Terminal Market had brought forth an abundance of crisp apples, pressed cider and hearty squash soup.

The Schuylkill River rippled from grey to silver as she merged onto the 76 Expressway and maneuvered the length of its curving stretches. The streets widened as she entered Montgomery County, drove deeper into Lower Merion Township and turned onto a shaded knoll.

Grand old homes winked like loot recovered from the flotsam of pirate ships until the stretch of the road ended abruptly into a grove of oak trees. The very last pair of gateposts was capped with broken lanterns. She slowed the car, drove carefully up a long driveway and stopped before the house.

She turned off the ignition and stepped out of the car. Vines curled defensively around a stone Tudor stone façade in the absence of Halloween decorations. It was as massive as it was beautiful, and as beautiful as it was misunderstood. It was a witch house that roused the curiosities of neighborhood children to their wildest potential. One that accommodated their cruelty in a daily show of sportsmanship but wept every night in solitude. One that had an abundance of candy to share but always wound up eating it alone.

The cobweb she pulled aside before ringing the doorbell was real and not the cotton variety from Michael's that was so plentiful that time of year. A few moments passed before the heavy wooden door creaked open slightly.

A woman in her sixties opened the door. She had a tangled mop of greyish blonde curls and a glowering energy in her blue eyes that wasn't exactly unkind but unaccustomed to entertaining novelty.

"Odette?"

"Dr. North? I hope I'm not too early."

"Of course not. And please call me Jana. Come in."

She stepped carefully over a broken stoop and followed Jana inside. Tall ceilings and dark wood flanked the entranceway of a stately home that was a tad overdressed by modern standards.

Odette took in the beauty of the carved paneling, winking chandeliers and crown moldings. She chose to ignore the staleness of the air around her.

"What a beautiful house."

As she stared at a chandelier, her scarf slipped away from her neck and fell onto the floor. She felt Jana's eyes linger at the hummingbird at her throat. She bent down to retrieve the scarf as quickly as she could and hastily wrapped it around her neck. An uncomfortable silence followed.

Jana's sculpted arms grasped the handle of Odette's bag with the agility of a yogi. "Let's have a cup of tea before you get settled into the guest room. It always helps me relax when I'm in a new space. After that, you can rest, explore the house, take a hot bath, get some work done, whatever you'd like, really. I know you didn't travel far, but I want you to feel at home."

"I'd like that."

She fell into step behind Jana through the living room, down a dark hallway, and past a panorama of stained glass windows in the dining room to the kitchen. Odette was surprised by her pace.

"Please sit down." Jana motioned to a nook in front of a bay window. Odette sat.

Every window in the house seemed to overlook the garden. Partly cultivated but mostly wild, it surrounded the house three quarters of the way around and rambled on for several yards in all directions, only stopping at the back of the house at the border of oak trees.

A pair of mushroom shaped salt and pepper shakers rested on the nook. They looked as if they had been untouched for forty years. When she picked them up to admire them, she accidentally knocked the salt shaker on its side. Tiny grains spilled across the windowsill. She brushed them into a neat little pile with her thumb.

"How are you enjoying Philadelphia and your new role?"

"I went to college there, so it feels like I picked up where I left off, in some ways. Nina and the rest of the faculty are making me feel right at home."

Jana placed a tea cup in front of Odette. Then she opened the cupboard to the left of the stove and took out a plastic mug in the shape of Wile E. Coyote's head. It was filled with sugar cubes.

"I haven't met Nina. She's Spiree's friend, right?"

"That's right. Nina's my boss."

"Spiree's a dear old friend of mine."

Odette nodded.

"Have you been to Warmdaddy's?"

"I don't think so."

She placed a tray of pastries on the nook in front of Odette. Odette selected a croissant.

"Delicious."

Jana picked up a silver teapot and filled Odette's cup before refreshing her own. "Do you remember Zanzibar Blue? Same owners. They're old friends, and they're feeding us all weekend. Actually, they've been feeding me since Russell's last trip to the hospital. So kind. I never get out much to see anyone anymore. To be honest, I really don't get out at all."

"I am so sorry for your loss of your husband. And I know it's late, but I can't even begin to tell you how I felt when I heard about Calvin. We never got to know each other very well, but I liked him. Our class was small. We were all connected."

Jana sipped her tea. "That is so kind of you, dear. Thank you."

They watched the sun and wind playing through the glass panes and sipped their tea in silence. Odette tried to stay alert, but the croissant in her stomach did little to distract her from the fact that she was very tired.

"I think I need a nap. Can I help you with anything before I step away to recharge?"

"You get some rest and we'll catch up later on tonight. I'll show you to your room."

Jana led Odette up the wooden staircase to the guest room and set the weekender bag down at the foot of a four poster bed.

Odette brushed her fingers against the ivory bedspread. "How lovely!"

"Does it feel cold in here? There are extra blankets in the storage chest."

"It's perfect."

In the corner alcove, a desk was positioned in front of a window overlooking the wild garden outside.

"I could get lost in my work for days here."

To the right of the alcove stood a tall bookcase. Hanging above it was a framed movie poster from *The Song of Freedom*. Odette scanned the names of the authors that were stacked neatly on the shelves. Zora Neale Hurston. James Baldwin. Herman Hesse. Walter Mosley. A pile of movie scripts was stacked horizontally near the middle. Odette picked up the top script, *Ganja & Hess*. She opened the cover and read the inscription.

To Russell. Thank you for everything. My best, Duane Jones

"Wow. I'm actually a big fan of Duane Jones."

"You've heard of him?"

"I lost count of how many times I've seen *Night of the Living Dead*. Your husband knew him?"

Jana nodded. "Russell mainly handled civil rights cases, but lines got crossed sometimes. He was a consultant for Duane and the Black Theater Alliance in the seventies. He was also involved in a handful of entertainment contracts over the years. Sealing the deal and that sort of thing."

She put down the script and picked up *Space is the Place*. She opened the cover and read the inscription.

To Russell. Peace on Earth. Saturn, too. Ever, Sun Ra

"His real name was Herman Blount. Russell was one of the contract attorneys. We saw him perform with his Arkestra a few times in the eighties, too."

She picked up a script from *Chico and The Man*. "So your husband sealed Chico's deal, too, huh?" She opened the cover and read the inscription.

To the incredibly hot and sexy Jana North! Looking Good! Freddie Prinze

"Nope. But fangirl here sure wanted to."

They giggled.

Jana led Odette into an adjoining bathroom with a large soaking tub.

"Nice!"

"I hope you'll take the time to pamper yourself."

Odette sat down at the vanity table and lovingly examined item after item.

"This is amazing! I can't believe you saved all of these."

"I guess I like to hold onto things."

"Ponds made peach cold cream? No way! Is this really a vintage bottle of Maybelline Moisture Whip Makeup? As worn by Lynda Carter? The one formulated with the highly maligned PABA, or as the seventies kids used to call it, Padimate O?

"It really is."

"What's the general medical consensus these days for keeping a thirty year old product containing Padimate O?"

"Still fresh as the date of manufacture. Because parabens. And if Lynda Carter's current beauty secret involves marinating in her leftover stash, I'm not too worried."

They giggled.

A flush crept into Jana's cheeks as she continued to relax.

"Wow. I can't believe you saved all of this! This is a total trip."

"Wait until you see the backup supply."

A collection of shampoos, conditioners, and various toiletry products lined the bathroom closet shelves. Most of them were sealed and unopened.

"Earth Born, Dimension, Deep Magic, Milk Plus Six. Where did you find these?"

"I always liked trying new ones."

"I remember them all! Short and Sassy?"

"Took a brief ride on the Dorothy Hamill wedge train when it first left the station. Total disaster."

"Perma Soft! I remember that smell like it was yesterday. Afro Sheen made a shampoo?"

"As I recall, it was a pretty good one, too. I might need to revisit it."

She looked at the bodies peeking out from a wire basket of vintage magazines on the bottom shelf. Donyale Luna. Marisa Berenson. Margaux Hemingway.

"Or you could join me in the present day. I've got some Qhemet Biologics and Miss Jessie's for you to try."

"I'll check them out, but come see the wardrobe first."

Odette gasped aloud when she saw the walk in closet. Rows and rows of dresses from the late sixties through the mid-eighties were among the many pieces in Jana's collection.

She clapped her hands and threw her head back with laughter. "Stop it right now!"

"It's my doll house for living dolls. You can wear anything you want."

"Halston and Stephen Sprouse? Jana! You have Gloria Vanderbilt jeans in every color. Stop it!" She looked through drawers lined in velvet that were stuffed with accessories. "Brett Somers wore those glasses on Match Game."

"There's jewelry too. And if you're in need of entertainment after you've bathed and dressed, there's also a collection of VHS tapes."

"It's a museum, Jana. An interactive product and clothing museum. Do you know how many people would pay to experience it?"

"I had a feeling you'd like it."

"How many fundraisers crash and burn in per plate wasteland? There's so much to discuss. When I'm ready for my close up. But first, I must nap."

"Rest. Play. Meet me downstairs when you wake up." Jana

blew a kiss and closed the door behind her.

Outside the window, the wildflowers danced interpretatively in the breeze. A small group trick or treaters sported colorful costumes and frolicked like an eddy of leaves in the distance. She drew the curtains shut and wondered if they would be lucky enough to score candy three nights in a row.

She nestled under the ivory bedspread and breathed deeply. For all its vintage opulence, the room bore an air of loneliness similar to the vine-covered stones outside. As she fell asleep, she imagined what it felt like to be a soap opera star in the seventies. Or Norma Desmond.

The Persian carpet felt soft under her bare feet when she woke up a few hours later and headed to the bathroom. She took a quick shower and pulled on a turtleneck and yoga pants. Suddenly thinking the better of it, she opened Jana's closet and peered thoughtfully at the pieces inside before changing into a pair of navy lounging pajamas and wrapping a paisley ascot around her throat. She checked her appearance in the vanity mirror and she dabbed her wrists with a single drop of Chanel Cuir de Russie before heading downstairs to join Jana for dinner.

"You look lovely! Did you get some rest?"

"Thank you! I had a very nice nap." She handed Jana three bottles of wine. "I got you these. I wasn't sure what you liked, so I brought Chardonnay, Cabernet and Zinfandel."

Jana took the bottles of wine and looked at the labels. Folie à Deux Vineyards.

"Thank you. That is so generous of you. I'll put them in the cooler for later."

"Can I help with dinner?"

"There's nothing to do but eat. We're having fried green tomatoes with rémoulade, softshell crabs, quiche, salad, and crème brûlée. Oh, and some kind of mixed cheese and olive plate."

"Lagniappe."

Jana's eyes sparkled. "That's right." She held up an open bottle of Chardonnay. "Cuvaison, too. Let's fill your glass, shall we?"

The dining room was set up with disposable chafers. They filled their plates, took their places at the table and began to eat.

Jana motioned to Odette's neck. "She gave me one, too, you know."

Odette brought her fingers to the ascot and looked down at her neck.

"Calvin and Russell buried it in the garden. I know it's just a coincidence." She looked down into her wine glass and avoided Odette's eyes.

"Please don't be upset, Jana. I don't want to put you on the spot or embarrass you, but I understand. I do."

"In what way?"

"I know about what happened in Orange County. I know about your daughter."

Jana shook her head and laughed resignedly. "That was a long time ago."

"She's not entirely here, but you brought her to this world."

"Please don't, Odette, She's not real. I get it."

"Yes, she is."

"I know it's an anthropomorphic delusion brought on by unresolved grief. I'm a doctor. Was, anyway."

"She's real. Her name is Ester. I know her. I think Calvin knew her, too. She saved my life."

An odd twitch crept from Jana's mouth as the two women joined hands across the table.

"She first came to me when I was a little girl. She held onto my pain and fear for me, but I've trapped her. She can't get free until I let go."

Jana rocked back and forth slowly and absorbed her words.

"Are you okay?"

"Seems we have a bit in common, you and I. I never expected anyone to hold onto the pain for me. Somehow it's all become too much. I understand. More than you know."

"Maybe we could help each other make it better."

"How?"

"Maybe we could take it back so she doesn't have to carry it anymore."

They paused and looked at each other. Jana emptied her glass, picked up the bottle and refilled it. She tipped it in Odette's direction. Odette nodded and held out her glass.

"I have something to show you. Upstairs. Bring your glass."

She led Odette up the wooden staircase to the second floor and the second staircase leading to the attic bedroom.

"I don't come in here often. I've pretty much left it the way he did. I've barely touched it since he passed away."

Odette stood in front of the dresser and examined the items that littered the surface. Two crowns made from integrifolia and dental floss lay amid a collection of antique puppets, Pysanka eggs and cassette tapes.

"Samhain, Odette."

"What?"

"In two days. Sunday. It's the day Russell and Calvin found the hummingbird. It's the day I gave her up."

Jana observed her reflection in the dresser mirror. With trembling fingers, she grasped Ells' Celtic cross pendant from its hiding place inside her t-shirt and placed it outside her sweater. She took one of the integrifolia crowns gently into her hands and placed it on top of her head. Hands still shaking, she turned toward Odette and crowned her with the second.

Odette faced the mirror and stared at her reflection.

"All Saints' Day, too." She brought her fingertips to the fragile crown.

"What?"

"Is Monday."

Their eyes met each other's in the mirror. Jana's lips curved into a smile.

"Lagniappe."

She dreamed that a conjoined twin who lived behind her back fell ill and died, leaving her alone to face the world with an identity that had always been a part of her but wasn't hers to claim. As she drifted awake, a faint stream of moonlight illuminated the wildflowers outside the guest room window and cast floral shadows across the ivory bedspread. She screwed her eyes shut to hold onto the prescient state for as long as she could, knowing it would evaporate as soon as it was exposed to light.

In the library, she tucked her grey blonde curls behind her ears and placed the stylus at the edge of a record. Jackson C. Frank's *Milk and Honey* rose from the stereo speakers as she curled up in a red leather chair. The scent of the music was tender, pure. Even the scratchy pits between verses were soothing. She stared at a canvas bundle on top of the desk and fought the urge to grab a cigarette from the nine-year-old pack of Chesterfields stashed away in the top drawer.

She drew a bath, eased herself into the tub and lingered in the perfumed water. She took her time styling her hair and applying touches of bronzer, mascara and gloss. She chose an orange satin robe and a tortoiseshell belt from Jana's wardrobe and paired them with her own maroon leggings. She adjusted the floral crown before giving herself a final once over in the mirror and heading downstairs.

She stood up from the chair, cut the burlap twine with scissors and freed the parcel from its canvas wrapping. All these years later, the marble of the Celtic cross she chiseled at the women's retreat glowed brighter than she remembered, but she told herself it was the heightened contrast against the evening sky. She brushed down the front of her lavender bias cut gown, drew her grey pashmina tightly around her shoulders, and straightened her crown before walking toward the sound of footfall on the steps.

"Has anyone ever told you that you look like Carol Kane?"

"A few times. You look beautiful."

"Thanks."

"Did you sleep well?"

"I did."

"Dinner's ready. I hope you like lamb gumbo."

"I love it."

The air felt unseasonably warm as Jana lit tapers and opened the French doors. After dinner, Odette perused the record collection in the library and selected Dead Can Dance's *Within the Realm of a Dying Sun*.

Music rose from the library and into the garden through the outdoor speakers. She noticed Jana's nearly empty glass and picked up the bottle of wine to refresh it.

"You know what Peter Lorre would say right now, don't you?"

"No, what?"

Jana grabbed the bottle and filled the glass to the top. "Don't be so stingy!"

They laughed. Jana raised the glass and brought it to her lips.

"I don't know what to say."

"Neither do I."

"Ready, then?"

"Yes. Let's go get my bird. Follow me."

They carried a large box, two shovels and an empty suitcase to a clearing at the base of the garden in front of the oak trees. After they set the box down, Jana felt inside of it and pulled out a crayon drawing. It had been waterlogged at one point and was stiffened with age. She studied the image of a healing forest and yellow moon.

"We're at the right place. This is Finn's healing forest. My bird is buried right here." Jana pointed out a stick marked by a tattered and filthy shred of fabric.

They each grabbed a shovel and started digging.

Something thudded under their shovels a few minutes later.

Jana thrust her hand into the cool dirt and unveiled a weathered pine box with cracked purple paint.

"Here it is." She handed the box to Odette, who placed it carefully to the side.

When the hole was deep enough, they spread a blanket on the ground, sat and rested.

Jana opened the suitcase and placed it halves up on the grass.

"Ready?"

Odette nodded.

Dead Can Dance's *Summoning of the Muse* blared from the garden speakers as they rose to their knees, reached into the box, and placed items into the suitcase.

Odette added the Queen of Clubs card.

Jana added Finn's drawing.

Odette added an astronomy book.

Jana added Calvin's antique Hungarian puppets and Pysanka eggs.

Odette added a Malibu Christie doll.

Jana added Calvin's Wile E Coyote mug.

Odette added sets of Earth Born and Dimension shampoo and conditioner, respectively.

"You know Courteney Cox was in a Dimension shampoo commercial before she got famous, right?"

"That was her?"

Odette added the bottle of Folie à Deux Chardonnay.

Jana added a bag of apples, pecans and carrots.

Odette added an envelope of instant oatmeal.

Jana fumbled with the clasp of the Celtic cross necklace that Ells gave her and added it to the suitcase.

Odette added her silver metallic scarf.

Jana added her stethoscope and lab coat.

Odette added the leather bound copy of Clark Ashton Smith's *The End of the Story*.

"Is that it?"

"Is it?"

"What about the love and peace notes?"

"Let's do it."

Jana reached into the box and took out a bundle of parchment paper scraps and a fountain pen. She wrote a note on the first scrap and placed it in the suitcase before passing the pen to Odette.

I love you, Russell and Cal - Peace, Jana
I love you, Mama - Peace, Odette
Forgive me Lonnie and Moose - Peace, Jana
Sorry about your ankle, Mollie - Peace, Odette
You're not my real Dad - Peace, Jana

They added the integrifola crowns to the top of the pile and latched the suitcase shut. They placed it in the hole and covered it with dirt. When they were finished, they marked the site with the marble monument, sat back down on the blanket, and waited. Jana was the first to break the silence.

"If we're going do this right, shouldn't we be singing?"

"Maybe, but I'm tired from all the digging. Want some more wine?"

"Of course."

They opened a second bottle and finished the leftover cheese and olive plate. Odette took out her phone and looked at Facebook. A distracted Jana prattled nervously.

"Maybe we should hold hands and do a circle dance around the monument. I'm serious. Aren't we supposed to get a sign?"

"I guess, but look! Cat memes."

Jana's face turned ashen.

"I'm just kidding. Don't get angry."

Jana pointed off into the distance. Odette turned to face the same direction.

"Holy shit."

A parliament of spotted owls guarded the entrance. They parted at the sight of Jana and revealed the access to a gazebo made from spider silk. Fireflies lit the structure like icicle lights. It attached itself to the spires of the house and stretched outward to the grove of oak trees where it knotted itself along the gnarled, ancient trunks. Grey spiders as large as cats hovered in random folds. Some extended the length of their graceful legs provocatively while grooming themselves. Others wrapped their bodies around quilted sacs to protect their glassy eggs. Beneath the canopy sprawled a colorful labyrinth of flowers and vines.

Jana stood up and led the way into the labyrinth. A chestnut colored spider extended a leg and waved it towards Odette.

"It wants to show you something. Give it your hand," Jana urged. Odette tentatively extended her hand. The spider sensed her fear and gently brushed against her fingertips with its downy fur before extending another leg to Jana. She grasped it timidly and allowed the spider to lead them deeper inside.

They staggered beneath the prismatic objects interwoven in the walls. Stethoscopes. Violas. Oversized martini glasses. A hummingbird flew out of the lattice and trailed a visible mist of silver and pearls before nestling itself comfortably on Jana's shoulder. She gently stroked the bird and put an arm around Odette.

"What is it?"

"I'm supposed to show you a message in the flowers."

The hummingbird flew to an orange blossom and waited.

"*Osmunda.*" Jana stepped aside as Odette pressed her nose against the bud. "Remember your dreams. *Adonis Vernalis.* Don't suppress or deny bitter memories. It never works."

She pointed to a vine curling into the giant web. "*Bearded Crepis.* Don't lead with fear. You're protected."

"*Carolina Rose.* Love is dangerous, but do it anyway. *Chorozema Varium.* Don't measure your worth by a love affair. Your value is internal."

"How do you know all this?"

Jana chuckled. "You're not my real dad!"

A halo of fireflies illuminated their terrifying beauty as they joined hands and spun around in a circle. They were two women waltzing madly in danger's court, no longer seeking solace in security, and looking eagerly towards the next dance. They reached the densest patch of the labyrinth at the blackest point of night. An emboldened vine buried itself into the small of Jana's back and coiled possessively around her like a wreath of armor. It scratched her temple with a pointed thorn and drew a blood drop that glistened black in the night sky.

"Ouch!"

Odette tried to pull it off, but Jana refused the assistance. She wrenched herself free with an audible succession of snaps and crunches.

The blood drop pooled onto a waxy looking cluster of pale yellow berries. "*Whortleberry*. You will come to know treachery. *Butterfly Weed*. Let it go. *Celandine*. Future joy will come."

They stopped to rest. The gazebo rocked back and forth as they stretched out on their backs. Intrigued, the spiders lowered themselves to have a closer look at their visitors. The weight of their bodies lowered a corner of the gazebo to the ground and created a makeshift swing. Jana and Odette carefully climbed inside. The spiders gently rocked them back and forth.

"Do you suppose she's happy, Jana?"

"She's not bitter, if you believe what the flowers say. She knew treachery, but she let it go. She looks forward to future joy."

"Where?"

"Back home, I guess."

The chestnut spider was busy weaving a bar cluttered with an array of oversized martini glasses. A second spider plucked two of the woven glasses and placed them on a tray. She approached the women politely and offered them a drink.

"It's official, Jana. We are officially certifiable. And scene."

Jana rolled her eyes. "Stop judging. It's our folie à deux. We can see what we want. And it's happy hour! Why complain?"

Jana took a woven glass from the tray and sipped eagerly. "Don't mind if I do." She scooped an olive from the bottom of the glass and popped it into her mouth. "Delicious!"

The spider lingered at Odette's side and offered her a drink. "No, thank you," she said. It bowed politely and began to crawl away.

"Wait! I'll take it!" Jana screeched. She threw her empty glass onto the woven tray and eagerly snatched up Odette's drink. She reached into her tangled mop of waist length grey curls, scooped out a handful of fireflies and threw them in the spider's direction.

"Thank you!"

The sun cautiously peeked into the eastern corner of the trees as Jana sipped the martini. "Future joy will come," she whispered.

"Did you say something?" Odette yawned.

"I used to think that if I followed the North Star, if I was lucky enough to catch it and pull it down from the sky, that's where she would be. Why do we always go at length to search for things when they end up being right under our noses? There'll be no future joy until I make things right." She looked down at her lavender dress and looked up at the sky. Her eyes filled with tears.

"Oh, Lonnie! I wish you could see the world today. The rainbows and pots of gold were so close! You just never got to find them because I got in the way. You were never the fool. I was. Still am. And I can't keep hiding forever. I have to face it. Will you help me, Odette?"

Odette was snoring gently. Trying to be as still as possible, Jana unfastened the shawl from her shoulders and nestled it around the younger woman's body. The spiders remembered their duties as the sun began to rise and gradually retreated back into the high corners.

"Pots of gold," she murmured. The martini glass slipped

through her fingers and stuck to the side of the swing. Sounds of morning filled the landscape from all directions as she curled her body against the swing, bowed her head and slept.

She awoke to sunlight a few hours later and gazed at the sleeping girl beside her.

"Morning."

"What time is it?"

"I don't know. You took the day off, remember?"

"Uh huh."

"How are you feeling?"

"Strange."

"Me, too."

"Jana?"

Odette examined the skin at the base of her clavicles with her fingertips. It was perfectly smooth without a trace of scar tissue.

"Let me see." Jana leaned in closer to look at Odette's throat. The scar was gone. In the distance, the unearthed painted box lay open and empty on top of the blanket.

"We did it."

Odette brushed down the surface of her orange satin robe and rolled up the sleeves. The deeply etched scars on her wrists were still visible.

She looked at Jana and shook her head. "But I don't understand. That can't be right. These aren't mine. I didn't do this."

Jana closed her eyes mournfully and extended her hand. Odette grasped it and continued to shake her head in denial. As her stomach carried the truth to the surface, the denial in her eyes gave way to confusion and acceptance.

"No," she whispered. Her eyes filled with tears.

Jana covered the younger woman's hands with her own and lovingly traced the scars with her fingertips before drawing her close.

"It's okay."

As she allowed herself to be rocked, she was overpowered by a sensation of resin that made her choke. The volume swelled deeply inside her chest and flowed inside her ears and mouth. She knew it would never go away completely. Because it was hers. And that was okay. There would be plenty of room for breathing once the curing process began. That's how resin worked, anyway. Or maybe it was mortar.

Jana wrapped her pashmina snugly around Odette's shoulders, unrolled the robe sleeves and covered her wrists demurely. "Let's get you inside. I'll make beignets for breakfast. And a pot of chicory coffee. Would you like that like?"

Odette nodded.

Jana led her out of the garden and into the house through the open french doors. She made sure she was settled at the nook in front of the kitchen window before quietly leaving the room.

In the library, she tucked her grey blonde curls behind her ears and placed the stylus at the edge of a record. Louis Armstrong's *When the Saints Go Marching In* rose from the outdoor speakers and filled the kitchen with song. The scent of the music was robust, exhilarating. Even the scratchy pits between verses cooled the breath inside her nostrils. She stared at the canvas wrapping where the marble cross used to be, opened the top desk drawer and threw the nine-year-old pack of Chesterfields into the wastebasket. Then she walked back into the kitchen and grabbed coffee, sugar and flour out of the pantry. She set them down on the counter and filled the coffeepot with water.

From her seat at the kitchen nook, a breeze outside the window lingered at her eyelids and chest. In a flurry of movement, it seized her chin and kissed her squarely on the lips. She cried out in surprise.

"Are you okay?" Jana was hunched down on her hands and knees in front of a large storage drawer. She emerged with an ancient cast iron pan and followed Odette's eyes to the scene outside the window. Together, they watched as the breeze floated away and joined the wildflowers in a frenetic dance around the monument.

"Strange." She stood up carefully. An odd smile escaped her lips as she wiped her mouth with the back of her hand and went to the refrigerator for milk and eggs.

Jana

"Odette?"

"Yeah?"

"How about living your dreams?"

"Tired."

"Rainbows?"

"Predictable."

"How about a music theme? Like *Come Together*?"

Odette set her textbook aside and stared at Jana.

"Nana. Seriously?" She queued James Brown's *Get Up, Get Into It, Get Involved* on her phone and started dancing in place.

"What's wrong with the Beatles? James Brown would be good, too."

"This is definitely going on the DJ's playlist."

"Should we make it the theme?"

"No."

"Why not? It's perfect."

"Maybe, if you're going for a forty-year-old PSA vibe. But with your luck, James Brown's estate will crash the party looking for royalties."

The look of horror that crossed Jana's face made Odette laugh. "I love paying homage to the seventies aesthetic. Heavily. But the project can't live there entirely; it has to step up to the present."

Jana dismissed her words with the wave of a hand. "There's no social relevance in popular music today."

"You could do a remix. How about, *Hey Soul Sister Get Up On The Floor Say Something Right Now Get Into It Na Na Na Get Involved Whatcha Say?* I'll leave you the fine tuning."

Jana scowled. "You think you're so clever."

Odette's cell phone rang. "Hold that thought."

She stepped out of the room to take the call. Jana continued to brainstorm.

She stepped back into the room. "That was Nina. I told her we were discussing themes. Her uncle suggested don't you want to be free?"

Jana sighed. "How about pots of gold?"

"Don't you want to be free?"

"I am free."

"Then don't name it."

"But there are so many factors. How do we tie them all together?"

"Leave them fractured. They'll come together on their own terms."

"Champagne, ma'am?"

"Thank you."

She couldn't help feeling a bit weepy as she took a champagne flute from the cocktail server's tray. She dabbed at her eyes with a cocktail napkin.

Oh, no! Did you smear it?

She watched the server follow a trail of sparkling balloons to a nearby cluster of guests.

It's waterproof, remember? Relax.

Thanks in large part to Odette and the faculty at Lincoln University, she was finally making things right. It had been fifty-six years in the making, but it was happening. Everything had turned out so beautifully. She could hardly believe they had pulled it off.

Not only was it an exceptional turnout, many guests had traveled a significant distance to attend. Spiree had flown in from Los Angeles with a group of her UCLA colleagues. A few staffers from *The Natchez Democrat* had shown up, too. She was beyond humbled.

The Philadelphia Museum of Art's Skylit Atrium was lustrous. A runway/dance floor paved with gold holographic coins sparkled in the mood lighting. Above the runway, three screens displayed images from Isaac Julien's *Fantôme Afrique*, Spike Lee's *Get on the Bus* and Shih-Ting Hung's *Viola: The Traveling Rooms of a Little Giant*, respectively. To the left, a woman in a sleeveless leather vest spun records in a DJ booth.

To the right of the screens, guests mingled within an interactive exhibit of wardrobe racks and tables set up with cosmetics and toiletries. Framed vintage advertisements, photos of designers and accompanying storyboards hung from standing backdrops. She leaned in closer to make out some of images. Ann Lowe. Scott Barrie. Cardinali. Arthur McGee.

She put her empty glass down on a cocktail stand and brushed down her dress, a sleek, emerald Stephen Burrows midi paired with vintage Yves Saint Laurent mod lace up boots.

"Hors d'oeuvre?"

"Thank you."

She turned around and took a mini bruschetta from the tray of a different server. Floral centerpieces adorned the long table set up for dinner. Across the lobby, Odette stood among the guests enjoying aperitifs at the bar. She looked ravishing in a floaty, multicolored Duro Olowu dress cinched with a vintage Norma Kamali wide jeweled cummerbund belt.

She felt her shoulders moving to the music as she waved to Odette and took in the scene around her. Maybe she was slightly giddy from two glasses of champagne. Perhaps it was because they'd pulled it off. Almost. She still had a speech to give, hence the two glasses of champagne.

When she thought no one was looking, she test drove an impromptu Mary Tyler Moore spin. Regrettably, her brakes were a wee bit rusty. Or maybe a bit too greased. In any case, she stumbled the tiniest bit and lost her balance. Fortunately, Spiree just happened to be passing by.

"Careful, girl!" Spiree caught her by the elbow and steadied her. "Those boots are smoking hot, but they weren't made for spinning. I'm so proud of you."

Spiree was dressed in a cream colored jumpsuit and dangling flower earrings. Jana hugged her. "Thank you. I can't believe you flew out during the middle of the week to be here!"

"Like I would've missed it for anything? Call me reckless!"

"Wearing white before Labor Day? Now, that's what's reckless, Spiree. And you, Mary Richards, are spinning out of control!"

They turned in the direction of Nina's voice. She wore an elegant black suit and a mixed metal Konstantino cross pendant necklace.

"I'm wearing open toed sandals, too, Nina." Spiree giggled. "Got the feds on speed dial?"

"No one's worried about your misdemeanor when grand larceny's happening over there." She winked and pointed.

Across the room, a beaming Lilith was front and center on the runway dance floor boogying to a Rihanna remix and holding a bottle of champagne. She wore a vintage strapless Halston metallic sarong gown. Her red mane defied both the visible color spectrum and gravity as the result of a fresh salon coloring and overnight braidout. She blew kisses as the crowd cheered her on.

"Girlfriend's still got it. Doesn't she, Spiree?"

"Tell me about it. She makes everything look so easy. She's

beautiful, brilliant, never fucking ages and has more energy than is humanly possible.

"She's got great genes. She's lucky."

"Sometimes I think she's an alien, Nina. I'm not even kidding."

———————————————

"You okay?"

"I'm fine."

When her name was announced, Odette squeezed her fingers. She walked carefully to her place onstage, took the microphone from the sound designer and remembered to stay calm.

"Thank you all for being here tonight.

Not being able to afford the New Year's Eve rate for this venue turned out to be a blessing in disguise. Not only are we here together to celebrate the first day of Black History Month, we're also together on the anniversary of Langston Hughes' birthday.

My name is Jana North. If you follow the regional news reports, you've possibly heard about my story. I'm a woman who despises the spotlight, but, for some reason, the crossroads of my life seem to garner attention.

I'm the widow of Russell North, a civil rights attorney. He passed away in 2010. We were married for thirty-eight years.

A month after my husband passed away, I went to the police and told them that my father was involved in the 1954 murder of Lonnie James, an innocent black man from Natchez, Mississippi.

After Lonnie's murder, my father lived out the rest of his days without ever being arrested, going to trial or serving time. When I finally went to the police in 2010, I told them how my father came home that night with the red mud from Lonnie's property caked on his shoes and bloodstains on his white hood. I told them how I ran straight back to Lonnie's house, and how the shoes of the police officer who threw me in the back of his paddy wagon and returned me to my father were caked with the very same mud. I submitted DNA evidence, too.

Now that I got that out of the way, thank you all for supporting *LONNIE*.

LONNIE, or *Loving Our Neighbor is the Nexus for Implementing Equality* is a community-led initiative against hate and bias crimes.

Thanks in large part to Odette Ridley, her network of colleagues at Lincoln University and an unexpected outpouring of support from various sources, we founded and launched the inaugural chapter in the Philadelphia Metro/Delaware Valley area. We're working diligently to launch chapters in Natchez, Adams County and New Orleans Metro area by 2013.

A long time ago, I went searching for answers and came across two men who saved my life.

Lonnie James was a brilliant creative and an optimist who found good in the worst of situations. He shared a story with me about surviving a tornado as a young boy and losing his home in the process. After his family members and dog were all safe and accounted for, he saw a rainbow and ran off to look for pots of gold.

I wish I could tell you he found them, but I can't. He paid the ultimate price. I did the unthinkable. I never made it right. His loved ones never knew justice. I could stand here tonight and make excuses about a faulty justice system, the racial climate of Mississippi in the fifties, or claim that it was someone else's responsibility to take care of it, but I would be lying. Despite marrying a man who committed his life's work to standing up for himself and others, I made a habit out of falling down and staying down. I never stood up and faced the truth. Until recently.

I can't change what happened that night back in 1954, but I can change what happens today. Every day of my life, every last bit of my energy and all of the resources that come my way going forward will be collectively dedicated to the implementation of impactful change. It's never too late to demand justice. It's never too late to create it, either.

There are dozens of cold cases spanning over a decade's time that are linked to the Silver Dollar Club, the Natchez-based hate group of which my father was a member. It is my hope that the families of every single victim will finally be able to know justice, closure and peace.

Thank you to the Philadelphia Museum of Art for the use of this venue and the delicious catering. And thank you to Lincoln University's Visual Arts and Criminal Justice Departments for curating our interactive makeup and fashion museum experience and putting together the runway show. All museum items are up for silent auction tonight. We will be drawing the winning raffle numbers shortly, so hold onto the tickets you received at the door. Thank you. Enjoy the rest of the party!"

Odette met her with a glass of champagne as she walked offstage and the DJ resumed her mix.

"That was brilliant."

"I love you so much, darling girl."

"I love you too."

Odette sipped her champagne. "I checked your messages. An agent reached out and wants to know if you're interested in writing an autobiography. Alcorn University wants to know if you can speak at a conference."

"Wow. Well what do you think?"

"That you need to learn how to retrieve emails."

"Meow!"

"You wanted the truth, right?"

"You'd give me anything else?"

"That's just for starters. Eventually, you'll need to hire an assistant. Between work and my thesis, I'm pretty much swamped. And the arc of Lonnie's rainbow is widening. Two pots of gold and counting."

Jana sighed. "You're absolutely right, and I apologize if I've leaned on you too much. I guess I haven't realized the extent of outpouring or understand why anyone would want to associate with me. Deep down, I don't expect anyone to forgive me."

"But what happens if they do?"

A man approached Odette. "May I have this dance?"

"Sure."

Jana gave Odette a knowing smile and stepped out of the way.

"Back soon. Oh. And before I forget, this package came for you." Odette handed her a clamshell box and headed to the dance floor.

She opened it carefully. Nestled inside a protective mound of tissue paper was a fragile, yellowing playbook. She read the title.

Don't You Want to Be Free?

She opened the cover gingerly and read the inscription.

To Mercer Baldwin. Best wishes, Langston Hughes

She stopped and looked around, confused. Nina happened to be passing by.

"Hey, Nina?"

"Hey, girl."

"Do you know where this came from?"

"Yes."

"Who's Mercer Baldwin?"

"My uncle. He's with the alumni chapter."

"Have I met him? Do I know him?"

"Funny you should ask that. He's from Natchez, too. Small world, huh? The folks back home call him Moose."

Jana looked stricken. She grabbed Nina's hands and held them tightly. "Moose is your uncle? Moose is still alive? Could you help me get in touch with him? Do you have his number?"

"I could, but why don't you just ask him yourself?"

Nina pointed. Across the room, an elderly man wearing a tailored blue suit sat amid a group of people at the bar.

A sudden wave of dizziness caught Jana off guard. "You did this, didn't you?"

Nina smiled and held out her elbow. "As I was saying, there's no time like the present. You ready, girl?"

She couldn't help feeling a little bit punked as she linked arms with Nina, but she held her tongue. She would get over it. More than anything, she was grateful.

The world wasn't really spinning; it had just slowed down around her. She could certainly stand to get off for a moment. Two moments, even. Regrettably, the ladies' room was in the opposite direction of her destination.

A man standing in the crowd behind the barstools leaned in close to Moose and tapped him on the shoulder. Moose stopped what he was doing and turned his head in Jana's direction.

Is this what they mean by missing time?

Despite the slowed down world, her feet were still operating in real time and she couldn't feel her legs. This created a centrifugal effect of sorts. It shouldn't have come as a shock when they buckled underneath her, but she was full of surprises that night. Her recovery rivaled a level of grace on par with that of a henhouse chicken, which was a pretty low bar to clear. Thankfully, Nina's strong arms held her up without missing a beat.

"I caught you, girl. Those vintage YSL boots are smoking hot, but they really weren't made for walking."

Fifty-six years without justice. And yet, after all this time, you still allow your fear to lead. He saved your life. Stop it!

She thought she could see the slightest tremble in his jaw as they approached the halfway point to the bar. She couldn't be sure, but she could certainly relate. Her TMJ was always in overdrive, even at the best of times. There was so much territory to bridge and her mind was drawing a blank. Perhaps her tongue wouldn't betray her. If only she could get it to move. It really was a toss-up at this point. Maybe she could communicate with her eyes instead. Yes. That's exactly what she would do.

Two men at the bar placed their hands at his armpits and shoulders and gently helped him rise from the barstool. He steadied his own hands against a brass knobbed cane and turned his body in her direction. The hands lingered supportively at his back. His mouth moved. The men nodded and the hands moved away.

"We're moving. You're moving. Almost there, girl."

Don't you dare look down! You look him straight in the eyes. He deserves your utmost respect. All of it.

She could really see him as she moved in closer. The contours of his face had relaxed over the years. His hair was thinner and completely white. And he was frail. Painfully so. But it was him. It was Moose.

What can I possibly say? Where do I begin?

His eyes never left hers as she made her way towards him. They communicated the wisdom of a true educator. One who remained teachable and not focused on controlling the moment. One who made a habit of looking beyond the obvious.

Deep down, I don't expect anyone to forgive me.

One who understood that true growth comes from weathering a tangled, reeking stench of experience and not from cherry picking a pretty bouquet of hand-selected soundbytes.

"And we made it! Uncle Mercer. Jana."

One who understood the difference between that which was best left buried in the past and that which was worthy of welcoming back into the present.

But what happens if they do?

She glanced at the book in her hands and stood in front of him.

Answer him.

Answer the question.

Give him an answer.

Answer his question.

Just answer the man's question.

Why don't you answer the question?

Can't you just answer the question?

Forgive me. Please.

Yes.

Ester

A turn of the tide lifted her from the crater bed and propelled her into motion along the hairline quark that delineated the present from the past. Time-weathered spheres hunched together and watched. Arrogant young comets wagged their tails obliviously.

In Bucks County, Margaret's phone fell from the bedside table to the ground beyond her reach. A fatal convulsion took hold of her body. She cursed aloud at her son and longed tearfully for Magyar.

In Anaheim, Lasse sat naked and giggling on an examination table with a tourniquet wrapped around his arm. A woman dressed in a naughty nurse uniform held a syringe filled with a lethal cocktail of morphine and adrenaline. "Time for your shot," she said, licking her lips suggestively. He groaned excitedly and held out his arm.

In Philadelphia, Bela ignored the phone ringing inside his dilapidated apartment and perched at the window to watch a troop of Girl Scouts laughing in the street below. They were happy in the moment and excited for the future, now that cookie time had arrived. His lips parted slowly, revealing lupine, greying teeth.

In Los Angeles, Hans waited for the automatic gate that surrounded his home to open before driving his vehicle inside.

The full moon disappeared behind a murky curtain of clouds as a woman staggered out of the passenger side door. He turned off the ignition, walked to her side and placed one of his hands at the small of her back. The other stayed firm on the knife inside his pocket.

The Samhain ritual in the night garden had certainly raised her spirit. What better way to accept their accolades than by staying out all night and dancing with the flowers and stars? She couldn't think of any. But when Louis Armstrong's velvety bass rang through the air the next day at that ungodly hour, she immediately knew something was amiss.

She bypassed the crumbling gateposts in favor of the backyard. The doors off the kitchen were wide open. The wildflowers were curly and giddy, as if they'd been watered with vodka. She couldn't help but feel as if they were in on the secret. They were fun to dance with, but you couldn't trust a word they said.

Now that Jana lived alone, she never woke up before eleven o'clock. But there she was, down on her hands and knees, lugging a pan that she never used from a drawer she never touched. This was troubling. There was no need for cookware anymore. A successful meal was finding a breakfast bar in the pantry, ignoring the expiration date and dunking it into her coffee. Why was she doing this?

She decided to make herself comfortable in her usual space, the nook at the kitchen window, but it was taken. Odette was there, watching the wildflowers dance around the monument. The sight of her sitting in the chair carried an unexpected sting. Something was different, but she wasn't sure why. In order to figure it out, she would have to see what Odette was seeing and feel what she was feeling. So she poised herself and tried to look behind her eyes. But she couldn't get in.

She was still tipsy from the night before; that's all it was. But a second time passed, and she was still unable to get inside, so she tried again. And again. And again.

A sense of ownership had taken root inside of Odette. The chasms she had once slipped into so easily were now filled with curling sprouts. She couldn't see them directly, but she could make out their tiny, upside-down reflections inside her sunlit irises. They looked delicate, but they were impenetrable, like forest garland armor.

She saw the puddle of salt at the windowsill and scoffed. Silly old wives' tale. She tried again, but it was futile. There was simply no way in.

Was it happiness she felt as she lingered outside the kitchen window and kissed her goodbye? Not really. Bittersweetness? Even that was generous.

There was nothing left to do but leave.

In Phialind, the beryl hills and valleys were shrouded by an awning of sunlit fog. Singing bowls called from herb-covered caves in contemplative odes of devotion. Spotted wild horses abandoned their grazing and ambled towards the sound at their leisure.

In Barterlind, the skyline was awash with light as she fell into step behind a late night crowd. A smartly dressed group of young women screamed when they noticed her lagging behind them. She ducked into the back of a black sedan and fell back against a buttery leather seat. Security guards shooed the women away as the driver sped off into the night.

In Sceptrelind, the house at 7 Storyville Lane was abandoned. Shutters hung from broken hinges and the windows were shattered. The furniture was covered with sheets, the kitchen cold and empty.

In Glaivelind, yellow eyes pierced the blackness as the car approached the forest. The bird elves sprang to attention immediately and assumed their positions in the air, wings elevated in the line of duty. They ignored the odd trespasser or two that attempted to bribe them with handfuls of fresh worms and colorful vials of nectar.

When they reached the Kaspare River, the driver opened the passenger door as she stepped out into the dank, mineral atmosphere. The North Wind whistled in welcome upon seeing her and gently nudged the trees and river to remind them of their manners. Elspeth turned an ear towards the sound of the car, pulled her woolen shawl tightly around her hunched frame and hobbled outside to welcome her.

"Land's sake, child," Elspeth scowled. "Do I have to send messages into the cosmos reminding you to eat your dinner? You're really just a ghost of a thing, aren't you?"

She clutched the girl to her chest and stroked the back of her head. Ester allowed herself to be held, but her hands remained stiffly at her sides as she gazed up at the stars.

Elspeth called into the night sky with her polished agate recorder. The bird elves appeared before the girl with a plate of oysters, figs and crusty bread. She pushed the plate away, ran to the water and vomited. The bird elves appeared stricken.

"There have been invitations to parties and interviews." Elspeth began warily.

Ester wiped her mouth and stood motionless at the edge of the river listening to the voices in the sanguinary water. "Just a ghost," she repeated.

"You should rest before you accept new cases."

"No."

The minatory tone that slithered from her parted lips curdled Elspeth's blood and reverberated to the outer edge of the forest. She drew her shawl tightly around her shoulders, stepped away from the girl and fled to the shelter of the hollowed oak tree. The North Wind ceased its prattle and warned the trees and river to hold their breath and listen.

When it was finally quiet, the dam that carried her pain and sorrow disintegrated into a whorl of hot ash and imploded in a series of hisses.

"They don't need me anymore."

A lurid glow emanated from her eyes as she slipped out of her garments and stood naked at the edge of the river. The black water waited patiently. A lone bird elf licked the length of her spindly, trembling fingers.

Safe within the fused branches of the hollowed oak, Elspeth turned her head away and closed her eyes respectfully. It was hardly her place to interfere with the girl's fate, and she was too old and blind to do much anyway. It was the natural flow to be nearing the end and awkward to linger without purpose. It was more dignified this way. It would be graceful.

The startled bird elves flapped into the sky as she shook the placid water with a violent swan dive. The force of it sent bubbles to the surface and filled her lungs with water and soft mud.

She sank deeper and deeper into the abyss, past the tangle of seaweed that claimed her hair and the school of fish that claimed her eyes. Soft ivory bones eventually settled into the mud where the bottom feeders dwelled, but her whispering soul continued to sink unencumbered until it reached that elusive realm where the water and mud eventually give way and reconnect with the sky and stars again.

She leaned against the surface of the North Star and allowed its warmth to pervade her senses until she stopped feeling numb. When she gazed down at herself, she was surprised to see that she was simply a ball of light.

A ghost of a thing, really.

Just a ghost.

———————————

Or was she?

She was subtle, not exaggerated or brash. A phosphorescent gleam that pulsed in the darkness. An expansive, constrictive paradox capable of superseding both the densest liquid and the tiniest grain of salt. But with a hell of lot more sparkle, like a sequined dress onstage at blackout. Shoulder shimmies. Jazz hands.

I want to keep going.

But I'm supposed to fade away now.

I don't feel like an anthropomorphic delusion.

But for everyone else to be happy, I must meet a tragic demise and selflessly fade into oblivion because I'm not supposed to exist. Those are the rules.

I stayed in the periphery and played nice the entire time, which was exceedingly accommodating on my end and far more generous than any of them deserved. I kissed Odette goodbye when I really wanted to bite her. I'm tired of hiding behind the mask of third person. It's time to use my real voice.

Why don't I stay here in the North Star forever and fuse myself into its surface so that people can see my face on nights when the sky is clear?

Why should I hide behind a star?

Why don't I resume my role as an alien and continue living the same lessons over and over again in the name of pseudoscience?

That isn't how I end. There's more to me than that.

What more is there? Before this, I was just a little girl in Sceptrelind.

I was around a long time before that. Back when I was older.

Older than Lilith?

I'm the Queen of Wands.

Is that where it began?

Focus on what's ahead. An eternity filled with endless shapes.

I really should stay here.

I really should get some rest.

I'll get some rest.

I'll stay.

But only for now.

ACKNOWLEDGMENTS

Momma: Thanks for letting me ponder the scenery outside the window while you kept a grip on the steering wheel. Now that you're riding shotgun, I will always do my best to keep you safe.

Daddy: You continue to lead the marathon with an abundance of style and grace. No one will ever have a stride more elegant than yours.

To the late Alfred Cahn, the late Maisha Baton, Ph.D, the late Neil Kosh, Doris Fields, Ph.D, Richard Borth, Ph.D, and Maricela Valencia: You are the finest teachers ever, and learning from you was a privilege. Your perspective was a valuable gift; I'm humbled and grateful for it.

Kamal John Iskander, Kristin Tiry, Mateen Kemet, and Buford Davis: I give you many thanks.

ABOUT THE AUTHOR

Ka Newborrn enjoys quad rollerskating and
kickboxing, Ethiopian food and barrel aged stouts,
Philadelphia soul and San Francisco sound, forgotten
pop culture and cranky feral cats. She divides her time
between Los Angeles and Las Vegas. This is her debut
novel.

www.ingramcontent.com/pod-product-compliance
Lightning Source LLC
Chambersburg PA
CBHW020947260626
47169CB00006B/1860